The Impossible Fairy Tale

The Impossible Fairy Tale

A Novel

HAN YUJOO

Translated from the Korean by Janet Hong

Graywolf Press

This publication is made possible, in part, by the voters of Minnesota through a Minnesota State Arts Board Operating Support grant, thanks to a legislative appropriation from the arts and cultural heritage fund, and through grants from the National Endowment for the Arts and the Wells Fargo Foundation. Significant support has also been provided by Target, the McKnight Foundation, the Amazon Literary Partnership, and other generous contributions from foundations, corporations, and individuals. To these organizations and individuals we offer our heartfelt thanks.

The *Impossible Fairy Tale* is published under the support of Literature Translation Institute of Korea (LTI Korea). The translation was undertaken with the support of the PEN/Heim Translation Fund and a PEN Samples grant.

Published by Graywolf Press
250 Third Avenue North, Suite 600
Minneapolis, Minnesota 55401

www.graywolfpress.org

Published in the United States of America

ISBN 978-1-55597-766-5

2 4 6 8 9 7 5 3 1
First Graywolf Printing, 2017

Library of Congress Control Number: 2016938176

Cover design: Kapo Ng

Cover images: Shutterstock

Each of us carries the mark of all that has ever been written.

—Botho Strauss, "Scribbles"

Contents

The Impossible Fairy Tale

I

Dog.
See the dog.
See the dog drifting by.

2

See the dog, swimming, following the current of the river.

Perhaps the dog is doing nothing more than being swept down the river, but it looks as though it's swimming, as though it's following the current, heading toward the dam where two rivers meet. No, it looks as though it's being swept down the river. Since the dog cannot speak, no one knows how it ended up drifting in the current, and even if it were able to speak, bark, or cry, the noise would get swallowed up by the water, and silently, it would be washed away with the dog. The dog is black and large, but because its soaking wet hair is as black as black can be and its large body is mostly submerged, its blackness and largeness aren't immediately apparent. The dog is submerged in water, the water is moving, the dog is moving, and so the river is moving. The dog's name, the dog's age, the dog's sex, the dog's breed, and even the dog's language are unknown. The dog that is far, right now so far away, even if it had a language, even if it were a dog's language, there is no truth that can be known about the dog. It's a dog, just a dog. A dog that happens to be swimming.

The dog is swimming wordlessly.

All of a sudden shouts ring out from the riverbank where frost has yet to form. Three or four people are gathered there, shouting at the dog. Video cameras. Microphones. Reeds. Wind. Summer. Four in the afternoon. And a point just past that. No one knows why the cameras are there. A small, run-down boat moored across the river looks as though it's adrift. Before the dog is carried to the dam, before it's cast away, before the water meets the barrier, it must be scooped out. If it were winter right now, if there were a cold snap and the harsh days continued until the air froze, until the whole river froze, then the dog could simply slide across the top of the thick ice. No, if it were a dry season instead, if the dry days continued until the sand became dust, until the river dried up, until the bottom of the river creased and cracked like wrinkled lips, then the dog could simply walk across the bottom of the river, on its four legs, without leaving any paw prints behind.

The dog moves on.

The dog isn't interested in crossing the river, or it looks as though it's not, since it's not fighting the current and just continues downriver. On and on it goes, front paws, back paws side by side, paws crisscrossing, on and onward. Someone shouts its name, but it seems unreasonable to the dog to call its name in a language not its own, and so it doesn't respond, it doesn't look back, but stares straight ahead—no, somewhere a bit higher than that—and keeps swimming, with its head pointing above the surface of the water at a thirty-degree angle. The dog is swimming calmly, but who can know how calm it really is? The people standing on the riverbank begin to walk in the direction the dog is heading. Quickly or slowly. Only if the dog could walk on water, only if it could run on water . . . While someone shouts again, while someone anxiously calls its name again, while its name is on everyone's lips, it acts as though it can't hear anything, or it pretends it can't, and with the bottom half of its drooping ears submerged in water, it moves on and on, westward and westward. The dog that is just a dog will sink before it sinks. It's a strange way to put it, but there's no other suitable expression. When its blackness and largeness are no longer in anyone's sight, it will disappear. The dog and the river, the river and the dog.

The dog must cross the river. There are cameras waiting to record that moment—the moment it crosses from that side of the river to this side—and there are people standing safely among the reeds, not entrusting their bodies to the current, who are hoping, no, who had hoped it would cross the river. The reason someone was able to become the dog's owner was because he or she had given it a name, and as a result, he or she had told it to cross the river, or perhaps had commanded it to cross the river, and after fastening a metal collar around its neck, had pushed it into the water. Perhaps the weight of the collar will cause the dog to sink to the bottom of the river. Therefore the cameras standing by across the river will also have to sink. Therefore the dog's name and the dog's language will also sink. The spot where the dog should have landed has already disappeared from the dog's sight and is disappearing from everyone's sight. No one knows why the dog doesn't cross the river, why it doesn't cut across or sail across, or how it has come to drift with the current. The dog isn't crossing the river and the dog isn't swimming. The dog is drifting by.

See the dog drifting by.

The dog is there.

The dog is not there.

3

The child is lucky.

Before we talk about her good luck, because several other children will soon be entering the scene, we need to address the matter of her name. The child's name is Mia. It could be Min-a, Mi-na, or Min-ha, or it could be A-mi, Yu-mi, or Yun-mi, but since she thinks of herself as Mia, let's just call her Mia.

Mia is lucky. One day, she receives a set of seventy-two German watercolor pencils from one of the two men who consider her to be their daughter. Mia has two fathers. One is not yet aware of the other's existence, or pretends not to be, and the other is aware of the one's existence, but chooses to turn a blind eye for some unknown reason. When a person discovers a truth that no one else knows, every surrounding relationship will change drastically. Nevertheless, even though they both function as fathers to Mia, only one of the two had given her a set of seventy-two German watercolor pencils. Because these pencils were manufactured in Germany and were not cheap ones made in China, they satisfied her taste and interest, enabling the father who gave the gift to gain leverage over the other father. Red, fuchsia, crimson, blood red, rose, yellow, orange yellow, citron, tangerine, flesh color. And light green, emerald, forest green, grass green. With such an overwhelming array of colors spread before her, lucky Mia gains the innocent and childish confidence that she'll be able to draw every object around her with seventy-two colors. When Mia traces the outline of an object with a gray pencil, when she is coloring the skin of an object with a blue pencil, Mia's mother realizes that her daughter has become larger than her own shadow. Mia's mother loves Mia, and Mia was sick often, and each time she got sick, five shades of color would appear on her face—red, yellow, violet, green, and black—and Mia's mother made herself absent during her husband's absence. There would be a square of chocolate and a glass of orange juice by Mia's pillow, but not Mia's mother. Wet with sweat, in bed with a cold, Mia would rouse herself briefly to drink the orange juice and fall asleep again under the damp blanket. When her mother would return late at night and gaze down at her sleeping daughter, because Mia is lucky, she would stir awake and ask her mother for a glass of cold water. After this sequence was repeated several times, Mia's face would once again turn white as milk and smooth as a baby's bottom, but when Mia's face turned dark as water and red as fire, when she recognized vaguely that the scene she was witnessing was losing some unknowable thing, the colors of objects became unfixed and began to waver. Therefore the early morning would become dark-blue rage, the afternoon would become crimson resignation, the evening would become gray silence, and the colors would, all at once, turn dark as night. These things happen whenever Mia is sleeping, whenever she is opening her journal, whenever she is engrossed in watching television, whenever she is climbing a jungle gym, whenever she is being warned that she is too young to drink coffee, whenever she is passing a note to the student sitting in front of her. And whenever she distractedly looks away, the objects return to their original color in perfect order.

When I grow up, I'm going to buy a fountain pen, says Mia. Do you know you can kill someone with a fountain pen? she asks. I got that from a book. If you drop the pen from high up at the right angle, the pointy tip will pierce right into the person's head. It's because of acceleration. It was in a detective story.

But of course, Mia has no desire to kill anyone; in fact, she doesn't understand the words *death* or *kill*. She is a lucky child, and she lacks the passion, let alone the opportunity, to kill someone; she doesn't yet know that people kill even in the absence of emotions such as hatred. She doesn't yet know that rather than trying to aim the tip of a fountain pen at someone's skull from a tall building, it is far more effective to drive the pointed metal tip into someone's throat, a fact she would have learned if she had read more books. But she is interested only in detective novels, and because there are more things she doesn't know than she does know, her world is simple; and for that reason, she is lucky. Anyhow, I'm going to buy a fountain pen when I grow up, she says. I like the way it sounds. Fountain pen.

Mia, who more or less has everything, who was always told she could have anything she wanted, thinks she could construct her world exactly the way it is with seventy-two colors, that she could fill in the shadows of already existing objects, each with its own shade, that she could erase even the shadows, that she could perhaps kill a person. If she has the power to kill, she equally has the power to save. Therefore, nothing is impossible. Mia, who has everything, or could have everything, thinks she is able to do anything. Of the two of Mia's fathers Mia's mother alternates between, one father is unaware of the other's existence while the other father is aware of everyone's existence. Mia moistens her lips with the tip of her tongue. Because she doesn't yet have a clear understanding of acceleration, she has no concept of the speed at which an incident breaks down once it takes place, no concept of the velocity at which emotions expand once they begin to swell and, ultimately, explode. She remembers seeing on television a reenactment of how space came to be; the Big Bang, that beautiful, round thing like a wreath. She tried to draw the scene with seventy-two color pencils, but no matter how many lines she drew, there were always two colors missing and she, who had no concept of the colors she lacked, proudly showed her drawing to her fathers, and perhaps even to her mother, and one father thought Mia had drawn a flower bouquet and the other thought she had drawn the entrails of a beast. While she moistens the tip of her forefinger with saliva and erases the light's outline, the smear of colors and their shadows become submerged in darkness. Naturally.

It's not yet known if Mia will receive a set of 120 German-made color pencils next year, or a pair of leather shoes adorned with exquisite ribbons instead of a pair of running shoes illustrated with a cartoon character. She has two fathers, enough people to give her presents, and so the piano, silver bracelet, doll, fountain pen, wool coat, her bright, sunny room, and the large window with mold growing in its every crevice will remain hidden, overtaken by the shadows of all that she will receive. Not even the speed at which the white-blue-and-black mold is infiltrating the room will be seen, not yet. She can have everything, and because she is merely twelve years old, there is indeed time yet to have everything. She must always prepare for the future. Just like they say, she must become the main character of the next century. Because she is important to everyone, Mia's mother may take her as a hostage in court, one of the two fathers may use Mia to gain leverage over everyone else, and the other father may want to use her as an excuse to turn an affair into a nonaffair, but, apart from these, Mia is involved in an infinite number of scenarios, and until the number of all these scenarios becomes null, she must not die or disappear.

Soon the emotions that are being launched in Mia's blood vessels, eyes, mouth, joints, and bones will rise and fall simultaneously, but when? How? A thirteen-year-old Mia may want, as the other girls do, to cut her hair in a bob like that of a middle school student, or to go to school in Adidas running shoes. Bobbed hair, Adidas shoes, and things like this will be given to her easily enough. While her mother pulls back Mia's long hair in a ponytail, Mia grimaces, despite herself, and doesn't forget to mention that she wants a new sweater—the one hanging in a store window that had caught her eye the previous afternoon; the one she saw as she passed the shopping arcade on her way home from her after-school academy; the one with five different shades of green and five different shades of blue; the one with a small deer knitted on the chest. White psoriasis blooms around Mia's mouth while Mia's mother, who has now pulled Mia's hair in a tight knot, turns Mia around to place a kiss on her cheek. Mia's mother tells Mia that it will soon be spring, that there will be no need for sweaters; and because she's a growing girl, she won't be able to wear it for long anyway. She pleads with her mother. Her mother says no. Mia writes in her journal: Mother tied my hair too tightly. So my head hurt. Mia says, I'm going to ask Ageosshi to buy it for me, because it might be gone ten days from now, by the time Dad comes home. The sweater that is still hanging in the window, the sweater that is much too large to be a child's sweater, the sweater that Mia will get or will not get, will be blacked out from her memory in several weeks in any case, blacked out even if it's not black or red or yellow. Since there is no lack of substitutes and there is more than enough to substitute for even the substitutes, Mia could have anything, as long as there is time.

Mia pulls her left arm out of her sleeve and hides it under her pajama top. She sits at the breakfast table with the empty sleeve dangling from her still-flat chest when her mother asks, Now what are you supposed to be? Mia responds by saying, My arm disappeared. It ran away, because there's no deer sweater.

Toast, milk, and apples are on the table, but Mia's fathers are not there at the head of the table. My right arm says it's going to run away tomorrow, too, and my chest might run away the day after that, says Mia, who uses her right hand to spread jam on her toast.

Her mother stares blankly at her daughter. Though no one had ever taught her, Mia always knew how to wheedle and whine in a reasonable manner, to a reasonable extent. While nibbling on her toast

Mia says, My friend—and as she begins to plead again, Mia's mother throws away the empty plastic bread bag and recalls the phrase *phantom limb pain*, forgotten until now. Her chest sometimes hurts when she thinks of Mia. And yet, there is no lack of substitutes. There are even substitutes for substitutes. Mia's mother could have another child—it was still possible—and even if she didn't want another child, she could have a substitute thing instead of a child, but if a substitute wasn't possible, she could have something else, and if she could have something else, she could also lose something; and so Mia must not be allowed to want anything. The more we want, the more we lose. But she is still young, so she is more interested in the things she can have than the things she can lose.

My friend wanted a doll so bad that she didn't eat for two days, says Mia. You don't see me doing something like that.

In the end Mia gets the green-and-blue sweater with the deer, but it is unclear who buys it for her. What is certain is that she could not buy it for herself. Dad bought it for me, she says. Dad bought the sweater for me, she writes in her journal. I like it so much that I wore it to bed last night. Tuesday, March 3, 1998, the second day of school. Weather: Clear. On her desk is a neat stack of new textbooks and notebooks. Her mother wraps plastic over the cover of each textbook, still fresh with the smell of ink. Mia has two journals: one she's been using for a year and one that's new; one that conceals secrets and one where secrets are revealed. But she can't conceal, reveal, cover up, or even expose her secrets. Her writing is too immature. Mia, who is wearing an adult sweater, looks even smaller and more childish than usual, and since the sweater has no pockets, she can't hide anything—not a single hairpin, not a morsel of a secret, not a container of pencil lead. Because she hasn't yet menstruated, grown-ups say that there is enough time for her to grow taller.

That there is enough, enough time, still. Before the sweater begins to pill.

Mia's new desk mate at school twirls a mechanical pencil between her thumb and index finger. She draws a big heart in a corner of her notebook and says to Mia, If you can color the whole heart black with just one lead, the love of your dreams will come true. But your lead can't break until you're done and you can't have any lead left at the end. You can't run out either. Like her desk mate, Mia draws a pretty, round heart on the last page of her notebook with her new mechanical pencil and new lead. The two girls concentrate on coloring their hearts until the end of lunch, but their lead keeps breaking. Who are you thinking of anyway? The two girls giggle. How about you? And they each lower their gaze. When their lead breaks, they can't draw hearts on paper they've already used, so they must begin anew each time with a new heart on a new page with new lead, but the lead keeps breaking, and their minds get crushed by failure. The boys, who had gobbled their food so that they could play soccer for the rest of their short lunchtime, return from the playing field, emitting a faint smell of sweat. Mia and her desk partner hastily shut their notebooks and put their pencils back in their cases. Mia's legs fidget below her long sweater, and she clasps her hands, which peek out from her rolled-up sleeves.

After school is out, the children scatter in all four directions from the school gate toward the district 2-1, toward 3-12, toward Suite 303 of Building 109, toward Solar Arcade, toward the Cheongpa Institute, melting their shadows into the afternoon's. The pencil cases that hold containers of pencil lead rattle inside the backpacks of these twelve-year-old girls, girls who have just been allowed to use mechanical pencils. Mechanical pencils were thought to ruin penmanship, so they were encouraged, perhaps even forced, to use wooden pencils until the fourth grade, and although grown-ups said they could use pens once they were in middle school, it was no use, the children already had poor penmanship; whether they used pencils or pens or mechanical pencils, they would not have neat, fine handwriting until they were no longer children.

If you're going to write about love, write it in pencil.

The children didn't write their love and the grown-ups said their love wasn't right. As the children drew and filled in their hearts with thin pencil lead, they believed this was love, but the lead kept breaking, and at semester's end, there was not a single child who managed to complete a black heart, not one child who kept the notebook with her failed hearts. Things like notebooks tend to disappear in a moment, even if you don't purposely throw them away.

Mia's desk mate had transferred to this school the previous year. Her hair went down to her shoulders. She pinned it back with hairpins. In every class there are several girls with this same hairstyle. In Mia's class there are many Kims, Lees, Parks, Chois, Songs, Kangs, Shins, Hwangs, Chungs, and Yangs, but these children who sit in rows according to birthday or height, or who are perhaps arranged in alphabetical order, will soon have to rearrange themselves based on their biological classification: species, genus, family, order, class, phylum, and kingdom. The children are half-plant and half-animal. The high temperature for early March hovers around the freezing point, and wherever new greenery as thin as eyelashes sprouts up, winter dies. Nothing is born a second time. When the previous summer returns like a phantom, today's spring becomes ill and the seasons die out repeatedly. Wherever children die, other children are born. When this year passes, the next will come, and when next year passes, the year after that will come. When it's past noon, three or four street vendors selling chicks gather in front of the school gate, and inside the newspaper-lined plastic buckets, yellow chicks grow sick. Sometimes there are chicks whose napes are dyed red or blue. They still look healthy, but the moment they leave their plastic nests and are gripped by clumsy hands, they begin to die. To the vendors, it's not important whether the chicks are male or female—they simply happen to be one or the other. The chicks inside the buckets of these vendors will die well before they can develop secondary sexual characteristics, before they can assume their general functions, before they can reach puberty, before they can mate, before they can reproduce. This one here, is it a female? asks Mia's desk mate. In an indifferent tone, the vendor replies that it's a male. In front of the elementary school gate, the price of every object is relatively the same, and the price of a chick is the same price as an ice cream cone, and the same number of coins jingle inside the children's pockets. Some children buy ice cream and get white and yellow stains down the front of their shirts, and some children buy chicks and drop them one by one from the apartment's rooftop. Some hope the chicks will fly away, since they have wings after all, and some hope that the chicks will die, since they have life. The boys carrying soccer balls and basketballs under their arms shove Mia and her desk mate aside, and peer down at the chicks, but the chicks don't cry *cheep, cheep*. No, to be honest, the sound coming from their beaks, beaks the size of a pinky nail, can't possibly be written *cheep, cheep*. It can't be called crying either. Mia doesn't buy a chick, but this is perhaps a good choice because the moment she gains a chick, she will lose something, something that has the same value as the chick.

The boy who sits in the row next to Mia bought a chick. With her mechanical pencil, Mia writes in her journal: I didn't buy one because Mom doesn't like animals. I don't know the boy's name. I want a puppy, she adds. She closes her journal and returns her pencil to her flat, metal pencil case, decorated with strawberries and bunnies. Her mother has not come home yet. It is a clear day on Wednesday, March 4, 1998, and laid out on the four-person table is dinner for one: fried rice, kimchi, and water. Mia doesn't eat carrots, but this doesn't mean that she eats every kind of food that doesn't contain carrots. Her mother often forgets that she doesn't eat carrots and chops them into every dish. Carrots are slow to go bad. Mia isn't yet hungry, and that's because she and her desk mate bought a snack after school instead of buying a chick. It's not yet certain if Mia will lose something because she bought a snack; nevertheless, she has lost a chick, as well as three or four coins. It would be nice if she no longer lost anything, but she is a lucky girl, and the things that she has lost so far amount to less than her own weight.

Once, she had two ten-dollar bills given to her by an uncle who had returned from the United States. At the time, a ten-dollar bill was worth around 8,000 won, but when the economic crisis continued, the value of her two ten-dollar bills shot up to more than 20,000 won. You're the only person making any money in this house, her mother had said, half-jokingly in a voice that was also half-sigh. Her father was away at the time. When the official currency exchange rate was 1,887 won for every US dollar, she went to the bank and exchanged a ten-dollar bill and got 18,680 won back, but the price of buying money with money was different than selling or receiving money. If she had decided to exchange the money one week before, she would have been able to get two 10,000-won bills. Although it is uncertain where she used her 18,680 won, ten-won coins rolled under the bed or disappeared down the drain; and although the speed at which the bills disappeared might have been a little slow, nevertheless, all of it eventually disappeared. At that time, Mia had to listen to the daily nagging about her being a picky eater, and the reason was that if the whole country were to go to ruin, she might have to skip meals regularly like children in Africa. But even then, she refused to eat carrots and in the end her country escaped ruin. As was the case with Mia's family. While the children in Africa were being used in treacherous, manipulative misery, Mia's mother didn't skimp on the cost of carrots, and while carrots were served without end at the four-person table, Mia's father held firm his position by being resolutely absent. The fried rice is orange, yellow, and white. Carrots are good for your eyesight, her mother liked to say, but Mia thinks, What more am I supposed to see? Mia takes off her green-and-blue sweater and changes into her pajamas. The sweater is folded carefully and put into the closet. Soon she won't be able to wear it anymore. Perhaps the day will also come when she will not be able to wear the pajamas. She might grow twenty centimeters overnight, her mother might permanently forget to pick up the clothes she had left at the dry cleaner's, Mia might grow tired of her clothes, or another more extreme scenario might come to pass. A trivial mishap could set off a fire in Mia's home, Mia's mother could suddenly go missing, Mia could spontaneously decide to run away from home without taking any clothes, or Mia could suddenly die. None of these scenarios, in fact or in theory, is impossible. No one knows what might happen to Mia tomorrow. But the same goes for anyone. So why is it that we are continuing with Mia's story? Perhaps by chance, perhaps by necessity. Just like how the boy in Mia's class who had bought the chicks asked whether they were male or female and no one knew, no one knows if it was Father 1 or Father 2 who bought Mia's sweater, and even if someone knew, these are the kind of questions for which no evidence can be produced. In truth, no one knows the truth.

After Mia falls into a deep sleep her mother comes home, but even when she comes home, Mia's mother isn't there. Mia's name was made by combining a syllable in her father's name, *ah*, with a syllable found in her mother's, *me*. Around the time Mia was born, it was popular to name children by this formula, and her parents each explained to their parents that Mia's name meant "beautiful child." They didn't explain that it also meant "lost child." And, just as her parents had hoped, Mia was considered to be a beautiful child by both sets of grandparents, even though she doesn't see them anymore. Mia's maternal grandparents are now dead and Mia's mother isn't welcome in the home of Mia's paternal grandparents.

By chance, both of Mia's fathers' names contain the syllable *ah*, but she doesn't call them by their names, she calls them either "Dad" or "Ageosshi." However, whenever she talks about them to her friends or writes about them in her journal, whichever father it is, she calls both "Dad," and because her sensibility of what is appropriate or inappropriate has grown dull with time, Mia's mom reveals more and more to Mia, who, because she is still young, doesn't know anything. Or so her mom wants to believe. Some say that Mia is all grown up, and others say she is still a little girl, the ink of her name barely dry in the family register, but in reality, the entry for Mia's register must be amended. If you're going to make an entry in your family register, write it in pencil, because if you make a mistake, you can use an eraser to wipe it clean. Mia's mother sits at the table, eats the cold fried rice, and feels like laughing and crying at once. She could simplify and amend her own family register if Mia didn't exist, she could even justify her own absence, but because the only person who could be proved to exist in this home was Mia, and Mia alone must receive love, Mia's mother must maintain her position. All children must receive love. Mia's mother puts the empty dish in the sink, turns on the faucet, and rinses her mouth. The leftover words that she couldn't wash out, they stay and torment her.

Mia's desk mate borrows a yellow Post-it from the student sitting in front of her and takes out a marker from her pencil case. There is a tiny label on the end of the marker with the name of Mia's desk mate: Kim Inju, 5-3. Even a single label has a thickness like every other object and so Mia's desk mate must squeeze the lid onto the end of the marker, but as the label is pushed, the words Kim Inju, 5-3 become slightly wrinkled. With the marker, Inju writes on the Post-it: Phone Mom. She must call her mother at lunch. Why? The reason isn't important. Kim Inju took out the marker to write something because her name had to be revealed. Inju sticks the Post-it to the corner of her desk and glances around the classroom. Kim Injung sits like an island beside the teacher's desk, his desk set at a different angle from the others. He is absorbed in coloring. Inju cringes. Diagnosed with a mental disability, Kim Injung, who knows only two phrases, "Stupid" and "I'm not stupid," will be transferring to a special needs school instead of middle school. During class, instead of sitting at his desk, he plays alone at the back of the room, and because Kim Inju and Kim Injung are such similar-sounding names, belligerent boys bring up Injung every time they make fun of Inju. You're Injung's sister, aren't you? Or are you his wife? Or his girlfriend? More than the words *sister* or *wife*, Inju can't help but feel shamed by the word *girlfriend*. The teacher is not there, it is rest time, but the children don't rest. Mia has dozed off with her head on her desk. Inju gazes at the dark brown lock of hair that comes down past Mia's shoulders and at the small mole on Mia's neck that is easily missed if one isn't looking closely, and Inju has the sudden urge to poke that mole with something sharp. It occurs to Inju that it could be done with the tip of a compass, a mechanical pencil, a stationery knife, or the fountain pen that Mia was talking about earlier, but because this thought only flashes briefly before disappearing, there is no chance for it to be revealed to anyone. Not even to Inju— Inju who had the thought and who just as soon forgot it. And there isn't enough time here to reproach Inju for that original thought because immediately after the thought, the boy sitting in the next row begins to speak in a loud voice. I killed all four chicks I bought yesterday. I dropped one out the window, I put one in boiling water, I flushed one down the toilet, I left one on the bus, and even though I didn't kill it myself, it probably died anyway. Someone could have kicked it by accident or it could have been mistaken for trash and been swept up. At once, all eyes and ears turn to the triumphant boy. Most of the girls scream and the boys whistle and shout, these children who are half-plant, half-animal. Someone shouts, Hey, stop lying! Someone says, Hey, Park Yeongwu, are you joking? When Yeongwu shrugs and sits back in his seat, the bell rings. The noise gradually dies down. The front door of the classroom opens and the teacher walks in. On top of Yeongwu's desk is a social studies textbook. Social Studies, 5-3, Park Yeongwung. Yeongwu liked to add an *ng* to the last syllable of his name, making it Yeongwung. Hero. As though unaware of all the commotion, Mia sits up, rummages through her bag, and takes out her textbook and notebook. She looks as though she didn't hear what Yeongwu had just said, her gestures and expression don't contain a hint of surprise. She gazes sleepily at the chalkboard. The dark green board, sometimes called a blackboard, is the same color as the metal box that holds Mia's seventy-two color pencils. The seventy-two colors inside the dark green box shade Mia's childhood. Gray, ink black, lead. When the teacher starts writing on the board, chalk dust falls like dandruff, and Kim Injung, in the middle of stretching, stirs the dust adrift in the air with his arms. He doesn't copy what the teacher is writing on the board into his notebook; perhaps he has never written anything in his notebook. The children had discovered a day into the new school year that Kim Injung was someone they could bully, taunt, or pinch. After gazing up at the teacher with a dumbfounded expression, he stands up and begins to ring the bell on the teacher's desk. The children's ears perk up, and the teacher puts down the chalk and stands Kim Injung before him. The sound of the teacher smacking him on the cheek rings louder in the children's ears than the ringing bell. Mia's face turns red. The chalk dust turns Kim Injung's left cheek white. Chalk dust falls, white and perilous, on the teacher's trouser cuffs, on his indoor shoes. The children are watching.

4

On their way home, the children see the first butterfly of 1998. This white butterfly has made an early appearance, late in the afternoon, flying low over the weeds that have begun to sprout between the cracks in the pavement. The children know the name of the butterfly. It is called a cabbage white. They also know the expression for the way a butterfly flies. The cabbage white flutters. Some of the children even know the significance of a white butterfly that appears in early spring. Even though the cabbage white fluttering through the air symbolizes the white mourning clothes for the first death of spring, there aren't many children who have tried on mourning clothes. These children are not familiar with death. Most children still chase balls or marbles, things that don't move on their own, instead of small white butterflies. The butterfly leaves behind a small black shadow, as though marking a dot, on the side of the road, but both the butterfly and its shadow are difficult to capture. Anyhow, butterflies will soon disappear. Their motionless shadows, no longer wavering, will be left like fossils on cement or asphalt. But even if every last butterfly disappeared from the city, the signs that foreshadow death will remain. A cracked porcelain bowl, a stained pillowcase, a withered insect stain on the ceiling, a sock with a hole, a button that's come off a shirt, the formation of dew, embers that don't die, flowers in full bloom, delicate shoots, a stopped subway train, a found wallet, chalk dust, an ink stain, broken pencil lead, threadbare sweaters, a busted clock, lost wind, lake water, tap water, dogs, birds, mice, and night and day—they will play the role of the white butterfly in spring. The children will die. Like specimens. The children will be born. Like specimens. They will die, quickly or slowly. The death of those dying speeds up. Everything is either quick or slow, one or the other.

5

The Child's eyes resemble the eyes of a fish. She doesn't see Mia, who says she will buy a fountain pen when she grows up. The Child's eyes reflect nothing, reveal nothing. She doesn't see Mia saying to Inju, Do you know you can kill someone with a fountain pen? The Child's eyes capture neither background nor foreground. Neither lucky nor unlucky, the Child is simply luckless. Pain begins to pulse from under her fingernails. Her nails are cut so short that the tender flesh beneath the nail is exposed. Usually she forces the stinging, burning pain aside by creating greater pain. But she can't bite her nails. She stares blankly down at her desk. Because of the pain in her fingertips, it takes great effort to grip either ordinary pencil or mechanical pencil. Every time she's able to forget the pain for a moment, time numbs, turning scarlet. That specific time must not be called "back then" because that time isn't beautiful. And even if she were to think again, even if she were to try to think differently, that time isn't beautiful. That time. Time. Time's grime. During that time, even time itself is shrouded with gray dust.

In the future, the Child will not remember anything. No trace must be left. She feels as though someone is always behind her, watching. She must not catch their eye. The sound of the pipe doesn't reach her ears. There are times a car engine sounds beautiful. With the tip of her pencil, she blacks out the scribble she had made on her desk just a moment before. Her fingertips sting. She doesn't use a mechanical pencil. She wasn't given one. With a pencil, she writes badly. She wrote badly from the time she learned to write. What had she scribbled on her desk just now? No one knows. It was all blacked out. She thinks today's scribbles can become tomorrow's evidence. Plus she writes badly. She wishes she could be erased. But every time she tries to erase herself, she only grows darker. Every day, she grows darker. Enough for her body to gobble up her shadow. At school, she exists like a shadow. Or she has become a shadow and is absent.

Once during a spelling test, she wrote *knell* instead of *kneel*. This was three or four years ago. Since that day, she doesn't want to risk hearing the kneel of her mother's anger. She knells and waits for her mother's anger to fade. She must always knell and make herself very small, like a dust mote, a grain, some kind of vermin. But even though she must grow smaller, the Child has the habit of wearing several layers of clothing to make herself look bigger. When she wears multiple layers, she feels less pain. Even when she is alone, she can't remove all of her clothing, because when she removes a layer, and then another, clothes that are red and blue persist. She could not be erased or grow dark, just as she could not remove her clothes—these clothes that cannot be removed, clothes that will follow her to the grave. Every day her blood vessels grow transparent. Protective coloration. The Child hears Mia say, If you drop the pen from high up at the right angle, the pointy tip will pierce right into the person's head. Absentmindedly the Child thinks that rather than aiming the tip at someone's head from high up, jabbing it firmly into the throat is easier and far more effective. Not wanting to find or be found, the Child doesn't open her closed mouth. Nevertheless, she must find. She must be found.

Beginning on the first day of the new semester, March 2, 1998, it is the Child's turn to be the class monitor for one week. On the next day, March 3, 1998, she is the first to arrive at school; she goes to the superintendent's office and fetches the Grade 5, Section 3, classroom key. During the lunch break, she leaves her food in her desk and slips out of the school and goes to a locksmith shop. Ten minutes later two keys jingle inside the Child's pocket. When school is dismissed, she goes back to the office and hangs the original key on its hook. There are sixty keys in the key storage cabinet. It occurs to her suddenly that she needs two months. No. She corrects herself; she needs more than two months. Because she must exclude Sundays. Because she must be trapped at home on days off. But more than anything, one key is enough. If she can't have all the keys, it is better to have just one. The superintendent sees the Child, who is standing idly in front of the cabinet. You, come over here. The Child flinches. The superintendent draws near and hands her a carton of coffee-flavored milk. To a child. She takes the milk and mumbles, Thank you. As she slips past the school gate, she mutters: Thank you, bless you, excuse you, screw you, fuck you. Thank you, bless you, excuse you, screw you, fuck you. The children, who are skipping their after-school academies, mash up the dirt on the playing field, and steal the ball from one another, over and over again.

The Child heads to the stands. The field that had been frozen all winter long is sloughing off its skin. The field, following the children's intricate web of movement, will become miry, soon, like ulcerous gums. The wind is chilly and the sunlight is strong, but the Child can't feel any warmth. She sits in the stands for a moment, feeling the sunlight and chilly air. The spring wind bites her skin, but her skin doesn't hurt. All of a sudden, she thinks that she must either drink or discard the coffee milk. Before the thought becomes a compulsion, she needs to dispose of it. Thank you, bless you, excuse you, screw you, fuck you. The Child must not take the coffee milk home. Why? She has no idea why. She thinks she simply must not, that she must not take home what she happened to acquire, that what she happened to acquire must not be spotted by her mother. The Child places the coffee milk on the bleacher and gets to her feet. That pyramid-shaped carton casts a 3:30 p.m. shadow in the shape of a crushed pyramid, creating evidence that she is there at that moment. All of a sudden, she thinks she is in an extremely conspicuous spot. No one is watching her. No, her shadow finds her. She turns abruptly and scans her surroundings. No one is there. She slowly walks toward the school gate. She remembers that she never ate her lunch. She must not take her uneaten lunch home either. Because the rice, the soup, the side dishes, all of it might get hurled at the wall, or at her face. For no reason. But anyone can easily conjure up a pretext. The Child must discard or finish her uneaten lunch before going home. She can't devote too much time to this task. Although she long ago became skillful at generating excuses, it would be better for her to avoid situations that require them, when possible. If you can avoid it, avoid it. Even if you can't avoid it, you must avoid it. The Child can't tell if her stomach is aching with hunger or with pain. She has heartburn. She learned the expression from her mother earlier than most children her age. She learned many expressions earlier than children her age. Expressions children hardly ever use. But she couldn't own as many things as the other children. She simply owned a sufficient number of objects that could suitably hide shadows or scars. A nylon jumper and sweaters, socks and hats. And countless words. She knew how to shed tears, how to wail, how to whimper, how to cry and then laugh; she was sad, blue, melancholy, lonely, anxious, distressed, scared to death, terrified, horrified, appalled, petrified, miserable, ashamed, embarrassed, frightened, rattled, in pain, in unbearable pain, in unendurable pain, in unbelievable pain, in unacceptable pain, in enough pain to want to die. She doesn't dare ask why. Perhaps there is no reason for pain. Aside from pain, she learned to feel nothing else. Her eyes must erase, rather than reveal, what she feels.

A cat crouches under a car, parked beside a stone wall. The Child sees it. From many past encounters, she knows that the cat will dart off if approached suddenly. She meows like a cat. The black-

and-white cat glares at her in silence. She takes out her lunch from her bag. It glares at her without moving. She removes each lid and overturns the containers onto the road, lining up the hardened contents. White. Red. Black. It glares at her with frigid eyes. She replaces the lids on each container, stacks them up inside her bag, and backs away. Until she escapes the cat's eyes. The food freezes on the road. The Child must return home. Before she freezes. The time has come. But she forgot that she had to have used the spoon and chopsticks. The cat flashes its fangs. The spoon and chopsticks are polished clean, glinting inside the lunch pouch. Although the Child is used to being searched, interrogated, and tortured, being used to these things doesn't lessen the pain. She is simply used to the pain. She must confess or admit that she threw out her lunch, or she must lie and say she ate her lunch with her hands. Regardless of the words she'll utter, she must once more swallow the fact that she is in pain. The spoon and chopsticks will be used in a way that is outside their intended purpose. The Child will hurt, and because that time is approaching, she is in pain, already.

6

Right now Mia, with an expression that indicates she has no idea what is happening, is knelling, no, kneeling in the living room before her mother. Mia's mother is glaring at Mia and Mia is about to cry, no, tears are already welling up under her lids. Why did you make up stories about someone else? Mia has no idea what her mother is talking about, but she doesn't dare talk back, because it's very rare that her mother gets this angry. Mia's lips twitch as she tries to speak, and even though Mia tries hard not to cry, it's too late. Drops of fat, swollen tears plop. She's crying. It was always better to laugh than to cry, and every time she laughed, she gained something. But what about when she cried? Mia didn't have much to cry about. She doesn't know the right way to cry. There is no artifice in her tears. She doesn't know how to calculate sadness. At the very least, she doesn't cry intentionally. Her shoulders and knees shake as she tries to hold back her tears. Did you see him kill the chicks? Did you see it with your own eyes? Mia gazes up at her mother's face, wearing an expression that says she's been falsely accused, as though she's become a half mute. But unable to bear her mother's blank expression, she soon lets her head droop lifelessly.

Only moments before, Mia's mother had received a phone call from Park Yeongwu's mother, and moments before that, Park Yeongwu's mother had received a phone call from Kim Inju's mother. In this way, women with similar backgrounds, who had in common the fact that they had children in the same class, made or received phone calls, and while a certain story was relayed from one phone call to the next, from one voice to the next, Park Yeongwu was now rumored to have killed dozens of chicks, exhibiting a brutal violence rarely seen in children. He was said to have killed one by putting it in the microwave, another by burning it under a magnifying glass in the midday sun, another by putting it in a rice cooker, another by kicking it while wearing soccer shoes, another . . . and another . . . These stories of Park Yeongwu killing more chicks than the number of chicks that exist in the world began to spread rapidly among women in their late thirties to early forties, women who had just begun to recognize one another at PTA meetings, women who considered themselves to be middle-class and who assessed each other by glancing at one another's clothing. The very first one to relay the story of Park Yeongwu and the chicks to a mother with somewhat childish exaggeration was Kim Inju. But the story began to grow, and when questions about the origin of the story swelled to uncontrollable proportions and came back, and whenever phone calls came for Park Yeongwu's mother, who had unshakable faith in the son she had birthed, and whenever she herself made phone calls, spewing curses without consideration for who was on the other end of the line, Kim Inju, scared as a child could be, ended up saying that she had heard the story from Mia and that Park Yeongwu had said no such thing. Sickened by the sight of Mia sobbing wordlessly, Mia's mother goes to her daughter's room and begins knocking over objects at random. But as everyone knows, Mia doesn't have anything she must hide. Whether it be an object or memories that are entangled with the object, whether it be the past or the future, whether it's there or not, it is Mia's mother, rather than Mia, who has things to hide. No, there is one object that Mia has hidden; it is one of the two journals, which Mia's mother manages to find just then—that flat object stuck upside down in the corner of the desk. Mia is naive. She hasn't read stories like "The Purloined Letter," and she hasn't yet learned how secrets are found or not found. There is no one to teach her such things. Mia is lucky. Is she lucky? Mia doesn't yet know how to hide secrets, and so Mia may not have any secrets, and therefore Mia is lucky. Mia's mother finds the second journal and begins to riffle through the pages. Dad . . . sweater . . . chick . . . Inju's house . . . Dad . . . Mom . . . Parents who have birthed a child are able to kill it, and things like this happen because they think the child is their property; things like this happen whenever a child's overgrown secrets are found—secrets parents are unable to accept, unable to accept that a child they had borne holds secrets, that the child has overstepped its bounds.

Dad bought the sweater for me. I like it so much that I wore it to bed last night. Mia's mother flips through the journal. Dad bought the sweater for me. I like it so much . . . She suppresses the anger that's surging up and reads through each page. Not knowing whether the flush in her face is caused by a rush of rage or a certain shame, she lets her right hand, which had shot up as though she were going to strike someone, drop listlessly. I want a puppy. (I'm going to ask Dad to buy it for me.) Mom doesn't like animals. (I went to the aquarium with Mom and Dad. I saw a strange-looking fish. It was called a moray eel.) I had ice cream with Inju. I felt cold. (Dad gave me a stamp with my name engraved on it.) I went to the bank by myself and opened up an account. It was because Mom told me to save up my allowance. (Mom didn't come home. I was bored and scared.) I fried an egg today. I spilled the oil on the floor, so I had to clean it up with a rag. It was hard work. (Mom said I can't get my ears pierced.) Mom tied my hair too tightly, so my head hurt. (Dad called in the evening.) Mom said no. (Dad said yes.) I got in trouble with Mom. (Dad made me feel better.) There's a kid in my class who has a fountain pen. (Dad said only grown-ups can use fountain pens.) I told Mom that I wanted to cut my hair like a middle school student. (Dad said he would buy me a fountain pen when I grow up.) Mom said no. (I had a nightmare.) Mia's mother holds the journal upside down and gives it a shake. The sentences that had been harboring secrets, secrets that have not had a chance to bud, begin to fall on the desk, the floor, and the top of Mia's head. The chicks are dying. Dad bought me color pencils. Dad and I ate hamburgers together. Dad said he would wire money into my bank account. Dad drew me a picture. Dad said he would buy me a puppy, too.

Mia's mother would rather be denied, but she was already in denial, and Mia had two fathers, and so Mia could perhaps feel twice the denial that other children feel. For an instant, Mia's mother wishes that Mia wasn't the daughter she had borne, that her real daughter had been stillborn or kidnapped, that the child who was crying behind her had been switched without anyone's knowledge. But because Mia's forehead, Mia's lips, Mia's eyes, Mia's knuckles, and Mia's expression are all there and nothing is absent, their kinship cannot be denied. Not even for an instant. The child she could not desert, discard, disown, or disclaim is standing behind her. White psoriasis has bloomed around Mia's mouth. Mia didn't hear anything and she didn't say anything. But Mia's mother knows from experience that there are many people who have a lot to say, even though they don't hear or say anything. Without a conflict, there is no story. At the very least, there are people who think so, many people. Mia's mother thinks she is experiencing an unusual amount of conflict; these conflicts have gradually started to be revealed to the outside world, and once they penetrate everyone's ears, her face—her many faces—will sink and fall. It's chilling. Mia's mother puts down her daughter's journal and turns to look at the sniffling girl. Mia will probably stop crying soon, but Mia's mother senses that everything began to go wrong a long time ago, and that everything will continue to go wrong. Dolls, books, pencils, and color pencils are scattered all over the floor. Mia is growing and Mia's mother stopped growing a long time ago. Mia's crying subsides. Without a word, Mia's mother bends, kneels on the floor, and begins to pick up Mia's things, one by one. Mia goes to her mother and says in a whisper, Mommy, I didn't do it. Mommy.

7

Surprisingly, the key inside the Child's pocket might remain undetected. If she is interrogated as to why she is in possession of an unfamiliar key, she has rehearsed several answers: her homeroom teacher sent her to make an extra copy of the classroom key; the class monitor must keep the extra key; she found the key on the street. But the Child must first provide an excuse for something else. An excuse for why her spoon and chopsticks haven't been used when the lunch containers are completely empty; licked clean. And she does. She manages to invent an excuse on the spot. An excuse that is quite plausible. When she relays her few words, as clearly as she can, she is let off more easily than she expected. Nothing happens today. Not yet. When evening comes, she will be left alone at home. Then she will be able to breathe easy. But until then she must hide. She goes into her room, with her head bowed. But she must not bow her head too much, or raise her head too much. She must not tread too heavily, or too lightly. She must not draw too much attention; she must draw a moderate amount of attention. From the opposite room, she hears the ticking of the wall clock.

A wall clock also hangs in the Child's room. Next to her bed is an alarm clock. She can distinguish the busy ticking of the second hand of all the different clocks. Time is passing. She hopes that time will pass quickly, that time will burn out at the fastest possible speed. She is twelve years old; she stopped growing before she turned twelve. She has never gone hungry. But the grains of rice that she has forced down have not become blood and bone, no one knows where they went. The Child will grow no more. Probably. Her face has already fallen. To the bottom, to the pit. Her face sinks and falls, over and over again. The top corners of most of her books and notebooks are torn. She habitually eats paper. Without being aware of it, she tears the paper into little pieces and puts them in her mouth. Paper tastes like paper. She can't sense the taste of paper. Even though paper simply tastes like paper and only paper, she doesn't know how much of the tasteless paper scraps she has swallowed. All that is certain is that she has grown up on paper, and that she has already finished growing. The torn corners that are perilously missing give evidence to that end. That is probably why she sometimes looks like a paper doll. Like a paper doll, though she is half-plant or half-animal, with the face of an herbivore. But she isn't seen. No one sees her. The children don't know her name or they don't care to know it. She is crumpled up like a piece of paper. Her fingernails and toenails grow very slowly, but even before these slow-growing nails have a chance to grow out, they are cut short, so short the flesh underneath becomes exposed. She sometimes wishes that mice or ants would eat her nail clippings, just like in the old stories, and transform into her image, and then appear before her. The Child hopes that many children, many who look like her, will become her and take her place. She hopes that these children who appear in the old stories, in fairy tales, will wear her clothes for her. Then she would be able to hide herself. She would not have to grow darker. She would be able to disappear forever. She never cries. If she cries, crying becomes the reason she can't disappear, and if she doesn't cry, not crying becomes the reason she can't disappear. The reason why one scar buds on top of another. The Child, who had grown up floundering between these two states, ultimately forgets how to cry. She waits for the mice, for the ants. After setting aside everything that is beautiful, she waits for the mice and ants. Things that are beautiful are useless. You can't forget anything with them. You can't heal anything. The Child has never seen anything beautiful. She has never understood what people call "beautiful." While her nails are being painfully clipped, she opens her eyes wide and wordlessly accepts this punishment. The mice and ants flee and disappear before they can even come to her, as though the Child's hands are a trap. Her fingertips hurt so much that she can't write. In any case, she records nothing about herself. No trace must be left. She must disappear instantly, as though she has never existed, not even for an instant. She, too, writes in her journal. But she records nothing. Nothing about herself. Every time the journal is returned to her, she learns how to camouflage more and more words with other words. *Cheek* with *leaf, bruise* with *wind, blister* with *light breeze, fingernail* with *butterfly, curse* with *song, calf muscle* with *stick, tongue* with *ice cream, palm* with *moon, hair* with *stars, sigh* with *whistling, grip* with *tree branch, shoe heel* with *footprint, glass shard* with *sky, spine* with *dog, thigh* with *cat, stick* with *streetlight, crying* with *bird, pain* with *bright colors.* When I opened the window, a light breeze blew in. I wanted ice cream, so I went to the store. There was dew on the green leaves. I saw the yellow cat's family. It was strange that their eyes were green.

The Child's journal is filled with the most beautiful words; the mice and ants have been erased and are nowhere to be found. Nothing has been transformed and nothing looks familiar.

I looked up into the sky on my way home from the after-school academy and saw many stars. I could even identify some constellations. The moon was very large and very round. But it appeared more red than yellow. Because the sky was black, the stars were more visible. The constellations were scattered everywhere. I learned how to find the Big Dipper.

Every time the Child gets her journal back, there is the same comment. No concrete story. But she doesn't know how to write a concrete story. No, even if she knows how, she must not write that kind of story. Although there is no concreteness in her story, she herself is concrete. But most of all, what is concrete is her sense of pain. I saw a white butterfly. Butterflies don't leave any footprints. It seems that spring is here.

The Child could not write anything, but still, she must write something. Her inability to speak, her inability to write, paint her redder and bluer and yellower and darker.

The Child sticks her hand in her pocket and checks that the key is there. She hears the thud of the front door opening and shutting. She's been left alone. She slips out of her room and begins to inspect the apartment. As though checking to see if someone who's been watching her has really left, as though she couldn't be certain unless she checked. She opens the kitchen window and peers down at the parking lot. Soon a car with its headlights on pulls out of the parking lot. She whistles. No one is home. She is able to accept the fact only after she's checked every corner of the apartment, again and again. She must hurry. She doesn't have much time. She quickly puts on her jacket and running shoes, and steps out of the house with a flashlight. It is about a fifteen-minute walk to school. She runs. Her breathing grows heavy. She reaches the school gate and takes a minute to catch her breath. The flush fades from her face. She passes through the gate, wearing a dark face. She knows where the open window is. Before heading home that afternoon, she had carefully and unobtrusively left a hallway window open on the ground floor. She walks quietly toward the back of the building. In the distance, the field is sunk in twilight. All of a sudden, she is curious whether the coffee milk she left on the stands in the afternoon is still there. Also the food she had left in front of the cat—is it gone? She must hurry. She walks toward the window she had left open. She opens it. She hears metal slide over metal. She grabs the ledge with both hands and lifts herself up. She crawls over the windowsill. Her hands smell of metal. When she gets home, the first thing she must do is wash her hands. After climbing through the window, she lands softly on the floor. She tiptoes down the hall toward the stairs. She walks up. No one is there. On an ordinary evening in March, no one expects someone to sneak into the school. The teacher on duty is probably watching television in the warm night-duty room. The Child passes the second and third floor and continues up to the fourth. Her classroom is located in the middle of the fourth floor. She stands in front of the door to Grade 5, Section 3. She puts her hand in her pocket and touches the key. It's safe. She takes the key out of her pocket and before she pushes it into the keyhole, she scans the hallway once more. No one. It's dark. Even though the shaking of the thin wooden door echoes louder than the turning of the key, no one hears. She carefully opens the door. She slips into the classroom. She carefully closes the door.

The desks inside the classroom glare at her. The clock hanging on the wall glares at her. The organ placed at the front of the classroom glares at her. The chalkboard eraser placed on the ledge of the chalkboard glares at her. Kim Injung's desk, set at a different angle from the other desks, glares at her. The bell on the teacher's desk glares at her. The children who are not present glare at her. The teacher who isn't present glares at her. The timetable hanging beside the chalkboard glares at her. The Child looks blankly at the objects glaring at her. She approaches the teacher's desk. The attendance book, documents, and textbooks are piled neatly on top. The students' journals are stacked on the floor under the desk. The Child snatches a pencil sticking out from the teacher's pencil container, crawls under the desk, and turns on the flashlight. Her face becomes dappled from the light. Beyond the light is shadow. Her ears are turned toward the hall outside the door. Because her hearing was as good as an animal's, even if a mouse or ant should pass in the hall, she would probably be able to hear it. She picks up the journal on the top of the pile. With eyes that resemble the eyes of a fish, she spreads open the notebook. The flashlight shines on the child's bad handwriting.

I went to the market with Mom. I wanted to eat spicy rice cakes, so I asked her to buy me some, but she didn't. But she made them for me at home. I hope spring will come soon. I realized today that a sudden frost is harsh. (Spring doesn't come. Spring that doesn't come is passing. Spring is blue, yellow, red, black, white, and murky.)

I practiced the violin all day. The sheet music looked really easy at first, but it's much harder than I thought. The competition is coming up. My violin teacher said that my right hand is too tense. I have to practice again tomorrow right after school. (I don't want to play the violin. I want to throw it away. I don't like my violin teacher. I hate her. The bow is long. The body of the violin is hard.)

It rained a lot. All the other moms were waiting behind the school gate, but only my mom wasn't there. But I still waited for her at the gate. I was really cold. She didn't come, so I just walked home. Then I realized my mom has never come to meet me with an umbrella. I'll always carry my umbrella with me now. (It didn't rain yesterday. My mom will never come to meet me. An umbrella is hard. A broken umbrella is useless.)

I kicked a ball without realizing my shoelaces were untied and tripped. The field was hard, so I skinned my knees. My mom saw my ripped pants and got angry. She sewed up the holes. She said she wouldn't buy me new pants, because I was going to rip them again anyway. (The field isn't thawing. Mom will get angry again. Shoelaces hurt. A needle is pointy.)

A boy who sits in the next row bought a chick. I didn't buy one, because Mom doesn't like animals. I don't know the boy's name. I want a puppy. (The boy's name is Park Yeongwu. Park Yeongwu killed the chick.)

I want to kill a chick, too. (I want to kill, too.)

The Child uses the flashlight to read the children's journals and adds a few sentences to the end of their entries by imitating their bad handwriting. Most children don't have secrets. Or perhaps, most children don't know how to properly reveal or hide secrets. Or perhaps, the Child doesn't consider the things that children consider to be secrets as secrets. She puts the journals back in their proper place and crawls out from under the desk. She pictures the expressions on the children's faces when the journals are returned. She could have been a little more daring. She could have written sentences that were a little worse with her bad writing. But she doesn't have much time. The wall clock that is half-submerged in darkness indicates it is 8:15 p.m. Her pulse isn't used to running this fiercely. Her shadow, which objects have gobbled up, jolts fiercely, but without sound. She heaves a low breath. She doesn't have to rush. She has about five minutes to spare. No sound comes from beyond the classroom, but she must be careful. If she is found and the news reaches all the way home, she will probably have to endure pain that is incomparable to anything she has experienced until now. She might not be allowed to go to school. She already had many experiences of being locked up, and each time, her shadow seized her throat. Without thinking, she covers her throat with her hand.

Before switching off the flashlight, the Child inspects the classroom once more, and wipes the pencil she had been holding with the hem of her shirt. No trace must be left. In the future, the Child will remember nothing. The sound of the pipe will not reach her ears. The mouse will not appear. Even if it were to appear, it will not appear in the image of the Child. Nothing can take her place. The Child will simply, just as she always has, disappear without a word, without a sound, without a trace. She must wait for that time. That time. Time's grime. The Child goes back home, retracing in reverse the steps that had brought her to the school. There is no one at the gate. The streetlights that dot the alley leading to the distant main road are lit. All of a sudden, she wonders if the cat ate her lunch for her, but she thinks it's better to hurry home, rather than waste time on something like that. It probably ate her lunch for her, and would have grown for her by a corresponding amount. The coffee milk would have now turned to ice in the shape of a pyramid. Except for that, nothing has happened. Not yet. The Child will cause more things to happen. More things than what has happened to her so far. And yet, she probably won't catch anyone's eye. She must believe that. She must not catch anyone's eye. Her dark face slips out of the alley. Her shadow urges her on. She begins to run. Toward home.

8

The children are choking one another at the back of the classroom. They call this "the fainting game," but because they are given only a ten-minute break, no child has actually fainted yet. Ten minutes isn't enough time for a victim to step forward. Plus the homeroom teacher rarely leaves the room at recess. The children wait only for him to leave. More incidents than one can imagine occur at the back of the classroom. All kinds of fun things. The children exchange meaningful, significant looks, but there is neither meaning nor significance here. They merely want to see someone collapse. They merely tear the wings off butterflies, they merely kill chicks. Without meaning or significance. They merely choke one another for fun. And they call this "the fainting game."

Inju hands Mia a pen. It's a pink pen, filled with pink-colored ink. Mia's face is still a little puffy. Mia removes the lid and sniffs. Inju is sorry, but she hides what she feels. She thinks she could make amends with a single pen. It's possible, of course. Can I have it? Mia asks. Sure, I have two anyway, Inju answers. Mia asks nothing else, because she doesn't know Inju was the cause of yesterday's incident. Inju won't say anything to Mia, and what Mia doesn't know today she won't know tomorrow. Mia is lucky . . . Once again, Mia's mother has tied Mia's hair back too tightly. Mia wants to cut her hair in a bob like a middle school student. She wants to wear thin nylon stockings like a middle school student, not thick tights. She wants to wear a uniform of starched shirt and plaid skirt like a middle school student, not a child's dress with lace and frills. She wants to wear a tie and

Adidas running shoes like a middle school student. These things have not yet been given to her. The time for these things has not yet come. Mia must wait two more years. Two years later, Mia will want to grow her hair long and wear knee-high socks and curl her lashes like a high school student. These things also have not yet been given to her. The time for these things has not come, not yet. Mia must wait. It's not yet certain whether Mia, who has gotten a pink pen today, will lose something tomorrow. It could be said that so far she has merely lost yesterday's journal. All she has lost so far is yesterday's journal.

A girl in the back makes a choking sound. She gasps. Her face grows pale and she falls forward. The children buzz. Buzzing, they crowd around the collapsed girl. The Child, who had been cleaning the chalkboard, looks at the girl splayed out on the floor. But the Child can't see, because the children's shoulders are blocking her view. Her hands, white with chalk, still smell faintly of metal. Even though she had washed them for a long time. Looking shocked, Mia and Inju also get up from their seats. Everyone steps toward the girl on the floor. Everyone except Injung and the Child. Someone shakes the collapsed girl's shoulder, but she doesn't respond and continues to lie limply on the floor. However, when someone offers to get the teacher, the girl bolts up right away. The game is over. Looking embarrassed, she returns to her seat. The other children return to their seats, looking both relieved and disappointed. Their breathing goes back to normal. Mia goes back to her seat as well. Mia is wearing a white headband with a bow on it. For an instant, the Child sees that white thing. I want to kill a chick, too. I want to kill, too. The Child knows that Mia's name is Mia. Mia doesn't seem to know the Child's name or she doesn't care. It will soon be Mia's turn to be the class monitor for a week, and her hands will also become white and streaked with chalk. Before spring ends. Mia's hands are fairly white, but they will become completely white, even whiter, and she'll be able to have hands that are whiter than white.

Do you want to come over to see my puppy? Inju asks Mia. Can I? Mia says. That day, friendship that is the size of a pen buds between Mia and Inju. They will soon forget about yesterday's event. The Child doesn't look at Mia and Inju. She can't grip chalk or pen because of the pain in her fingertips. Still, she must write something. Sentences that are not hers. She hears Mia and Inju whispering. I want to kill a chick, too. I want to kill, too. For an instant, the Child isn't sure what she wrote in Mia's journal. I want to kill, too. I want to kill, too. The Child brushes the chalk dust from her clothes. Every time her black clothes get covered with white streaks, her hands grow darker. At that moment, Injung, sitting at his desk that was placed beside the teacher's desk well away from the other children, holds out a piece of tissue toward her. For an instant, shock spreads over her face. Injung flaps it at her. His eyes resemble the eyes of a fish. His eyes resemble the eyes of an animal. He raises his black eyes and looks at her. She thinks she has seen those eyes before. They reveal no emotion. Perhaps they contain no emotion. Without thinking, she takes the tissue from him and returns to her seat. The chalkboard is wiped clean. There isn't even a smudge of chalk. The Child wipes her white hands with the white tissue. Her hands grow darker and darker until they are transparent. Her face is still as dark as ever. Injung is gazing blankly at her. She avoids his gaze. With her dark face, she turns and sneaks a look at Mia. Mia doesn't look at the Child. The white bow on Mia's headband flutters. It flaps up and down. The bell rings. The Child turns around. All of a sudden, she thinks of Mia's last sentence. She has forgotten all the other children's last sentences. She thinks of Mia and Mia's last sentence. Mia must look at the Child. Mia will soon look at her. She will look, even if she doesn't want to look. Mia is lucky . . . We must continue with Mia's story. Look at Mia.

9

Everything sinks. The children go home, stomping on flower petals. Flowers wither. Spring doesn't retreat until it has killed the last flower. The hunger of spring is desperate and murderous. The children don't know the names of many flowers. Yellow, pink, white. The children pass through them on their way home, but their futures will have a different hue. Their futures that are neither red nor yellow are standing by somewhere beyond their gazes. The road in front of the school gate splits into three paths. A forked road always symbolizes the future. Most of the children walk home past the hospital's back gate. The school is situated on top of a big hill, and the hospital is on top of a small hill. Sometimes children dash into the road to retrieve a ball that has rolled down the hill. They come to a stop. The emergency room and morgue. The parents failed to move the hospital entrance somewhere beyond their children's gazes. But they needn't fret so much. Because the children will inevitably pass through these places one day.

Mia and Inju head toward Mia's home. A certain Wednesday in April 1998. According to Mia's schedule, she had language arts, mathematics, social studies, and biology that day. On days when there were no afternoon classes, the children tossed their unopened milk cartons on patches of sunlight, milk flowed and splattered, and with every step they left behind dirty, white stains. The pencil cases in Mia's and Inju's backpacks contain identical pens of the same brand. The sound of pens clattering inside the pencil cases can barely be heard, buried by the din of traffic and the wind caused by atmospheric instability. At the end of class, Mia and Inju wrote the date of their field trip next month in their agendas. May 12. There's a month left still, mutters Inju. A month is an extremely long time to Mia, Inju, and other children their age. In one month, some will grow taller, some will learn curse words, and some will break their legs. Some will play soccer, some will kill chicks. Some will tell lies. And some will . . . and some will . . . and some . . . and something new every day . . . something new . . .

And then there are the tests we have to take, grumbles Mia. The two girls let out a sigh at almost the same time. Their shoulders tremble in a somewhat exaggerated fashion, but this practically goes unnoticed, hidden by their backpacks. My mom told me to come home early, Inju says. You can always call her later, Mia says. Inju's grandmother is ill. Inju thinks about her grandmother for a moment. More specifically, she thinks about her grandmother's lump of greenish stool. That happened this morning, but it also happened yesterday, and will happen tomorrow as well. Inju's grandmother whose mind comes and goes often forgets to flush the toilet. Her grandmother holds her head up like a bird, large, baggy clothing always covering her small, thin frame. Set in her face are many black stones. Inju has never once thought, You could play Gomoku if there were white stones too. It was Mia who has had this thought. Many times Inju has heard her parents talk about her grandmother. Maybe a year, maybe two. Inju's mother sighed. Inju realizes that her grandmother doesn't have many years left. But whether it's one or two years, it seems like a very long time to Inju. The only thing Inju's grandmother has relinquished is her grip on sanity. Every single cell that composes her body still has a tenacious grip on life. Inju doesn't know or care about every desperate effort her grandmother makes to get to the bathroom to relieve herself. When Inju turns eighty, she will naturally lose her memories of being twelve years old. Often her grandmother rummages through Inju's schoolbag and takes new notebooks or nice pens and pencils. This is how Inju's grandmother tries to replenish what has been erased from her life, while Inju's father puts money in Inju's hand without his wife's knowledge so that she can pick out whatever notebooks, pens, and pencils she wants. Perhaps a year, perhaps two. Inju's grandmother was born in 1919. It's a mysterious number to Inju. Perhaps even to Inju's father. Perhaps even to Inju's mother. Mia doesn't have a grandmother. No, Mia's mother no longer takes Mia to see her grandmother. Mia thinks Inju is lucky. I haven't seen my grandmother for a long time, Mia says. I wish someone would take mine, says Inju. Mia glances at Inju. I'm just joking, Inju says. All of a sudden, Inju recalls how her grandmother had secretly turned on the stove and peered into the blue flame as though possessed. Inju's mother had run out and turned off the stove, with her face deathly pale and hand raised high as though to strike Inju's grandmother. Shocked, Inju screamed. The dog who had been sleeping under the couch dashed out and began to bark, and Inju's grandmother copied the dog, baring her teeth and barking like a dog. There are bite marks on that day's expressions. The expressions suffer from the wind. One day when Inju is a grown-up, she will recall that day.

Inju wants to talk to Mia about her grandmother. About her curled fingernails, her wrinkled earlobes, and her loose greenish stool. And about herself, who must, every day, look at ugly, dirty, filthy things. At vile, ancient things. My grandmother is . . . Inju struggles to find the proper word to describe her grandmother. *Pitiful* isn't exactly the right word to describe her. Neither is *pathetic*. And it seems wretched for a child to call a grown-up *wretched*. My grandmother is . . . , says Inju, who finds, just in time, what she considers to be a suitably grown-up phrase . . . She's in poor shape. Mia cocks her head. And the two children forget for a moment what it means to be in poor shape.

Mia and Inju enter the apartment complex through a side gate.

The roses have not yet budded. There is no one inside the security booth. Blooming dandelions and pansies fill the flower bed. Yellow and purple. Several days later, into this very flower bed, onto the flowers and soft grass, two middle school girls will plunge. The flowers and grass are soft enough to break the necks of the girls at once; they are cozy, like the grave. Yellow, purple, and green ram into and pry open the girls' clasped fingers. But this hasn't happened. Not yet.

Mia and Inju head toward Mia's home. Mia has been to Inju's home several times and she's even patted Inju's dog, but this is the first time the reverse has occurred. Building 110, Suite 904. Mia takes out a bunch of keys from the front pocket of her backpack. Mia's mother is not there. Mia's father is also not there, but this has nothing to do with the couple's fundamental relationship and is simply a coincidence. Inju, who is setting foot in Mia's home for the first time, sits primly on the sofa that faces the small, dark living room wall, and looks somewhat awkward, disguised as a polite guest. Mia heads straight for the refrigerator, gulps water right from the bottle, and then calls out to ask Inju whether she would like something to drink. On top of the table, a meal for one is already set. There is no note. Inju begins to straighten the books scattered on the coffee table and discovers *The Biography of Diana*. Strewn below the face of the woman who had once been the princess of the British Empire are several cheap, worn books with titles like *The Diamond of the Moon* and *A Grand Expedition into the Earth*, and on the covers of these books are stickers that read "4-2 Classroom Library." While Inju leafs through the pages, Mia, who has brought a cup of cold water, says in a small voice that contains a hint of laughter, I stole those, you know. White psoriasis has bloomed around Mia's mouth. Inju knows instinctively that she shouldn't criticize or condone Mia's behavior, but because of the morals shaped by her sloppy education and because of the friendship that has just begun to bud between the two girls, she doesn't know what expression she should wear. Inju only shuts her mouth and, in doing so, becomes Mia's accomplice. Mia heads toward the balcony and draws back the curtains. Thick sunlight cascades onto the floor. Inju glances again at the woman with the golden hair. Mia, who has come close to Inju, says, Isn't she pretty? My mom says she was the princess of England. Mia turns on the television. On the cartoon channel, the last episode of *Galaxy Express 999* is on. A planet is being destroyed. It collapses. Everything is collapsing. It collapses. It's collapsing. The citizens of the planet that is being destroyed say over and over again, as though they're singing a round, that everything is collapsing. It collapses. It's collapsing. While they panic, the buildings sink and the roads twist apart. There is no way to save them. The planet's queen no longer possesses the means to revive her planet, despite the fact that it is her machine body. The planet will remain extinct, until the very last trace testifying that this planet once existed disappears, until no one remembers the word *fate* anymore. It collapses. It's collapsing. It has collapsed. It cannot be said that everything has collapsed. Because after everything has collapsed, anyone who could have used the past tense would not exist. Because anyone who could remember the past, or anyone who could recall the past, or perhaps even the word *past*—none would exist. One day when Inju is a grown-up, the last words of this old anime film that had aired long ago will come alive once more inside Inju's head. It's collapsing, everything, everything is collapsing.

This is boring, Mia says. Inju wants to see Mia's room, but Mia doesn't offer to show Inju her room. Mia opens the door to the master bedroom. Let's play inside my mom's room, says Mia. A commercial for an insurance company appears on the television screen. Does your old age welcome you? Mia and Inju's old age is neither welcoming nor unwelcoming. Nothing is certain. Not yet.

10

The Child straightens her slumped back. On her desk, a small cal-
endar, pencil holder, pencils, textbooks, notebooks, and a few memo
slips are neatly arranged, and on the surface where the Child's arm
that's supporting her chin rests is a long, sharp scratch. It has the
same look and shape as the marks on her back and shoulders. The
same depth. The Child is neither lucky nor unlucky. She is simply
luckless. She crawls under her desk and carefully collects the dust
with her hands. Her dark hands turn ashen. Ash. No trace must be
left. Dust is bad. Dust leaves footprints. Pens are bad, too. Letters
written in pen cannot be erased. Rain is good. Rain erases footprints. The sound of the rain erases the sound of crying. Wind and
rain erase memories. The Child lets the dust that has pooled in her
hand drift into the trash can. She suddenly looks back. No one is
there. But she still feels uneasy. The dust she has shed now takes
her place on the chair. Dust casts no shadow. The Child flinches,
but the movement is unreasonably quiet, too quiet to disturb the
air. The Child looks like some kind of vermin. But not in the usual
way one might use the word to describe someone; the Child knows
how to make her body small and flat, like a cockroach. The Child
is neither erased nor transparent. The Child alienates herself from
the marks, traces, and stains. For no reason. Everything has a reason, but the reason the traces—left on her body as stains—have
not been erased, even by the rain, has not been spoken. Even as she
cries, she must not cry. Even as she speaks, she must not speak. It is
impossible to describe the Child's expression or voice. Every second

as she twists apart and collapses, she merely maintains the smallest shape. Despite how many times something has collapsed, it is always possible to collapse again. Until now. Inside a fairy-tale world, everything is already determined and everything is already given. There is no need for the main character to wait. Every time the main character puts out her hand, whatever is needed is put into it. But the Child must wait. She doesn't yet know the word *silence*. Her closed mouth, her veiled eyes, these words testify that the word *silence* exists somewhere. White psoriasis blooms around the Child's mouth. It is milky and murky like pollen. The Child scratches her back. When she's not looking, dark crusts of dried blood fall from her back.

11

The children's journals are on top of the teacher's desk. The children whisper among themselves. The sentences they could not and cannot write are on the teacher's desk. The potted plants on the windowsill complain of hunger and thirst. Small, yellow leaves hang from limp, feeble stems. The teacher is silent as he gazes down at the children. The bell on top of his desk has been removed. And Kim Injung, who sits beside the teacher's desk, has not been removed. Kim Injung doesn't write in his journal, or at the very least, he doesn't turn it in. In every one of the children's journals, except for Kim Injung's, sentences have been added. (I despise you.) But no one, not one, admits to doing (or committing) such a thing, and no one, not one, admits when that thing was done (or executed). Looking perplexed, the teacher interrogates the children in silence. (I hate you.) His dilemma is that he can't even understand what has happened here. (An umbrella is hard.) No one is missing anything, no one has stolen anything belonging to anyone else, no one has hit anyone, no one has tricked anyone. (A needle is pointy.) The children sit in their seats with downcast eyes, looking as though the situation is unfair. The teacher scrutinizes each child's face. (A fire is hot.) A black stain marks the floor in the middle of the classroom where a furnace has just been removed. (A long and hard thing.) He thinks this incident is a first. His platform and desk have been in the same spot for more than twenty years. Incidents and accidents both big and small have occurred here, and some children have developed, some have fallen ill, and some have died, but these things have always happened within the radius of his expectations. (It hurts.) Most of the children have bad handwriting. Their penmanship is not yet polished. Most of the children don't have secrets, but even if they did, their secrets would be quickly discovered. The children submit their journals once a week, and when the journals come back with short comments, the children either read or don't read the red letters that cling to the pages—the superficial comments about their thoughts or actions—and soon forget about them. (It hurts so much I can hardly bear it.) The children don't know exactly why they must keep journals. They don't even know exactly why their journals are checked. (I want to kill, too.) The children sit with vacant eyes. This incident will not take a long time. Perhaps in thirty minutes or an hour at the most, the children will head home, choke one another in some obscure location, or kick a ball around the field.

Everyone, close your eyes, the teacher says. The children obediently close their eyes or perhaps pretend to close their eyes. Who did this? he asks. The children's pulses speed up simultaneously, but no one moves. Who did this and why? he asks again. When? But not a single child responds. (I despise you.) (I hate you.) (I want to kill.) We may just have to go to the police station together, so you better raise your hand now, he demands. The Child flinches, but so do the other children. Mia is on the verge of whispering something to Inju, but she doesn't. Inju squints at Mia. The Child is sitting in the aisle next to Mia and Inju. From where the Child is sitting, she can't see Mia's or Inju's face. (I want to kill, too.) The Child's dark hands smell faintly of metal. No trace must be left. In the last month, after it had grown dark, the Child had carefully snuck into the classroom three or four times. She could have been more daring. She could have erased all the sentences in the journals and replaced them with her own. She could have imitated their bad penmanship. But there wasn't enough time. (It hurts.)

The Child isn't discovered. She must not be discovered. Not yet. The Child must grow a little more, before the pain that is left in her back, her thighs, and her shoulders covers itself with a crustacean shell. The Child must cast off her skin. The teacher senses that no child will come forward. In the end, the incident itself isn't that serious. But it angers him. Who, what, when, where, why, how. In every language arts class, he stressed the five Ws and one H. Writing must be clear and concise. The meaning must be understood immediately. All that is certain in this case is the sentences that have been plastered into each journal. (I hate Mom.) (I despise Teacher.) (Long, hard things are all bad.) (Bad things are painful.) (Painful things are bad.) The teacher glares at the children whose eyes are shut. Thursday, April 1998. Who, what, when, where, why, how. The incident angers him. But he can't keep interrogating the children. He can't hit or punish them either. There is only one item that is certain out of the five Ws and one H: what. But until now, *what* has always been the problem. What? A chick. What? A wallet. What? A desk mate. What? An eraser. What? Homework. What? A watch. But this time, nothing is missing, nothing has gone missing. Only the sentences with no source and no clear meaning remain. The teacher has no real reason to detain the children. Several of them begin to cry. The time to slip out of the school has passed. Most of the children will be able to tell the truth at home or at their after-school academies. This is what happened at school. We don't know who did it. I didn't do it. The teacher got angry and wouldn't let us go, that's why I'm late. But the Child must come up with another excuse. The Child, like other children, could possibly tell the truth. But what truth? The only thing the Child can tell is the outcome. And it's better not to say the possible outcome. If you can avoid it, avoid it. Even if you can't avoid it, you must avoid it. The owner of the sentences that have ruined the journals will not be discovered.

You've heard of a lie detector, haven't you? says the teacher. If you don't want to take a trip to the police station and get interrogated, you better come forward by next Monday. Interrogation. The children's hearts sink. The trivial lies they've spewed carelessly until now come to life in their heads. The children quickly grow unhappy. More children begin to cry. The crying spreads. Kim Injung, who is in his seat and has no idea why they're being detained, bursts into tears. A light breeze blows in through the half-open window at the back of the classroom. With eyes tightly closed, all Mia thinks about is going home. Her journal also contains one of the Child's sentences. I want to kill, too. Mia is wearing the sweater with the deer knitted on the chest. (Dad bought it for me.) Mia wipes her eyes with her too-long sleeves. Inju taps her foot nervously. Interrogation. Integration. Degradation. Decimation. The Child mumbles. *Interrogation* is a bad word. It brings other uncomfortable words to mind. The children cry louder. Exhausted, the teacher shakes his head. Open your eyes, he says. Journal, journey, the Child mumbles. The Child, too, has a desk mate. But the desk mate is so overjoyed that they're allowed to open their eyes that she doesn't hear the Child's low, quiet voice. Kim, Lee, Park, Choi, Chang, Kwon, Moon, Kang, An, Shin, Yoon, Na, Yang, Hwang, Hong. The children who have stopped crying begin to pack up their things noisily. They busily reclaim their happiness. With his index finger, Kim Injung smears the tears that have dripped on his desk. Mia and Inju let out a sigh. The children will forget about today's incident. At least until next week. The Child looks both anxious and relieved, but no one, not one person, is looking at her face.

12

For some time, the Child sits hunched over in a corner of the bleachers facing the school field. Since she's already late, it might be okay to be a little later. The field is quiet. The ice on the field has melted and disappeared. In the distance, beyond the magnolia trees, two children are hanging upside down from the chin-up bar. Without thinking, she slips her hand inside her pocket. *Clack.* Her hand touches the cold key. She must throw it away. Because it's becoming more and more difficult to hide it. The air is dry. She becomes a part of the arid landscape and wonders where she might hide the key. She didn't think she wouldn't be discovered. However, she hasn't been completely discovered either. She can't find a suitable place to hide the key. If she can't hide it, she must throw it away. She stands up. She can no longer see the children hanging from the bar. Perhaps the magnolia trees, perhaps the wind, is blocking her view. Anyhow, she doesn't see the children. She quietly heads toward the school gate.

The road in front of the school gate splits into three paths. A car is parked in front of the stationery store. She notices something move under the car. It's a cat. She crouches down and peers under the car. The cat glares at her with yellow eyes. The Child meows like a cat. Without budging, it glares at her. She does the same. She goes on meowing like a cat. The black-and-white cat cocks its head and slips out from under the car, hiding from her. She stands up. The key inside her pocket emits the smell of metal. Faintly. Her face crumples.

As she heads home once again, she runs through the possible excuses one by one. Devoid of children, the alley is quiet. She walks past the glass shop and the hardware store. The shutters are lowered at the wallpaper and linoleum store. The sand and small rocks that are scattered on the concrete path crunch under her feet. One, two, three, she counts. The marks on her neck and the left side of her back from three days ago are still there. One, two, three. Three days later there may be new marks on her neck and the right side of her back. Mark, bark, dark, stark, she mumbles. She doesn't mumble, It hurts, it hurts. *Scar* is bad. Because *scar* looks like *scare*. *Ash* is bad, too. Because it rhymes with *slash*, *crash*, *mash*, and *gash*. Women with black purses squeezed at their sides pass by, casting disinterested looks at her. She mutters, even as she passes the supermarket and hair salon. There are people inside every shop, but there's no one inside at night, she thinks. I wish there was a place that kept its lights on even at night. In the middle of the night and early in the morning. *Hair* is all right. Because *hair* rhymes with *bear*. Mama bear, Papa bear, and Baby bear. The Child doesn't sing. *Legs* and *hips* are bad. Because they rhyme with *begs* and *whips*. *Fingers* and *toes* are just as bad. There aren't many good words. The best word is *eye*. Because it's the same even when you read it backward, and it sounds exactly the same as *I*. But maybe it's not good after all, because it rhymes with *die*. But *die* has more than one meaning. And there's also *dye*. I throw a die. I swallow dye. I die.

The Child swerves into the left alley. Because the earth is round, if she kept going, even backward, in the opposite direction from her home, around the earth, she would be back home. It would be nice if it took forever to go home, then she wouldn't have to go home, ever. Time. Chime. The Child can't escape from home. Her mechanical feelers must stretch toward home. Her gaze, which had been sweeping over the shopping arcade's three-story, rectangular structure, suddenly falls on the shrubs beside the security booth. The stalks shake. Something is moving. She peeks inside the booth, but it's empty. Slowly she approaches the shrubs. There is a kitten between the overgrown weeds. Their eyes meet.

The small kitten meows at the Child. She moves slowly toward it. Hi, Kitty, Kitty, she says. Here, Kitty, Kitty, I won't bite. It arches its back. But it doesn't seem especially wary. The Child's running shoes crush the grass. Slowly she bends her knees while keeping her eyes on it. Here, Kitty, Kitty. The striped kitten moves toward her. You must be hungry, she says. It fixes its yellow-green eyes on her. Carefully, she brings her backpack around to her chest and takes out her half-empty bento box. It watches her without moving. Inside one of the side dish compartments is some leftover spicy dried squid. She picks some up with her fingers and holds it out. The kitten backs away for a moment and then returns and begins to lick her fingers. Eat it, even if it's spicy, she says. It begins to greedily devour this unexpected meal. Carefully, she stretches out her other hand and begins to pet it. Its spine is hard and narrow. She slowly strokes its spine. Nice Kitty, she says. Nice Kitty, pretty Kitty.

All of a sudden, the kitten's small, sharp incisor pierces the Child's finger. She flinches. But it clings to her hand, as though planning to chew and swallow the finger, as well as the squid. She snatches her hand away. The kitten, dangling from her hand like a crescent moon, flops to the ground. In the middle of her thumb is a small, round hole. Blood wells up from this hole that's like an inverted cone. The kitten looks up at the Child with pretty eyes as though it has no idea why the Child has snatched her hand away. Kitty cat, kitty cat, Kit Kat, kat. What does *kat* mean? Or *kit*? Tool kit. Tools hurt. Hammer, wrench, screwdriver. The Child stops thinking. Hit. Pit. Her thumb begins to throb. Grimacing, she offers the rest of the dried squid. The kitten goes back to devouring her bleeding finger and the squid. The kitten, which looks to be a month old, is so small and light that the Child can easily pick it up with one hand. Now in the Child's arms, it is completely engrossed in eating. She hides it inside her jacket and looks around. Two middle-aged women and three or four children who appear to be about her age pass by, but no one is watching her.

Where should I go? the Child mumbles. The kitten digs its claws into her shirt as though to shred it. The Child must not draw attention to herself. Should I go to the rooftop? she wonders. She heads for the apartment building directly in front of her. She gets into the elevator and presses the button for the fifteenth floor. The rooftop is only one flight up from there. She has been on the rooftop three or four times before. Should I jump? the Child had thought. Which side of the building would hurt more? she had wondered. It's useless, she had backed down. There is no one on the rooftop. Not even a mouse or an ant. Even up there, the Child seeks out the darkest corner and only then puts her backpack and the kitten down. The kitten, which has finished eating, stares up at her as though it's still hungry and licks its mouth. You're wrong, you're wrong, the Child says. There's no food left. It doesn't answer. Sitting idly on the edge of a shadow, it starts to rub against the Child's feet. She strokes it. Its hair, curved like smooth wire, tickles the Child's wrist. (It hurts.) Her thumb still hurts. Should I jump? she asks the kitten. I bet you'd survive if you jumped, wouldn't you? The kitten doesn't answer.

For a moment, she gazes at the exquisite shadow cast by the kitten and then opens her bag and takes out her pencil case. Inside the pencil case is a stationery knife. The knife is long and sharp and pointy. It sometimes hurts the Child. But not today. With her right hand, she slides the blade out from its plastic handle. The sharp, thin metal slices the sunlight. The yellow-striped cat that is folding itself into her hand closes its eyes into slits and tries to sleep. Its nape under her left hand is soft and slender and delicate. She waits. Shadows pant in the patches of sunlight. One minute, perhaps two. The kitten grows quiet. The Child swallows and parts the hair at its nape, revealing the delicate flesh. It is trembling ever so slightly. The sound of the pipe doesn't reach her ears. There are no mice or ants. She has heard that a cat has nine lives. In some book of fairy tales. But she has never owned a book of fairy tales.

She tightens her grip on the knife and slashes the nape of the sleeping, defenseless cat. One. It writhes violently. Two. But she has a tight hold. Three. It extinguishes its breath without a sound. Its hair turns red. Red sweat trickles from the Child's forehead and neck ever so slightly. The kitten sags red. Her dirty running shoes are sprinkled with blood. One sprinkle, two sprinkles, three sprinkles. Hey Sprinkles, she calls out to the kitten. The kitten doesn't answer. The Child puts it on the ground and wipes the blood off the blade on its tail. Its tail turns red. The Child pants. Cold, red sweat trickles down her back. A long, narrow stream of blood stretches between her and the kitten. A cruel blood tie. The trail of blood suggests nothing. After gathering her things, she gets to her feet and suddenly looks back. No one is there. No trace must be left. She checks her clothes, hands, and trembling legs. Only her running shoes are sprinkled a little with blood. The dead kitten will not be discovered for a long time. People hardly ever go up to the rooftop. It's all right, sorry, it's all right, sorry, the Child mumbles. The dead kitten doesn't speak. A cat is an animal that doesn't speak, and what's dead doesn't speak. Sorry, that's enough, stop it, stop it, stop. The Child stands motionless for a moment until her breathing returns to normal. Her shadow stretches over the kitten. Soon the darkness will fall and nothing will be seen. What's dead feels no pain. Only what's alive feels pain. Until it dies.

The Child returns to the first floor and runs toward home. She is out of breath. The key clinks in her pants pocket. She's really late. She must hide the key. Because she's so late, the Child thinks she'll be forced to strip off her clothes when she gets home. Sweat surges from her forehead, the bridge of her nose, her spine, and trickles down from there. Gravity and acceleration. It's because of acceleration. Suddenly the Child recalls Mia's words and just as suddenly forgets them. As she runs home, she puts her hand in her pocket and takes out the key. As she runs home, she turns her head to check behind her. She who was lost. She who will be lost. Behind her, a harsh silence gathers. Where is everyone? How can there be no one? Has everyone died? But that's impossible. The Child hurls the key she's been clutching at the balcony window on the second floor of an apartment building. *Ca-clang!* The explosion of metal hitting glass echoes through the air. It's a good thing it's not night, because if it were night, it would sound so much louder. The Child is scared that someone will open the balcony window and shout at her. But no sound comes. Everyone has died, everyone. The Child runs and runs some more. *Ca-clang.* She likes that sound. *Ca-clang* can be used as both onomatopoeia and a mimetic word. They say onomatopoeia portrays a sound and a mimetic word portrays an action. Next time, I'm going to throw something bigger, heavier, and harder, she thinks. Something bigger, heavier, harder. The Child knows of many such things. Something longer, pointier, sharper. She knows of many such things as well. A window, a window, a window is bad. It's cold and transparent and breakable. Every beautiful thing cracks and shatters and collapses and crumples and bleeds. If not now, it will eventually. The parched April sunlight pursues the Child's shadow. Her shadow shrinks and expands, over and over. There is no key and there is no cat, she thinks. So it's all right. Things that have disappeared don't follow me. (I want to kill, too.) One of her shoelaces becomes untied. She steps on the loose lace and falls before she can catch herself. Her chin, chest, and left knee hit the concrete. It hurts. Friction spreads through her whole body. But she doesn't have the luxury of feeling pain. Blood oozes from her chin. It hurts, it's all right, I can say the blood on my shoes is from tripping and falling. Her face crumples from holding back her tears. I shouldn't cry, I shouldn't laugh either. She struggles to compose her face. I can say I tripped over a rock on the way home, and that's why I got hurt, and that's why I'm late, at least today.

She runs. Today of all days, her home is an eternity away. This is like a dream, she thinks. No matter how far I run, I feel as though I'm running in place. The square landscape retreats from the running Child. Is this a dream? she wonders. Perhaps it is. But it's a dream that will wake her.

13

Monday arrives. That afternoon, none of the children comes forward to confess. The teacher waits until the bell rings at the end of the last class. The children open and close their bags noisily as they get ready to go home. Most of the children have forgotten about last Thursday's incident. Do you want to come over today and do homework together? Inju asks Mia. We can play outside with my puppy. Mia becomes excited at the thought of seeing the dog. Sure, Mia answers brightly. Mia's voice reaches even the Child's ears. The Child turns and looks at Mia without thinking. Mia's long hair is held in place by a green hair tie. The Child doesn't think, It's green. When all the children place their bags on top of their desks, the teacher speaks. I will give you until Friday. If no one comes forward by then, we will take a trip to the police station together. Several children breathe sighs of relief. There are even some half-witted children who ask, What? What happened? Park Yeongwu whistles. Looking uninterested, Mia and Inju secretly change out of their indoor shoes into running shoes under their desks. Friday, police station, interrogation, fingerprints. The Child stands up, looking as though she has received a blow to the head. To her, a blow to the head is nothing. But no one notices the Child's confusion.

Mia's green hair tie moves away with her. Gazing at it, the Child slips down the hall. No trace must be left. The Child goes into the bathroom at the end of the hall. She waits until the other children have left before filling up the sink with water and washing her face and neck. The cold, red water cools her heat. She doesn't lift her hot face. She doesn't look into the mirror. What she sees are her ten fingers attached to her open palms. Fingerprints. Fingerprints on the journals. Slowly she makes her way out of the bathroom and begins to walk down the stairs to the first floor. How could I forget that? she thinks. I can't get caught now. I still have so much to do. As she descends from the fourth floor to the third, from the third to the second, closer and closer to the first floor, her legs begin to shake. She grabs hold of the railing. She doesn't realize that the teacher's threat is empty. She doesn't yet know that the teacher isn't the type to disgrace himself by dragging a group of children to the police station, or that even if he were, the police wouldn't be interested in a problem that didn't involve death or injury, in a trivial issue concerning children's journals. Key. She thinks about the key that she had hurled at someone's window last week. Key. Flee. Key. She must find the key. Key. Plea. Key. Key. Mumbling, she slinks down the stairs. From the second floor to the first. But as she is about to set her foot on the last step, she trips. Oh feeble soul—but does she even have a soul?

The Child's hand, which had been gripping the railing, beats the air lifelessly. She tumbles down several steps. Key, key, key, fingerprints, fingerprints, fingerprints. Even while she lurches in every direction, she thinks only about the key and fingerprints. I have to find the key, she thinks. Her cheek throbs, pressed against the concrete floor. Because of the bloodstains on her running shoes, because of her cut, swollen chin, because of her torn palms, she had completely forgotten about the past weekend. Like all the other weekends. Like all the other days. She forgets even the past weekend, like today and tomorrow, like yesterday. In the future, she will not remember anything. She will not be able to remember anything. Wounds heal and scars fade. Memories get blotted out and there is no recovering them. Memories are dazed and forgetfulness blazed. Key, key, key. If you say *key* over and over, it sounds strange, she thinks. The cold that comes up from the icy ground cools her heat. Key, key, key. If you say *key* over and over, it doesn't seem like *key* anymore. I have to find the key. She sits up. Right then, someone thrusts a childlike hand in front of her face. She looks up at its owner. It's Kim Injung.

With small, black eyes that resemble those of an herbivore, Kim Injung looks at the Child. His eyes look similar to a cow's or goat's. But the Child has never seen a cow or goat before. Does it hurt? he asks. Does it hurt? Does it? The Child gets to her feet and dusts off her clothes. She doesn't look at him. Does it? Does it hurt? Kim Injung asks. The Child doesn't answer. He follows her closely. Does it hurt? She looks back without thinking. No one is not there. Kim Injung looks at her with eyes full of unknowable thoughts. Or perhaps eyes full of no thought. I'll blow on it for you, he says. One, two, three, four, the Child counts without thinking. There are four pockmarks on Kim Injung's face. Five, six, seven, she counts out of habit. There are three moles on Kim Injung's face. He stares blankly at her. Key, I have to find the key, she mumbles. Does it hurt? Key? Kim Injung cocks his head. A sudden murderous desire pulses from the tip of her tongue. You stupid retard, she mutters. Kim Injung cowers like an animal before slaughter.

The Child begins to walk quickly. She slips out of the school gate and walks past the stationery store, snack shop, wallpaper and linoleum store, and hardware store without slowing down. Kim Injung follows her. She turns and glares at him. Kim Injung cowers and asks, Does it hurt? Does it hurt? She resumes walking. The sound of the pipe doesn't reach her ears. Kim Injung follows her. She decides to leave him alone. It'll be okay, she thinks. He probably doesn't know what I'm doing anyway. I mean, what I've already done. The hair salon, dogs, middle-aged women and children, the supermarket and fruit stall follow her. Kim Injung won't know what she will do either. The street is covered with pale pink cherry blossoms. The crushed transparent petals don't retain the

Child's footprints. Walking quickly, she glances at Kim Injung's reflection in the window of the movie rental store. With his mouth hanging open and his gaze fixed on her back, Kim Injung is following her earnestly. Retard, she thinks, biting her bottom lip with her top teeth. You stupid retard, get lost. But she leaves him alone. Once again, there are people in every shop. Of course they wouldn't have all died. They were all alive. No one had died. This, too, is like a dream, she thinks. A dream where they come back to life no matter what. A dream where they don't die. Where they won't die. Sweat beads on the bridge of her nose. Is this a dream or a lie? *Dream* is a bad word. *Lie* is bad, too. That's right, every word is bad. Almost every word. She walks past the security booth. Behind the booth, between the tall overgrown weeds, nothing moves. She doesn't look in that direction. I forgot, I will forget. Then it means I haven't done anything, she thinks. Nothing happened. But the Child hasn't forgotten anything. She can't forget anything. Not yet.

She sees Building 101. She stops for a moment in front of the building but doesn't look up toward the rooftop. Kim Injung, who has stopped and is standing on her shadow, looks up toward the rooftop. She turns to glare at him and then resumes walking, looking for the spot where she had hurled the key. No trace must be left. But Kim Injung is following her. Anyone who could recognize the Child must not see this sight. The sound of Kim Injung shuffling his feet gets on her nerves. All of a sudden, she stops and turns to look at him. Get lost, she says. Does it hurt? Does it? he asks. (It hurts.) Get lost, you retard! she yells. Does it hurt, does it? he asks. (It hurts.) I told you to get lost! she shouts, stamping her foot. But he comes closer and gazes blankly into her dark eyes. Does it hurt? (It hurts.) She closes her eyes. Kim Injung puts his hand on her cheek. Does it hurt? he asks. She shakes her head. (It hurts.) He strokes her cheek. The pain that she had forgotten about comes alive. She shoves his hand away and begins to walk toward the spot where she had hurled the key. It will be fine, there's still some time left, she thinks. Mom said she'd be home late today, she told me to make my own goddamn food. She said I could eat or starve, for all she cares. Late for the Child's mother means after sunset. There's still plenty of time before the sun goes down. Before the shadows lengthen, before the shadows disappear, the Child must go into her room and sit as though she were dead. Retard, you stupid retard, I told you to quit following me, she thinks. She reaches the spot where she had hurled the key last Thursday. There isn't a single blemish on the large balcony window. There is no stain, mark, scratch, or scar. She steps into the flower bed in front of the balcony, below the clear glass that tautly reflects the sunlight. Kim Injung follows her in. While she tramples on the clusters of dandelions and pansies blooming in the flower bed, while she pushes aside the stalks with her feet, Kim Injung copies her ruthless movements. Key, key, key, she mumbles. Kee, kee, kee, Kim Injung mumbles. Keep, keep, keep, he mumbles. Keen, keen keen, he mumbles. She moves faster. Gradually she grows anxious. Budding lilac branches graze her body. Key, key, key, Kim Injung lisps into her ear. She flinches. Does it hurt? Key? Looking dazed, he thrusts a small metal object in front of her eyes. The key.

Kim Injung wipes the dirty key on the front of his jacket. The Child takes a deep breath. I've got it, it hasn't disappeared, she thinks. Good thing I didn't throw it down the sewer or in the trash. She takes the key from Kim Injung and looks around. Ordinary people are walking past an ordinary scene. An ordinary afternoon, ordinary sunlight, an ordinary time, the Child and Kim Injung draw no one's attention. She takes a deep breath. Does it hurt? he asks in a whisper. Avoiding his eyes, she doesn't nod. What should I do now? she wonders. The pain that she had forgotten about, the pains pulse again. (It hurts.) Kim Injung strokes her cheek. She twists her head away. Gripped tightly in her hand is the Grade 5, Section 3, classroom key. I'll blow on it for you, he tells her. Come to my house, I'll blow on it for you. One, two, three, four, she counts. Five, six, seven. There is still time before seven o'clock. That's about when the sun will set. The Child grips the key that has already grown warm. She smells faintly of metal. No trace must be left. She steps out of the ruined flower bed full of crushed flowers.

Three hours later, before the sun sinks below the top of the apartment buildings, two girls fall into the ruined flower bed that is full of crushed flowers. The flowers lose the sensation of pain. The Child's key doesn't become dyed with blood.

The Child narrowly misses witnessing that afternoon's dreary sight. Witnessing that scene is not her lot. Because a different scene will soon be prepared for her.

14

Mia steps into Inju's house. You're lucky you have a yard. Mia thinks Inju is lucky. Although Mia owns a set of German-made watercolor pencils, a sweater with a deer knitted on it, two journals, and two fathers, she could not own the flowering trees in Inju's yard or the dog that would sometimes bound out into the yard and trample on the flowers. Perhaps ten or even twenty years from now, Mia might somehow have a yard, a dog, and several flowering trees. But for that to happen, the fence must never become any taller than it is, the view beyond the yard must never disappear. Nothing must change.

Inju's mother greets Mia. She finds Mia's pretty face and childish demeanor pleasant. Inju's mother has forgotten about the incident from last March. Mia is friendly, and the gossip about Mia's mother has not spread. Not yet. Do you girls want a snack? Inju's mother goes to the kitchen. Inju and Mia, who has picked up the dog, go to Inju's room. Mia puts him down on the bed and uses the bathroom while Inju hurriedly puts away an object from the top of the desk. The picture of the woman who had been England's princess gets hidden between books on the bookshelf. Inju had ripped it out from the book in Mia's living room. Inju's face turns red. Deep inside Inju's desk drawer is a pearl brooch. Inju had taken it from the bedroom of Mia's mother. Inju's face turns a deeper red. Mia washes her hands and comes back to the room. Inju hugs Mia awkwardly. What are you doing? It tickles, Mia says, giggling. I'm just happy to see you, that's all, Inju says. Inju opens her wardrobe and takes out a once-treasured satin dress. Do you want to try it on? Inju asks. It's pretty, says Mia, but inside, she thinks the dress is child-ish and unsophisticated. Mia removes her thick cream-colored car-digan and beige T-shirt, and neatly places them on top of Inju's desk. Mia's smooth, slender prepubescent body is revealed. Inju, whose color has returned to normal, hands Mia the dress. The white lacy dress fits Mia loosely. Inju winds her arms around Mia's waist to tie the red ribbon. Oh, that looks so pretty on you, she says. She guides Mia to the mirror on the door of the wardrobe. They both gaze into it. You want it? Inju asks. It's too small for me now. I grew this much last year. She puts one hand above the other, forming a height of about a single hand span. It's a little big on me, Mia mumbles, tug-ging on the collar where the lace is flattened. Big. Mia wants to be bigger.

Inju's mother steps into the room with a plate of spicy rice cakes. Smelling the food, the dog jumps down from the bed and looks up at her, wagging his tail. Busan, stop it, she says. Didn't Mommy tell you not to beg? Inju's mother looks at Mia. Mia is wearing the dress that Inju had worn when she was younger, something she had pleaded for when they'd had to attend a relative's wedding. It fits you perfectly, says Inju's mother with a smile. I guess you have some growing to do. The dog jumps up and down, begging for food. He was born in Busan, that's why his name is Busan, Inju had once said to Mia. Thank you, Inju and Mia say simultaneously to Inju's mother. Busan begs, scratching Mia's legs with his front paws. With a fork in one hand, Mia tickles his scruff with the other. Make sure you don't give him anything spicy. Girls, I have to step out for a bit. Inju's mother leaves the room. Don't you have to call your mom? asks Inju. It's okay, she's not home anyway, Mia says, being careful not to get the sauce on Inju's white dress. After we eat, let's finish our homework quickly and play, says Inju. Sure, Mia says, nibbling on a piece of onion. Your mom's a good cook. Inju looks blankly at Mia. And suddenly, Mia's milky skin, her long hair, and slim body irritate Inju. (I hate you.) Inju's face turns red once more. Mia, wearing the dress that no longer fits Inju, wields the fork with a prim expression. Inju recalls the sentence in her journal, written in an unfamiliar hand. (I hate you, I hate you. I hate you so much I can't bear it.) Inju puts her fork down and shakes her head furiously. They said that hating someone, being jealous of someone, being prejudiced against someone, without reason, was bad. But the older Inju grows, the worse her thoughts become. Bad thoughts generate bad behavior. Inju has no reason to hate Mia. There is no room in Inju's heart for bad thoughts. Not yet. Much later, when she is a grown-up, she will suddenly recall this afternoon. While wearing the white dress, Mia nibbles at a rice cake. The dog sits at Mia's and Inju's feet like a sculpture. Inside Inju's desk drawer is a pearl brooch with a broken clasp, and hidden on her bookshelf is a picture of Princess Diana, as beautiful as a movie star. In a corner of her mind, the older Inju will think about the memories formed on this day, stored layer upon layer. Ten years from now, she will possess even more memories, memories that are both sinister and dangerous. Memories come to life once again. When that happens, there is nothing she can do. Everything collapses. Everything is collapsing. Inju is secretly jealous of Mia. However, Inju doesn't yet know the word *jealous*, or even if she did, she doesn't know how to use it properly. And so, Inju has no way to describe her own feelings. And even if she could express her feelings in words, Inju can't speak them. To anyone. Because it would be embarrassing.

Inju takes Mia to the living room. Hidden inside Inju's room are objects that the young, softhearted Inju has difficulty handling. Mia looks around the living room. Clear sunlight spills in through the window facing the yard. Many objects, a wall clock, a large family portrait, house plants. Happy home, happy life. Mia and Inju forget they're supposed to be doing their homework. Isn't your grandmother home? asks Mia. She's probably sleeping, Inju answers. The phone on the coffee table in front of the sofa catches Inju's eye. Hey, do you want to make a prank call? Inju pokes Mia in the side. Really? asks Mia. Let's call someone in America, says Inju. In America? Mia snickers.

Inju picks up the receiver and dials 1. Several more numbers are pressed at random. Mia holds her breath. There's a disconnected tone, followed by words in a language that Inju can't understand. After that, the line goes dead. No one's picking up? Mia asks. I don't think the number is in service. Again, Inju presses random numbers. A phone starts to ring. Inju nods gravely at Mia. Mia nods back. After five or six rings, someone picks up on the other end. Inju brightens immediately. Was it America? Was it an American? At the other end of the line, a person is saying something that Inju can't understand. Inju coughs and hands Mia the receiver. Shocked, Mia takes it. Hello, hello? It's the first time Mia has been on an international call. It's also the first time she's spoken to a foreigner. I can barely hear, Mia whispers to Inju. Say something! Anything! Inju says anxiously. Come on, what if they hang up? A smile spreads over Mia's face. Looking as though she found the situation funny, Mia says, *Doo yoo speek ing-gli-shi?* As soon as the words are out of her mouth, she bursts into laughter. She laughs hysterically. Inju snatches the receiver from Mia, but the foreigner has already hung up. Inju starts laughing as well. The two children can't stop. Why is it so funny? Inju finally says, exhausted. I don't know. It's just funny, Mia gasps, just barely managing to stop. And then the two children are sent into a fit of laughter all over again.

You idiots! someone shouts. Mia and Inju stop laughing at once. The dog that had been running around Inju's feet in circles freezes. Inju's grandmother is glaring at the two children. Couldn't you let me sleep? Inju's grandmother, as scrawny as a bird, hunches her shoulders. Mia wonders who it was that picked up the phone. Inju's grandmother comes closer. Inju takes half a step back. I'm sorry,

Mia says. It was just so funny. We'll be quiet now. Inju's grandmother, moles protruding from her face, glares at Mia. *Doo yoo speak ing-gli-shi?* Why did I say that? Mia thinks. As soon she has this thought, laughter spews from her mouth again.

Mia twists her body, struggling to stop, but it's as though an electric current were running through her entire body, tickling her. Mia covers her mouth with both hands. Inju pokes Mia in the side. (I hate you.) What's the matter with you? Are you crazy? But Mia can't answer. Snickers escape between her fingers. *Doo yoo speak ing-gli-shi? Doo yoo speak ing-gli-shi?* Mia can't hold back any longer. She guffaws uncontrollably. The dog licks Mia's toes. Why is it so funny? Mia wonders, even while she's laughing so hard that she can hardly breathe. It's so funny she can't bear it. Inju grabs Mia's shoulder and shakes it. What's wrong with you? All mirth has now disappeared from Inju's voice. It's just so funny, Mia gasps. The lace edging on the white satin dress flaps in the air. Inju, watching Mia with a baffled expression, discovers a small, red stain on the bottom hem of the dress. (I hate you.) Louder and louder.

Someone strikes Mia in the head. Ah! Mia screams and lifts up her face. From behind the latticework of black moles, the eyes of Inju's grandmother bore into Mia. Mia's eyes fill with tears. Inju looks in shock from her grandmother to Mia. Mia has stopped laughing. With eyes full of tears, Mia looks at Inju. (I hate you.) Inju's grandmother will die before long. Death is in her every wrinkle. The black dots on her face mark the hour of her death. You little idiot! Inju's grandmother shrieks. Mia trembles. One day, Inju will recall this incident. By then Inju's grandmother will be dead and gone. Perhaps even Inju's dog, perhaps even Inju's friends. And so one day Inju must recall this day. Such is Inju's lot.

15

The Child steps into Kim Injung's building. On the stair landing, Kim Injung rummages through his pocket and takes out a bunch of keys. Keys that don't belong to the Child. He unlocks the door with one of them. She doesn't ask, Are you sure no one's home? After removing her shoes in the entryway, she follows Kim Injung into the living room. No one is there. A cross hangs in the short, narrow hallway leading to the small kitchen. Above the cross is a wall clock. It's 4:27. Mechanically, she calculates how much time is left. There is time. No, there is no time. Kim Injung leads her to his room. Two desks are placed side by side and on the wall is a picture of a woman with her hair covered by a veil. It's the Virgin Mary. She glances at the books on the shelf. Math, ethics, and music textbooks. And spiral-bound notebooks. Do you have a brother? she asks. Kim Injung nods. He comes home later, he says. She is a little surprised that he knows how to answer properly. Before she has another thought, Kim Injung thrusts a notebook at her. This, he says, his finger on a spot in the open book. What is it? he asks.

The Child peers at the page. But the letters are not legible. The jumbled letters of the alphabet disturb her eyes. I don't know, she answers dryly. Kim Injung looks at her with dark eyes. Tell me. *Gieok, niun, digu.* My brother gets angry. Then it's scary, he says. *Riul, mium,* he says.* The Child's face crumples. Do you know how

* Here, Injung is mispronouncing the first five consonants of the Korean alphabet, which are *giyeok, nieun, digeut, rieul,* and *mieum.* Two of his mispronunciations happen to be actual words: *gieok,* which means "memory," and *mium,* which means "hatred."—Trans.

to talk? she asks him. This. Tell me. Stubbornly, Kim Injung shoves the notebook in front of her face. She's starting to get anxious. Hey, do you remember the key from earlier? she asks. Kim Injung's face briefly clouds over. He nods. Do you know what that key was? Kim Injung nods, wearing a blank expression. Her thoughts become snarled. Inside her pencil case is a stationery knife. It cuts up her tangled nerves. No trace must be left. She glares at him. He blinks. Key, home, I need the key, he says. If I don't have the key, I can't go home. If I can't go home, I'll be in trouble with Mom, Kim Injung says. The Child exhales softly.

Kim Injung opens a desk drawer, rummages through it, and takes something out. A half-eaten bag of chips. Kim Injung thrusts the bag at her. Without thinking, she takes it. Crumbs fall by her feet. I shouldn't leave any footprints, she thinks absently. But it's okay. It might be okay, because I'm wearing socks. She gets Kim Injung to sit in a chair and she sits in another one. There is still time. She's starving. Actually she can't tell if she's hungry or if she has a stomachache. Pencil, she says. Kim Injung grasps a stray pencil that is lying on the desk for himself and hands one to her as well. She opens the notebook to a new page. *Giyeok*, she says as she writes the letter. The page fills with a checkered pattern.

Giyeok, repeats Kim Injung as he writes. His letter is bigger and more crooked than hers. *Nieun*, she says as she writes the letter. He draws a similar-looking letter below the Child's. *Digeut*, she says as she writes. *Rieul*, she says as she writes. *Mieum*, she says as she writes. A tear falls onto the page. She flinches and jerks her head up.

She brings her hand to her eyes and finds it comes away wet. Kim Injung stops writing and raises his dark eyes toward her. Does it hurt? he asks. She shakes her head. Again, she says. Write your name. As though that were the only thing he knew how to do, he hunches confidently over his notebook. *Giyeok, ieung, jieut, i, i, u, mieum, nieun, ieung.* Kim Injung has the habit of writing the first consonant letter of each block, instead of completing one block at a time. The Child watches. His name appears on the page. But the letters that form his name are so mixed up that she can't decipher them. Again. Try again, she says, wiping off her wet fingertips on her pants. You need to write one block at a time. You need to write *mieum* under *gi*. Kim Injung, clenching rather than just holding the pencil, carefully writes his name. He then shows it to her with pride. So you do know how to write your name, she says. She struggles to remember when she first learned the alphabet. But she can't remember anything. She struggles to remember the first sentence she wrote. But she can't remember anything. She struggles to remember the first sentence she erased. But she can't remember anything.

Kim Injung starts to write something else. *Hieut, digeut . . .* Although he's writing in the wrong order as usual, the Child realizes what he's trying to do. She snatches away the notebook before he can finish writing her name. He drops his pencil. As it falls on the notebook, it leaves a mark on the page. The short, curved segment doesn't connect Kim Injung and the Child. If you're going to write about love, write it in pencil. Pencils are good. Words written in pencil can be easily erased. If you have an eraser. But when you write in pencil, you must not press too hard. An eraser can erase lead, but it can't erase imprinted writing. Kim Injung looks blankly at the Child.

Stop it. The Child's voice is threatening. Kim Injung's eyes grow wet. Stupid retard, she mutters. She rummages through her bag that had been thrown carelessly on the floor and takes out her pencil case. Inside the pencil case is a stationery knife. The pencil case clatters open. She takes out the knife and slides out the blade. No, I shouldn't. The Child hesitates. An incident that she cannot and will not understand has not yet begun. Not yet. A tragedy must not be explained. It is bound to become infinitely trivial the instant an explanation is offered. Kim Injung's eyes are ruthlessly clear and quiet. The Child can't stop thinking that he's hiding something behind those eyes. She thinks he might have followed her, and so might know what she had done at school, what she had done on the apartment rooftop, what she had done even at home. No trace must be left. And so, she must commit another act. She brings the knife to his throat. He winces.

On the left side of Kim Injung's neck is a small mole. All of a sudden, she wants to pick at it, to carve it out with a knife. But a stationery knife won't do. Something as small as a kitten can be killed with a stationery knife, but not a person. A knife, a kitchen knife, she mutters. Where's the knife? she asks sharply. Kim Injung, who had been crouched down on the ground, gets up. Cutting board. Knife. He leads her to the kitchen. On the table that protrudes out into the hallway is a meal set for one. Soup, rice, side dishes, and water. A fork is set instead of chopsticks. There is no note. Kim Injung walks past the table, opens the drawer under the sink, and takes out a knife. The lighting isn't good. The blade flashes but doesn't shine. He hands the large kitchen knife to the Child.

Knife, he says. Here. Her head empties precipitously. Her hand shakes as she takes the knife from him. *Kieuk*, says Kim Injung. *K*. Is a *k* onomatopoeic or mimetic? she wonders all of a sudden. Is it a kackle? But there's nothing funny. Kim Injung fixes his dark eyes with their large irises on her. She tightens her hands around the knife handle. But her grip is weak. Her dark hands grow pale. She looks back. No trace must be left. A blue jacket hangs on the back of a chair by the table. It doesn't belong to Kim Injung. It's too big. She raises her hands. Kim Injung looks dumbly at her. Many times, in the shadows of the stone wall surrounding the school, she has seen him get beaten up by the rougher boys. He would cover his face with his arms and sink into the shadows, screaming shrilly.

But today, as he stands before her, he shows no sign of being scared. No sign of terror, dread, or fear. The Child quickly grows damp. She thinks that the blue jacket hanging on the chair is watching her, that it knows everything that she has ever done, that at the very last second, it will run up to her and snatch away the knife and stab her instead. Deeply. Her blood, and not someone else's, will soak the floor, and her feet, and not someone else's, will leave behind footprints, and her small body, and not someone else's, will become the evidence. These will prove that she was alive, that she existed. No. She doesn't think about anything. She can't think about anything. Her hands quiver. Exactly like the word. Perhaps they are quavering. Just like the letters. The knife slips weakly from her hands. The knife drops to the floor. The long, hard, sharp object drops, coldly, as though it will carve out the linoleum floor. One strike of dull silence. Knife, says Kim Injung. And with the syllable still trapped on his tongue, the clock on the living room wall chimes. Five strikes of silence. The tip of the blade vibrates imperceptibly from the impact on the floor. By the time the knife has stopped vibrating, the Child is already gone. On top of Kim Injung's desk is his open notebook, and on the pages of his open notebook are the letters he had been writing.

Will we ever learn the Child's name? What will she be called?

16

We must not call that time "back then." The words *back then* attempt to make the past too beautiful, something to long for. That time. Time's grime. That time when every eye contained a glass shard. That time when I wanted to snap, trample, snip, cut, crumple, and ruin everything I saw. That time when even a narrow strand of light aimed for the throat like a knife. That time. That time when the slanted sun in the sky gripped a butcher knife. That time. That time when every beautiful thing was scattered and crushed and tangled, extinguishing every possible spark of future longing and regret. Because memories assault recollections, recollections return as memories full of objections. Therefore, no memories return without anticipation, without premonition, without sensation, without emotion. They are like a wide-meshed net, unable to catch anything.

Could I describe you with the length of a shadow? Could I explain you with the number of teeth I lost in those nightmare-ridden nights? Could I identify you by a fingerprint left on a surface? Could I estimate you with the thickness of a stack of notebooks? Could I recognize you by the wounds scattered like the Milky Way? The wounds loosed like a constellation? These things are beautiful. But we must not be deceived by their beauty. If they can be called beautiful. Beauty doesn't last. Only ugly, hideous things persist, doggedly, and sink people. They collapse. They are collapsing.

You are already being documented. You're not you and you're not like anyone else. No trace must be left. Because the traces you've left behind so carelessly will one day pursue and catch you and then scratch you. The footsteps you've left behind must disappear before they begin to chase you. But is it possible for you to completely disappear? What will you be called?

You must grow a little more, you must weigh a little more. So that you no longer fit into the clothes you are wearing, so that you can wear new clothes and hide your ragged body. Your feet, too, must grow a little more. You must change out of your bloodied shoes. The gaze collapses. There is no sentence that can save you. While you escape the page and are not seen, there is no sentence that can describe what happens to you. There is no sentence that can describe what you're thinking or feeling. You must keep moving. Then the sentences that don't yet exist will become your shadow. May those sentences never pursue you, attack you, kill you, or bury you.

17

The Child moves on. It's raining. The sun has set. She checks the time with great care. Thursday. She sticks her hand in her right pant pocket to check once again that the key is there. One hour will be enough. Enough to slip out of the apartment complex and run all the way to school, slide open the window she'd secretly left open on the first floor earlier that afternoon, creep up to the fourth floor, open the door to the Grade 5, Section 3, classroom, and walk up to the teacher's desk. One hour is plenty. No. She must also account for the time it takes to get back. She needs time to run home and catch her breath, to wipe her damp face, and to hide the redness of her cheeks. But still, one hour should be plenty. She doesn't need to write anything today. Now that she has thought about time, she must think about space. Where can I throw them away? she thinks. Should I burn them? But that would draw too much attention, because the sun has already set. More than anything, the Child wants to keep the journals. Rather than get rid of them. But there is no suitable location. She jogs slowly. She must be back by nine o'clock. She must be sitting at her lamp-lit desk, quietly reading her textbook. Then today's beating can be pushed back to tomorrow, perhaps the day after tomorrow. There isn't room on the Child's bookshelf for the journals. Not because her own books already crowd the shelf, but simply because objects that don't belong to her should not attract any attention. No. The names that don't belong to her, the sentences that were never once hers—they should not attract any attention.

Instead of carrying an umbrella, she covered herself in a nylon jacket and hat. She could have covered her face if she had used an umbrella. But she thinks she can't run quickly while holding one. She doesn't hear the splashing rain. She runs past pedestrians. They will forever exist as pedestrians. She doesn't look at their faces. They disappear from her sight. Should I burn them? But it's raining. I can't burn them in my room. Because ashes will fly around. But more than anything, the room would reek of burned paper. The key moves in her pocket, according to her movements. She is aware of the key's movement. I can throw it out anywhere. After I've wiped it clean. This time, it really doesn't matter if I chuck it into the drain. There are so many keys out there. There are probably more keys than doors in the world. That's right. Even if I throw it out anywhere, even if someone finds it, no one will know what door it opens.

The Child walks past a produce market and glances at the clock hanging above a pile of fruit covered in plastic. 8:05. There is still time. The cold April night air pushes out her breathing. She doesn't think, Will this be the last time? She doesn't think, Why did I do this? She doesn't think, Why did I think of something like this? While she thinks about the thoughts she doesn't have, the mice and ants pursue her noiselessly. The sound of the pipe doesn't reach her ears. From time to time, cars shine their headlights on her and her shadow, and drive by. Then each time, the procession of mice and ants behind her disappears in a flash. Like a lie. Like the lies she had to invent without hiding anything. Like the lies she forgot to prepare. I should have brought a flashlight, she thinks. No, I won't need one. Because all I have to do is carry them out. She tries to guess the thickness of the stack of notebooks. She won't be able to hold them all with one hand. But she must leave one hand free. She must shut the door and window, but more than anything, she must throw away the key. Should I throw the journals into the incinerator? Disposing of them that way seems to be the most realistic solution. But can a realistic thing become a real thing? The

Child steps into the alley. All the stores in the shopping arcade are dark. Streetlights illuminate the raindrops, making them transparent. But they hit the ground before they can be completely illuminated. She reaches the school gate and catches her breath. A raindrop drips down her nose. A diagonal line becomes etched on her cheek. Knife. She looks back. No one is there. She looks back only when no one is there. But is that really true?

The Child disappears into the school. She will probably stand on her toes and slide open the window at the end of the hallway, step onto the corner of the protruding brick to climb the meter-high wall, and slip through the window and land silently on the wooden floor. She will remove her shoes and carry them so that her footsteps will be silent, and after making sure no flashlight flickers at the end of the hallway, she will tiptoe up the stairs to the fourth floor. And from time to time, her hand will slip into her pocket to make sure that the key is still there. She won't be thinking about anything. The classroom door will open, she will head straightaway for the teacher's desk, and pick up the stack of journals that were collected the day before. After checking the time on the clock on the back wall—8:25—and without catching anyone's eye, she will once again walk down the hallway, once again descend the stairs, once again open the window, and once again set her feet on the ground.

She places the thirty-five journals on the window ledge and climbs over the window. Hidden in the dark, her face can't be seen. Rain drips from her black jacket. Her feet are wet. The raindrops she had dripped along the hallway will dry up by morning. Now back outside again, she briefly hesitates with the journals in her arms. If she is to go to the incinerator, she must cut across the field or go along the edge of the field at a right angle, following the sparsely planted magnolia trees.

She hesitates.

She stands.

She does not move.

She moves.

Tucking the journals under her arm, she heads toward the school gate. Journal, diurnal, dirge, purge, surge, submerge, urge, mutters the Child. At the school gate, she looks back again. Everything is bound to sink. The incinerator located at the opposite end beyond the field is shrouded in darkness. And no one is there. Incinerate, degenerate, eviscerate, obliterate, she mutters. She must hurry. Before she gets home, she must hide the journals. But will she have time? The road in front of the school gate splits into three paths. She moves like an automaton. The rain is letting up. A raindrop slides down her nose. She tightens her hold on the notebooks that keep slipping from under her arm and begins to run. Most children use pencils. If only they had written in their journals with water-based pens, if only the rain could erase their childish sentences. But most children use pencils. The Child, who has slipped out from the alley, stands by the side of the two-lane road. The sign hanging from the hospital rooftop is lit up. Green. The traffic lights are lit up. Red. While she waits for the lights to change, she rummages through her pocket for the key. She takes it out, and without hesitating, she hurls it into the drain. For a split second, the key catches on the grate and then falls somewhere beyond where she can see. It starts to drizzle. Even if more rain should fall, even if the streets flood and water flows into every house, the key will not float. The trait of metal. The weight of metal. She is safe. The key will never again appear. The lights change. A car drives over the stop line and stops. The Child starts to run. She passes the hardware store, the wallpaper and linoleum store, the flower bed in front of the after-school academy, and a bicycle shop. Several people holding umbrellas walk by. She can't see their faces. Pedestrians. As she is passing the ATM at the corner of the bank, her face lights up briefly. It's the light. Her black nylon jacket reflects white light for an instant. From there, the road goes steeply downhill. She braces her left arm in order to keep the journals from slipping. In the distance, the shops in her apartment complex begin to come into view.

Running past the supermarket, the Child bumps into someone's shoulder. She instinctively braces her left arm. Until it hurts. But it doesn't hurt. Without looking back, she tries to resume running. You! someone shouts. The Child looks back.

It's Mia. Mia recognizes the Child. We're in the same class, right? asks Mia. Mia's mother is standing behind Mia. You almost broke our eggs, Mia says to the Child. Mia's mother peers into the plastic bag. The Child bows toward Mia's mother in apology. I'm sorry . . . , she trails off. Mia's mother gazes down at her. You should be more careful, she says. What's that? Mia asks, as though curious. The Child glances sharply at Mia. What's all that under your arm? Mia asks. The Child flinches and backs away. Mia gives her a puzzled look. The Child backs away from Mia. To somewhere close, far, far away. Are you friends? Mia's mother asks Mia. She's in my class, Mia says. Do you live around here? What's your name? Mia's mother asks the Child. The Child turns around without saying a word. A drop of either sweat or rain runs down her back. It's cold. It's slippery. Mia's mother doesn't call out to her. Mia taps the ground with the end of her closed umbrella. The Child doesn't look back. She moves into the darkness. Her face that has turned white can no longer be seen. Where should I go? She walks blindly toward a spot beyond the gazes of Mia and Mia's mother. The rain has stopped. No trace must be left. But that is now an impossibility. A long and pointy triangle is drawn with the Child, Mia, and Mia's mother as the vertices. The Child moves. The triangle gets longer and steeper. Where should I go? the Child wonders. Right then, a large recycling bin catches her eye. Throw them away, the Child mutters. Throw them all away.

While the Child is throwing the journals into the recycling bin,

Mia and Mia's mother head home. So that girl isn't your friend? Mia's mother asks Mia. No, Mia answers absentmindedly. Mia and Mia's mother step into their empty apartment. Mom, can I sleep with you tonight? Mia pleads. Mia's mother, who had been putting the groceries into the fridge, looks at Mia. There she stands, wearing a pitiful expression. Fine . . . , Mia's mother trails off. Mia beams. As she goes into her room to change into her pajamas, her thoughts turn suddenly to the Child. Then she just as soon forgets about her.

No one is home at the Child's apartment. Not yet. Standing before the front door, the Child takes a key out of her pocket. She sticks it into the keyhole. But the key doesn't fit. The Child sways as though she were going to fall. The Grade 5, Section 3, classroom key is in her hand. A drop of either sweat or rain runs down her back. It's hot. It's slippery. There is no key. No, there is a key. A different key. Her entire body is wet. It's 8:52, the key that she has accidentally thrown away lies at the bottom of the dirty water. But she doesn't have the time or means to find the key. All of a sudden, she thinks of Mia and her mother. She doesn't forget them. Mia, Mia, Mia. The Child forgets nothing. She clings to the doorknob, hardly holding herself up. Is this a dream? No, it's not a dream. She won't be able to sleep tonight. Because she won't be able to sleep, she won't be able to dream. The Child tries to come up with a realistic way to open the door and go inside. But a realistic thing isn't realistic. A realistic thing has never once become a real thing. There she stands. She does not move. Even if it rains, she who is already wet can't get wet again. But still, we must go on talking about the Child. And though she may grow more dreadful, and though she may grow more wretched, and though she may grow more desperate, we must go on talking about her.

Look and see.

Look and see the Child.

18

Park Minsu remembers the bird. Pigeons and sparrows with no inkling of the fate that awaited them would sometimes fly in through the open window in the hallway. Anticipating such opportunities, the children carried slingshots in their pockets. Park Minsu was responsible for quickly shutting the window in order to trap the bird. The children loaded their slingshots with marbles, a marble bore through the bird, and the bird dropped to the ground. Then they put the dead bird in the slingshot, the bloody, nearly featherless pulp became a pellet to be flung, malicious boys aimed for the backs of girls' necks, and the girls who were hit shrieked. The boys laughed hysterically at this sight, unaware of the fate they would share with the bird, and were in turn beaten to a pulp by the teacher.

Lee Jiyeong constantly came across other children who had his name. For all of his twelve years but one, he was called Big Lee Jiyeong, or perhaps Boy Lee Jiyeong. Those with the same name were always girls, and if there weren't any who shared both his first and last name, there were at least those who shared his first name. The first time he didn't come across other Jiyeongs was when he entered the army. Shortly after starting his term, he was tasked with cutting iron pipes to make chin-up bars. He mixed the cement. A corporal cut through the bar with an angle grinder. The grinding wheel spun. Suddenly someone shouted, Pick up that skin! Hurry! As he picked up the corporal's skin that had become a sludge of dirt and sand, Lee Jiyeong was struck by the strangeness of the expression "pick up skin." The corporal lost 40 percent of his right arm.

For the rest of his time in the army, Lee Jiyeong heard no other news about the corporal.

Cho Yeonjeong remembers a certain concert. When it was announced that a popular American singer would be coming to Korea on tour, she and her friends cheered. After several days of pleading with her father, she was granted permission to attend the concert. But while she was there, her father saw a news bulletin that said the concert had reached critical capacity. He bolted to the venue and managed to find Cho Yeonjeong among the tens of thousands of spectators. She was dragged home, unable to stay to the end. But after she left, screams ensued, instead of a song. The stage had collapsed. The next day on the news, two deaths were reported.

Before the apartment towers went up, Park Yeongwu reigned as the king of the vacant lot. He and his minions didn't care about the chunks of broken brick or shards of glass; they played soccer or brawled until the sun went down. One day, a group of middle school boys came looking for Park Yeongwu. Without knowing why, he took a beating in front of everyone he'd treated like his personal servants. While being pummeled, Park Yeongwu saw a piece of rebar sticking out from under a plank. He pulled it out and began to whirl it frantically through the air. The nervous middle school students backed away. The other children looked on dumbly. That day, two boys suffered fractured skulls and a broken arm. Park Yeongwu's parents visited the parents of the middle school students fifteen times but were never forgiven.

Yang Yeong-ae received a bicycle for her tenth birthday. It was a child's bicycle with training wheels. Her mother stubbornly insisted that Yang Yeong-ae was not allowed to ride the bicycle unless she wore knee pads. Then why don't I just wear a helmet everywhere I go? she complained. She rode the bicycle into the elevator. On the way down, the elevator stopped and a man got on. After glancing at her and the bicycle, he grinned, saying that girls shouldn't ride bicycles.

When she asked why, he said that she'd find out when she was older, and she was filled with an unnameable shame.

Jang Minguk liked dogs. His whole family liked dogs. They had four. One by one the dogs died, starting with the oldest. When there was only one beloved dog left, his family decided to let it roam free in the house. One evening, Jang Minguk's family grilled meat inside, right on the dinner table. Drooling over the smell, the dog put its paws on a chair and barked. Jang Minguk's father said it should be tied up. No one objected. Even after it was tied up, it kept barking. Jang Minguk's father rummaged through the first aid kit and found a roll of white tape. He wrapped the tape around the dog's muzzle a few times. The dog looked at the family with mournful eyes, its long tongue dangling from between the tape. It wasn't given any meat. After dinner, Jang Minguk removed the tape from its muzzle. On the sticky side of the tape were its hair and whiskers.

The day before Arbor Day, Kim Jongho received moss rose seeds from school. When he asked why they were planting flowers on a day they were supposed to plant trees, his teacher didn't reply. Back at home that afternoon, Kim Jongho didn't know where to plant the seeds. He went to the playground. He failed to note the difference between soil and sand. He was eight years old. He dug up the sand under the slide and poured in the seeds. Starting the next day, he kept watch over the spot under the slide. Even after a month, the moss rose didn't sprout. Tired of waiting, he dug up the sand again. But where the seeds had been, he discovered two rusted coins.

Lim Ojeong didn't get along with her older brother, who was two years older than she. Somehow, things always descended to violence when they were with each other. It was Lim Ojeong's birthday. When the boy's mother reprimanded him, saying he should be more affectionate with his sister, he gave Lim Ojeong a model battleship as a present. She accepted the box with a puzzled look. She was too young to know how to put a model together. Her brother took it back, assembled and painted it, and then displayed it on his desk. On her next birthday, she didn't get anything from him.

Yun Kyeonghui liked to read. Christmas drew near. The kindergarten she attended had all the students write down what they wanted for presents. On a slip of paper she wrote the title of a children's book she had always wanted to read and then submitted it. The day before Christmas, the man from the business next door came dressed in a Santa Claus costume and took out a box with her name on the label from his large red sack. Heart pounding, she opened it. But inside was a different book. The book she had wanted was in another child's hands. Yun Kyeonghui remembers the name of that book. But she still hasn't read it.

Huh Namjun's family on his mother's side lived out in the country. His maternal grandparents, who raised three Jindo dogs, lived up in the mountains a little ways from the village. Whenever he visited, he was allowed to pat these ferocious dogs on their heads. During the winter break, Huh Namjun and his family went to visit his grandparents. But the dogs were gone. When he asked about them, his grandparents said they'd all been killed. The dogs had broken free of their chains and gone down to the village; there, they had attacked and killed all the village dogs. In turn, his grandparents' dogs were shot and killed. Huh Namjun could not tell the difference between "killed" and "were killed."

Kim Injung's mother remembers all the days he struggled with math. She taught biology at a middle school, and spent countless hours teaching him addition and subtraction. But he couldn't understand subtraction. If you take 10 away from 12, what are you left with? she asked. From 12, answered Kim Injung, blinking his dark eyes. She has never hit her son before. It was at the hands of Kim Injung's older brother that the beatings usually happened, when she was still at work. For the older brother, Kim Injung was a problem he could not solve.

Kim Taeyong remembers the summer he was ten years old. On the day his entire summer Bible school class went to an outdoor swimming pool, his bag, clothes, and shoes were stolen. He had to walk home barefoot. The asphalt was hot. He left behind damp footprints, at first from the water from the swimming pool and then from the sweat that trickled down his back. He wore only his swimsuit. One summer, he took his young daughter to an outdoor swimming pool. He kept an eye on both his daughter, who was playing in the water, and their locker.

Kim Inju lost many friends. During the winter of her first year in college, she took a trip to Gangwon Province with three of her school friends. One of them had borrowed a car from her father. The girls were all rather inexperienced drivers, and on the highway they encountered the heaviest snowfall ever. But heavy snowfalls always tend to be the heaviest ever. The car slipped on the slippery road. When Kim Inju woke up, the car was totaled and her friend who had been sitting in the passenger seat was already dead.

Lee Jun-gyu's grandmother enjoyed cultivating the small garden on the rooftop of their house. His family liked to keep pets. Tropical fish, hamsters, guinea pigs, cats, chickens, dogs. One day, he turned up his grandmother's vegetable garden to dig a pond. While he was busily digging out the soil with a trowel, he found the carcass of a small animal. It looked like a hamster or guinea pig. Grandmother, he called. What? she said. A piece of flesh that hadn't rotted away was stuck to the gray bones. Lee Jun-gyu flung aside the trowel. He felt as though his house were an old graveyard.

Lee Muyeong learned about cyanotypes in his third-grade science class. Lee Muyeong, who purchased a sun printing kit at a stationery store, sat in a sunny corner of his apartment building's parking lot and placed small trinkets on top of a photosensitive sheet that was the size of his hand. He waited for an hour. The clouds moved. While he wasn't paying attention, a butterfly alighted on top of the sheet and then fluttered away. He managed to obtain a print with the faint image of a butterfly. White powder from the butterfly's wings rubbed off onto his fingertip.

Whenever Kang Myeonghwa became angry, she locked herself in her room and refused to come out. And every time, she banged her window open so that her family would hear it, and hurled objects out the window, such as her melodeon or globe, things that would make a loud noise when they crashed to the ground. Day by day, her belongings dwindled. Once all the heavy objects had disappeared out the window, the lighter ones soon followed, one by one. Unable to stand by and watch any longer, her mother finally took the bedroom door off its hinges. Kang Myeonghwa slept in a room without a door until she graduated from senior high school.

Choi Mia had two fathers. She received twice as many presents as the other children received on birthdays and Christmas. She had no siblings. The other children were jealous of her face, clothes, and school supplies. She has never been jealous of other children. Choi Mia was not given enough time to learn about jealousy.

When Jang Kihyeon entered the second grade, he went to the house of his new desk mate. The girl's name disappeared from his memory long ago. She led him into her room. Her mother came in with a tray full of snacks and soon left the house. The girl coaxed him to play a fun game. She got him to lie down on the floor and then climbed on top of him. What are you doing? he asked. I don't know. I saw my mom and dad do this, she answered. Mom, my desk mate climbed onto my stomach today, he said to his mother when he got home. Is your desk mate a girl or boy? she asked. Jang Kihyeon's mother called his teacher and demanded that he be assigned a new partner.

Kwon Yeoreum's sole hobby was dancing. But her parents strictly forbade singing and dancing. They kept the television in a large wooden cabinet under lock and key. Whenever their parents left the house, she and her younger siblings would open the cabinet doors with the key they had secretly copied. They would watch television and mimic the singers' moves. Having determined the order ahead of time, they would take turns keeping watch from the balcony. This continued until Kwon Yeoreum became an adult.

Mun Suyeon recalls the yogurt drinks she was never allowed to finish. Because they were expensive, her mother had only one yogurt drink delivered to the house per day. Strawberry, apple, or grape. Mun Suyeon was forced to leave half for her younger brother. A fight ensued if she happened to take one sip beyond the halfway point. The yogurt drink tasted sweet and sour. She had to mark the container at the halfway point with a pen.

Kang Jiyeong recalls the orange juice. Once a week, her mother had a carton of Sunkist Family Juice delivered to their house. Every morning, she had to drink a glass. One morning before school, she dropped her juice-filled cup. It was a mistake. Her mother, who had been spreading jam on her toast, spat out a single command: lick it up. After hesitating for a moment, Kang Jiyeong got down on her hands and knees and lapped at the juice. It was sour. The family dog came running and started lapping juice alongside Kang Jiyeong.

Ahn Jonghyeok remembers the railroad tracks. He and Park Yeongwu often played near the tracks. They placed two coins on top of the rails and waited for a train to run over them. Their favorite was the Saemaeul train. When that train passed, the coins ended up as flat as disks. They did this again and again until they managed to get ones that were perfect circles. The spoils from these expeditions eventually disappeared. But the thin, flat coins weren't all they lost.

Song Ho-myeong wore shirts that were held together with safety pins instead of buttons. His mother had died before she could teach him how to sew buttons on his shirts. His father, who didn't care whether his son even wore a shirt, didn't notice that there were safety pins instead of buttons on his son's shirts. When Song Ho-myeong was able to buy shirts with buttons, he got a girlfriend. This girlfriend, who had gotten a divorce right before she met him, had a ten-year-old daughter. This girl taught Song Ho-myeong how to play chess. They played against each other on their mobile phones. He rarely won.

Shin Munhui was good with her hands. When she entered the tenth grade, sewing was popular among the girls. During breaks, the girls would gather in groups of two or three to sew makeup bags and handkerchiefs. Even during class, Shin Munhui secretly sewed under her desk. Shin Munhui! the geography teacher called. Focused on her sewing, her head bowed, she didn't hear the teacher call her name. Again, in a loud voice, the teacher called her. Shocked, she jumped to her feet. The needle that had been dangling under the desk stabbed her in the thigh and snapped.

Hwang Guenmo remembers Park Yeongwu. In fifth grade, Hwang Guenmo was Park Yeongwu's partner. Park Yeongwu began stealing Hwang Guenmo's change on the first day of class. Hwang Guenmo carried two sets of journals and notebooks. He did Park Yeongwu's homework. He also filled out Park Yeongwu's journal. Once when the homeroom teacher called Park Yeongwu's name during attendance, Hwang Guenmo answered for him without thinking. The next day, Park Yeongwu threw Hwang Guenmo's shoes into the incinerator. Hwang Guenmo had to walk home barefoot.

So Yeonghyeon had a close friend. The friend's name was In-kyeong, or perhaps Inseon. In-kyeong, or perhaps Inseon, had a brother who was ten years younger. A rumor began to spread that In-kyeong, or perhaps Inseon, breast-fed her brother. Even children from another class came up to So Yeonghyeon to ask whether or not it was true. It was ridiculous. But when all the children ended up believing this ridiculous story with the exception of So Yeonghyeon, she no longer needed to keep saying it was ridiculous.

Yu Huikyeong remembers the chicken. On a certain day in March, she bought a chick in front of the school gate. She kept it in a cardboard box she obtained from the produce market. Whenever it got too loud, Yu Huikyeong's mother would cover the box with newspaper. The chick then became quiet. It met a fate far different from the chicks in the fists of other children. The chick died before it could mature into a chicken. She didn't know whether to call it a chick or chicken.

Choi Hayeon remembers the piano. She hid a few trivial, but meaningful, objects inside the piano bench. When that spot was discovered, she opened the lid and hid the objects inside the piano. She wouldn't practice pieces that required her to hit high notes, since the weight of the objects on the strings prevented the higher keys from moving. Choi Hayeon was the only one in her family who was intimately familiar with the large, elegant instrument. The piano was never once tuned.

One time around Christmas, Wu Jina swiped Christmas cards from around her apartment complex. She stole perhaps a hundred altogether. A name was written on every card. She couldn't figure out a way to reuse them. Before her family could find out, she stuffed all the cards minus their envelopes into a mailbox.

Lee Dongju recalls the seagulls. Lee Dongju and his mother went to visit his aunt who ran a bed-and-breakfast on an island off the west coast. It was to be his first time meeting this aunt, as well as his first time on a boat. Shivering at the quayside, he ate some instant noodles. When the boat started to move, Lee Dongju, who had been standing by the railing on the top deck, heaved up everything he had just eaten into the sea. The seagulls circling overhead dove diagonally toward his vomit that was now floating on the waves. The same thing happened on the boat on their way back.

Na Yunmi had three friends. She began to receive an anonymous note every day. You're a sheep dressed in wolf's clothing. Die. Just die. Na Yunmi hid the notes in her textbook and refused to go to school. Her mother took her to see a child psychiatrist. The doctor offered only one answer: nerves. The sender of the notes was one of her three friends. Na Yunmi still has those notes.

Park Jihye recalls the time: 8:40. It was winter. After coming home from school, she fell asleep in the living room. No one was home. When she was startled awake by the chill that crept in, the hands on the clock were pointing to 8:40. Shocked, she hurried to the bathroom and washed her face. She then realized she hadn't done her homework, but she was already late. She put on her backpack and was hurrying down the stairs when she ran into her father. Where are you going? he asked. To school, she answered. Why are you going to school at night? he asked.

Jung Yongjun recalls that convenience store at night. When he was about ten years old, the first convenience store opened in his neighborhood. The lights of the store's sign never turned off, no matter how late it was. One evening on his way home from a tutoring session, he thought everything looked strange. What was it? Was the earth collapsing? he wondered. Even the store's blue sign that always shone brightly was out. The dusky street was quickly growing dark. Candles were lit at his house. There had been a power failure.

Oh Sora was a gifted ballet dancer. Or perhaps the ballet teacher simply flattered Oh Sora's mother. Starting a month before the ballet competition, Oh Sora skipped dinner. Every night, she fell asleep while thinking of all that she wanted to eat. On the night of the competition, she failed to win a prize. As she and her parents were driving from Seoul back to their city, they decided to make a quick stop at a highway rest area. Oh Sora wanted to eat a hamburger. But the only place where the lights were on was the bathroom. She demanded that her parents buy her a hamburger. Her mother, unable to cope with her own disappointment and exhaustion, slapped her. Oh Sora quit ballet.

19

The children's journals are not on the teacher's desk. The children are silent. The sentences that the children could not and cannot write are not on the teacher's desk. As always, the potted plants on the windowsill complain of hunger and thirst. The children have all committed sins large and small during their brief lives. Sin. It is only after they have committed a sin that they understand the weight of the word *sin*, or perhaps of *evil*. The sins, or evils, both large and small that the children have committed and will commit choke them. It's still April. Friday. Clear. Exactly 9:00 a.m. Cold spring air blows in through the half-open window at the back of the classroom. The children in the back rows wince. All thirty-five children have their mouths closed. Kim Injung raises his dark eyes and gazes at the teacher. The teacher turned forty-nine this year and also greeted his twentieth year teaching. He looks at the children. The children, whose gazes are lowered, stare blankly at the scribbles on their desks. He thinks this incident is truly the first of its kind and the first in every way. The journals the children had submitted have now disappeared altogether. He glances at the children's small heads. Who could it be? There is no way of knowing. Who in the world would do such a thing? He thinks that perhaps it's not a child's doing. He can't imagine any child who would dare sneak into the classroom with a stolen key and take only the journals. And yet. Nothing else, apart from the journals, is missing. And yet. No child he knows would be bold enough to trespass into the empty school in the middle of the night, and at least twice. That morning, immediately after he had checked under his desk, he had gone looking for the teacher who had been on night duty. After hearing the full story, that teacher gave a bewildered smile. Maybe a child played a prank on you when you weren't watching? Anyhow, he hadn't seen anything out of the ordinary. And yet, the homeroom teacher thinks there is something disturbing about the whole incident. The incident itself isn't so serious. But it's a rather elaborate act for a child to commit. There is no trace. The evidence has disappeared. And yet. The teacher thinks about the clear penmanship of the person who had added sentences to every journal. I hate you. It hurts. I despise you. A fire is hot. A long and hard thing. A needle is pointy. It hurts. It hurts so much I can hardly bear it. I want to kill, too. I want to kill. Bad things are painful. Painful things are bad. And yet, as far as he knows, there is no child in Grade 5, Section 3, with such penmanship. It didn't look like a child's handwriting. It looked more like a grown-up's handwriting. If it indeed had been a child, the teacher thinks he would have entered that child as class representative in a penmanship competition. And yet. The writing in the journals looked like the writer had intentionally imitated the bad handwriting of children. The teacher shakes his head. There is no longer any need to wait until Monday. At a loss, he stands on the platform at the front of the classroom. He doesn't have the nerve to become the piper himself and pretend to lead thirty-five children to the police station. It only takes about fifteen minutes to walk to the police station. Fifteen minutes isn't enough time to obtain a confession. The children's attention scatters. Their mouths are still closed. Looking bored, Kim Injung throws his head back. The Child glances at him. With his head tilted back, he is staring at her with dark eyes. She meets his stare calmly. *Gieok. Niun. Digu. Riul. Mium.* His tongue darts in and out between his open lips. Knife. He is watching her, and she is focused on watching Mia. Yesterday. Thursday. It rained yesterday. Rain is good. Rain erases footprints. She once read a book from the school library about a detective who lost the culprit's tracks because of the previous night's rain. Swamp. Mud. Quagmire. The detective, his assistant, and the police inspector, who dragged along a dog, all fell into the mud. While the Child read the book, the two-lane asphalt road came immediately to mind. Footprints can't be left on asphalt. And yet. At the end of the story, the detective finds the culprit. The detective possessed other evidence. Evidence that wasn't erased by the rain. Evidence that didn't drift away with the rain. Evidence that the culprit had carelessly left behind. The Child nearly shakes her head without thinking, but stops herself. She must not attract any attention. The detective was able to find the culprit because the culprit happened to be one of the characters in the story. Because every story needs a conclusion. But the Child isn't merely a character. She has no conclusion. At least not yet. Besides, she didn't leave behind any tracks, let alone other evidence. Her daring and meticulousness crush the teacher's chest. Tracks. Cracks. Backs. But the teacher doesn't watch the Child closely. He has never properly looked at her. Perhaps she has never properly revealed herself to the teacher. Or to anyone. Time is passing. The hands on the clock on the back wall are pointing to 9:05. Close the window, the teacher finally says. A child sitting next to the window slowly shuts it. The child's name is Na Yunmi. Child, child, child. Thirty-five children. The journals are missing, the teacher says. I trusted you, but now I don't know what to say. Kim Injung twists around in his seat and looks back at the Child. Knife. But her gaze is fixed on the scribbles on her desk. Mia, who is sitting diagonally from the Child a few desks away, looks absentmindedly at the back of the Child's neck. On her bluish neck is a distinct red line. This curved red line doesn't connect the Child and Mia. The Child's rumpled collar covers the end of this line. Something pops into Mia's head, but she soon forgets it. No, Mia finds the thought again. Inju, who is sitting next to Mia, hopes only that this moment will pass.

That class will start, that this time of forced silence, perhaps, this time of forced confession, will pass. I was planning to wait until Monday, says the teacher. But instead of confessing, you've stolen all the journals, whoever you are. This cannot happen. If you don't come forward by the end of the day, we will all go to the police station together. Or I will just have to find some other way to track the culprit down. The children whisper. The children stare at those around them. On each child's face is an expression akin to rage at having been pegged as the potential culprit. Now, the children must peg those around them as the potential culprit. The child sitting next to the Child stares at the Child. The Child stares back. The two have barely ever spoken to each other. Maybe an eraser had passed between them a few times. The Child glances at the notebook and textbook on top of the child's desk. Yang Yeong-ae. 양영애. 5-3. It's a name composed of o's. Calmly, the Child puts her hands inside her desk and pulls out her notebook and textbook. It's 9:10. The bell rings through the classroom speakers. It's journal time. Busily the children glance inside their desks. All of a sudden, the Child feels a pain in her neck. It happened yesterday. No. The day before yesterday, no, the week before, no, a month before, no, perhaps it had been happening for an eternity. The pain spreads down her back and hips. She begins to pant. Teacher! someone cries. Thirty-five gazes, including the teacher's, swivel sharply toward the voice and affix themselves on the speaker. The Child also turns to look. It's Mia. Teacher, Mia calls once more. Yes? the teacher says, as though he anticipates something. What is it, Mia? Looking embarrassed, Mia asks, May I go to the bathroom? As soon as she finishes speaking, the thirty-five gazes that were directed at Mia go slack. All at once. The teacher nods vacantly. Mia gets up from her seat, looking relieved. Inju looks up at Mia with a dazed expression. The Child's neck grows stiff. She turns to watch Mia, who slips out through the back door of the classroom. A vivid pain runs down the Child's back.

Through the classroom window, she sees the top of Mia's head as she walks down the hall toward the bathroom. Her hair, tightly secured with a green hair tie, sways from side to side. The Child's gaze is fixed on Mia's green hair tie. She must be careful about Mia. Perhaps Mia said that she needed to go to the bathroom for a reason. Perhaps it was a warning to the Child. Perhaps Mia has put everything together. The Child grows anxious, like a block of ice left out in the midday sun. Except she can't simply melt away and disappear. The teacher coughs. Kim Injung spreads open his sketchbook instead of his textbook and turns to look at the Child. Knife. She avoids his dark eyes. Knife. Every time she moves, pain digs into her body. Like a knife. Calmly, she moves her hands and opens her textbook. She hides her left hand under her desk, under her textbook. She has lost a fingernail. It happened yesterday. But no one notices that her finger is missing a nail. She has lost a key. It happened yesterday. On page 27 is an illustration of the Antarctic Research Station. Without warning, she ducks her head and plugs her nose with her right hand. But there is already a drop of blood on the white snow. One. Two. She tilts her head back. The trickle of blood runs down between her fingers and her bony jaw. Yang Yeong-ae, who is sitting next to her, looks shocked and rummages through her bag for a tissue. The long, red scratch on the Child's neck swells. The hand that is plugging her nose trembles faintly.

20

Mia and Inju head home. On a yellow Friday in April outside the school gate, the children scatter into three groups, each following one of the three paths that split off the road. I wonder who did it, says Inju. Was it you? Mia asks, peering at Inju mischievously. Inju jumps in protest. How can you say that? Inju, who can't help reacting this way, suddenly remembers the pearl brooch that is hidden in her desk drawer and Princess Diana's picture. Inju's face turns red. I was just joking, why are you so scared? asks Mia. Mia and Inju walk past the corner bookshop. Should we have some spicy rice cakes before we go home? asks Mia. Inju nods. They walk into the snack shop where children their age have gathered. A plate of spicy rice cakes is placed between the two children, who sit across from each other. Give me your hand, says Mia. Why? But before Mia even answers, Inju extends her hand toward Mia. Make a fist. Inju's fingernails dig into her palm. The fleshy part of her palm sticks out. Mia presses the base of Inju's palm. Two small bumps bulge out on the border between Inju's wrist and palm. What are you doing? Inju asks. They say if two bumps stick out like this, you'll have two kids when you grow up, says Mia. Really? Inju asks, somewhat skeptically. It's true. Mia nods, looking serious. Now you make a fist, says Inju, starting to reach for Mia's hand. No. Mia shakes her head and laughs. Hey, that's not fair! Come on, give me your hand! Steam is rising from the rice cakes. A few boys walk into the snack shop. Mia gets up, pours two cups of water, and brings them over. Inju looks at Mia's hand that is holding the cup. Five fingers. They are neither long nor short. They are neither pale nor dark. Mia's pinky catches Inju's eye. Mia grew just her pinky nail long. Mia, sitting back down in her seat, grips her fork and says, I tried, but I didn't get any bumps. She lets go of the fork and takes a sip of water. Really? Inju asks. Yeah, I didn't get any. But who knows if it's real anyway?

Mia and Inju say good-bye at the intersection in front of the hospital. Mia has to be home early that day. Mia's father is coming. But which father? Mia had told Inju only that her dad was going to buy her something delicious for dinner. That night Mia's dinner table will become one of many bridges. The two children wave at each other and turn away. As Mia turns, her hair that had been in a ponytail sways. On the way home, no butterflies can be found. This scene where no butterflies can be found, however, doesn't grow darker. It's already dark. Mia's green hair tie bounces with every step. A hard knot. With every step she takes, the physical world surrounding her changes in perfect order. A world for Mia, Mia's world. She has never looked back without thinking. She has never been suspicious of anything. Mia's world is perfect. There is no end to what she is given. Yet her world doesn't become bloated, because there is no end to what she loses or forgets. There is no lack. There is only forgetfulness. There is no lack of substitutes. But there is no time. No. There is time. There is still time. If there is still enough time, Mia could grow up and receive about forty desperate missed calls on her cellular phone while she's asleep, someone could climb into her window while she's out, she could temporarily ruin someone's life this way without realizing it. Because after all, Mia is quite pretty, and she could unwittingly use her innocent, dazed expression as a kind of device. And finally, no, tentatively, she could even settle for someone who would guarantee her safety. But none of this has happened yet. No one knows what will happen to Mia or the other children. Mia passes the hardware store, the wallpaper and linoleum store, the flower bed in front of the after-school academy, and the bicycle shop. She doesn't want to go to an after-school academy and she wants a bicycle. The outcome will hinge on how much she begs. Mia has two fathers, and one of them doesn't know what to do when Mia cries. As she walks past the supermarket, she doesn't bump into anyone. Her head is filled with thoughts of a bicycle. She no longer wants to ride a child's bicycle. She wants to ride a bicycle to school like a middle school student, or perhaps a high school student. In a brown uniform, in Adidas running shoes. Her mother might forbid her to ride a bicycle in a skirt. Anyhow, all of this will be given to her someday; time will provide. When the time comes. Mia has completely forgotten the previous night's incident. The new bicycle that she will gain exhibits great power, even though its existence isn't yet a reality. She doesn't know the name of the child she bumped into last night. Everything that exists has a name. Such is the case with the bicycle. Mia's bicycle. She may get a new one this month. She may even give it a name. This bicycle is entirely Mia's. She may grow tired of it in less than two months. But she won't forget something like its name. But she doesn't know the Child's name. And so, Mia doesn't remember the Child. The Child is blacked out. No. Perhaps to Mia, the Child has never existed.

In front of Mia's home, or to be exact, in front of the lobby where the elevator that will go up to Mia's apartment is located, Mia sees her two fathers. Father 1 is grabbing Father 2 by the collar. Father 2 is glaring at Father 1. Mia's mother is absent from this scene. At this moment. Mia drops her shoe bag. But her two fathers don't hear the bag hit the sidewalk. They swing their fists at each other, but because they keep each other at a distance, their punches beat the air. The security guard stands near them, beside himself with worry. Mia never anticipated an incident like this. This is to be expected, because Mia has never anticipated any incident. The two fathers are not aware of Mia, who is watching them with a dazed expression. They are too busy attending to their own needs. The security guard who had been trying to separate the two fathers ends up backing away instead. The week before, two middle school students plunged into a flower bed in this apartment complex. This incident has frayed the nerves of all the security guards. Friday. 4:00 p.m. It is a leisurely time, if one doesn't count the women going to the bank or market and the children returning from school. A woman who has come outside to take her dog for a walk watches from afar. Even a real estate agent and someone who appears to be his client, even a person skating by on Rollerblades, even the women carrying plastic bags with purses squeezed at their sides, watch from afar. Laundry hangs from several balconies. People reveal every intimate detail about their families by carelessly hanging out their laundry. Mismatched socks. An apron still faintly stained with blood. A shirt with its breast pocket betraying the outline of a balled-up receipt, which hadn't been removed prior to washing. During the scuffle, Father 1 takes off his jacket and hurls it to the ground. The moment the jacket falls, their dignity also falls away. They have never met one another. Until now. But it's not clear how they have come to put their pride on the line to engage in such a fight, the way it's demanded of male creatures, right in front of Mia's home, claiming some kind of ownership over Mia and her mother. If they hadn't met this day, they would have had to meet someday. Even in this case, people often use the expression "a matter of time." Mia is watching her fathers with a dumbfounded look on her face. Every last thought of the bicycle has disappeared from her head. Will Mia get a bicycle? But when? Look at Mia on a bicycle. Look at how she pedals, in her backpack and the sweater with the deer, look how she races away, her ponytail swaying from side to side! Will this scene ever exist? But when? Building 110, Suite 904. Mia looks up toward the ninth floor. No laundry hangs from the balcony of Mia's home. Not even a sock or scrap of underwear. There isn't even a small household item on the balcony, like a potted plant.

Mia's mother can be seen dimly through the bedroom window that looks out onto the balcony. Half-hidden by the curtain, she is merely watching the spectacle unfold below. As a complete bystander, she watches Father 1 and Father 2. There is no way of knowing whether or not she is aware of Mia. From where Mia stands, she can't see the expression on her mother's face. In the end, all things are a matter of seeing and being seen. Father 1 has never seen Father 2. In his world, he was able to swallow his rage while Father 2 was absent. But through some coincidence, or perhaps some necessity, Father 2 appeared before him. The opposite case is possible. Father 2 has also never seen Father 1. Until Father 1 appeared before him in the flesh, he was also able to swallow his rage or some emotion similar to rage. But they have run across each other. In front of Mia's home, in a spot where they could look up at Suite 904 of Building 110. The two cannot enter Mia's home at the same time. Only one can put his hand on Mia's shoulder and confidently stride through the lobby doors. One must back off. One must leave. And he must never again appear before the other three people. But neither of the men makes a move to flee. Father 2 also takes off his jacket and hurls it to the ground. The security guard, exhausted from trying to break up the fight, picks up the two jackets and brushes off debris. A piece of dry laundry from an unidentifiable source hangs over the guard's left arm. Mia tries to anticipate her mother's wavering expression behind her window. Mia's mother gazes down at the scene below, wearing an expression that Mia cannot name. The two fathers continue to beat the air in vain. The first person to land a blow will suffer a defeat. The two men, who have just entered their forties, know this all too well. They know that the person who takes a punch and drops to the ground will have a better chance of possessing everything. The amiable-looking security guard steps in between them. But the guard is much shorter than the men. The two men continue exchanging punches that keep missing the target as though they don't care if the security guard is there or not. One father ends up striking the security guard's face with his elbow. It's most likely an accident. The guard screams and clasps his face. The two jackets that had been slung over his arm fall again to the ground. At the same time, the dignity of all three men also falls away. No. They no longer possess any dignity to let fall to the ground. Mia, who had been watching in stunned shock until now, shouts. Dad!

When that happens, the two fathers both turn toward Mia.

And standing behind Mia is the Child. No. To be exact, standing in a spot Mia can't see, perhaps in a spot even Mia's fathers can't see, is the Child, hiding in the shadow of the lilac bushes. The Child has followed Mia from school, past the snack shop, the hardware store, the wallpaper and linoleum store, the after-school academy, the bicycle shop, the supermarket, and the apartment security booth. And so, being seen wasn't everything. The Child existed where Mia couldn't see, where you and I couldn't see. And now the Child is watching Mia. Mia isn't watching the Child. Mia's head, which had been filled only with thoughts of bicycles, is now filled with thoughts of her two fathers who are looking anxiously at her. The security guard rubs the bridge of his nose and looks at the fathers. Mia bursts into tears. The two fathers' shoulders slump. The cuckolded husband and paramour. But there is no way Mia could know this sort of expression. Neither father rushes to Mia's side. Mia sinks to the ground and begins to sob.

And there is the Child. Let's not forget about her. Without thinking, she touches her neck. A reddish scab falls by her feet. It's so small no one notices it. She looks back carelessly. No one is there. Into her memory she engraves Mia, Mia's two fathers, and Mia's mother, who can be seen faintly through the balcony window of Suite 904. And even the security guard who keeps rubbing his nose. The bystanders leave. And the Child must also leave. She turns and begins to run for home.

21

The weekend passes. Another Monday. The teacher doesn't speak a word about the stolen journals until the end of the last class. The right side of the Child's face is badly swollen. It happened on Saturday, or perhaps Sunday. Or maybe Thursday, or perhaps Friday. No one seems concerned about her face. The teacher assumes she has caught the mumps. No, the teacher doesn't think about the Child at all. No one approaches the teacher with a flushed face, even when the last class ends. He has no choice but to think of the petty authority and dignity granted to him as a teacher. He must take responsibility for his words, at a minimum follow through with his threats. But no one has come to him offering a confession, accusation, or excuse of any kind. He also has a child. But the fact that he has a child in middle school is no help at all right now. The children's expressions, the children's gestures, the children's speech, are a complete mystery to him. Even if he were to scrutinize all thirty-five students one at a time, he lacks the means to discover which child was capable of such an act. Which child. He decides to remain silent. For the time being. He decides to wait. For the time being. At the end of class, he tells the students on classroom duty to clean with greater care than usual. Those not on duty noisily open and close their bags, and escape from the classroom. There are eight children left. Awkwardly, Inju waves at Mia and leaves. Mia, the Child, and the rest of the children drag the desks to the back of the room. Mia, who spent the entire weekend crying, also has a swollen face. Mia has hardly spoken to Inju today. Inju had asked if anything was the matter, but Mia had merely given her the same answer—I'm fine—over and over again. The Child glances at Mia's face. With her mouth tightly shut, Mia is sweeping. Hair ties, erasers, and notes that were secretly passed in class get swept up by Mia's broom. The teacher isn't there. The Child thinks this is her chance to approach Mia. She must interrogate Mia. I hate you. I hate you. It hurts. I despise you. A fire is hot. A long and hard thing. A needle is pointy. It hurts. It hurts so much I can hardly bear it. I want to kill, too. I want to kill. Bad things are painful. Painful things are bad. I want to kill, too. I despise you. It hurts. I hate you. Dust rises from the end of the broom.

Stifling her anxiety, the Child observes Mia. Are you friends? Mia's mother had asked. She's in my class, Mia had said. The Child isn't Mia's friend. Mia would never pour out her heart to the Child. What she had seen. What she hadn't seen. Right now, Mia's head is filled with thoughts of her two fathers and mother. Mia's pinky fingernail catches the Child's eye. No one, not even the Child, can see the Child's pinky fingernail. It had disappeared from the Child's finger. It had happened last Thursday. The Child, quietly sweeping while watching Mia, looks back. No one is there. Do you live around here? What's your name? Mia's mother had asked. She hadn't answered. All she can think now is that she has been discovered by Mia and her mother. In her head, something keeps collapsing. Keeps collapsing. Something. Even though it seems impossible for something to keep collapsing. Having finished with the sweeping, the children begin to move the desks back to their original place. The Child is assigned the job of sweeping the dust and trash that have collected at the back of the classroom into a dustpan. Hey, the teacher has to check everything, someone says. Everyone's gaze swivels toward Mia, who's standing by the classroom door. Mia steps out, looking churlish. And just then, the Child's nerve, pulled impossibly taut, snaps. Her face grows pale. (I hate you.) Her darkness is exposed. With trembling hands, she empties the dustpan by tapping it against the trash can. The pile of brooms in the corner gives off an unpleasant smell. The smell of wet straw. The expression "wanting to grasp at straws." Perhaps Mia has gone to tell the teacher something else instead. (I hate you.) Mia never relinquished the duty of reporting to the teacher; she always did it herself. The Child leans back against the supply closet. She weighs every possibility. In her head. In her mind. Perhaps with all her body. The wounds on her neck grow darker. Like the protective coloring of a wild animal. (I hate you.) The floating particles of dust settle on the Child's nose and shoulders. She wishes she could turn into a fossil. She thinks it would be nice to turn into a fossil and be discovered a million years from now. But no trace must be left. Even such an infinitely long time as a million years will not be able to protect her. Right now, there isn't enough dust in the classroom to shroud her. It's because she has swept. And because Mia has swept. The Child must simply disappear. If not, the mice and ants that have been following her will erase her tracks and gobble her up. Someday. Even if a million years went by. Sometime. The children, who sat perched on top of the desks looking bored, start to choke one another. They call this "the fainting game." The only time the children can play this game is when the teacher isn't there. The child being strangled gasps, pretending to choke. The other children snicker. The Child looks blankly at Kim Injung's desk, which is set at an awkward angle beside the teacher's desk. Knife. She thinks about the afternoon she taught Kim Injung the alphabet. *Gieok* and *mium*. Memory and hatred. And knife.

Mia and the teacher walk through the classroom door, which had been left open. The children who were choking each other release each other in surprise. With flushed faces, they avoid the teacher's gaze. The teacher, who had been glancing around the classroom absentmindedly, makes eye contact with the Child. For a moment, he stares intently at her face. She stares back at him. Her legs shake. It's not that she's frightened of him. She knows from experience that it's always possible to be more frightened than frightened, more scared than scared, more terrified than terrified. Perhaps only death can put a stop to these things. Perhaps the teacher is only noting her swollen face. Perhaps. She struggles to look calm. Has it only been a second? It feels like an eternity. Mia packs up her bag, looking coy. You may go now, says the teacher. See you tomorrow. The Child expels a shallow breath. The children who had been fiddling awkwardly with the straps on their bags hurry out the classroom door. The Child also picks up her bag. It hurts. Her face, her neck, her back, her hips, her legs, her head, her shoulders, her knees, her feet, her knees, her feet, her head, her shoulders, her knees, her feet, her knees, her ears, her nose, her ears. She walks down the hall and goes down the stairs, panting, and looks back without thinking. Mia is walking down the stairs with a coy expression on her face. The Child's legs give out. She grabs on to the railing and collapses. She is shaking. The cold stairs are cold. The cold railing is cold. The cold Child is cold. All of a sudden, the Child tips her head back and plugs her nose with her hand. A cold trickle of blood runs down between the Child's fingers. The cold blood is cold. Mia, who had been walking down the stairs, draws near. Are you okay? asks Mia. The Child flinches. Several boys pass Mia and the Child boisterously. Once they're gone, Mia sits next to the Child and puts her bag down. Your nose is bleeding, Mia says. The Child says nothing. She is covering her face with both hands. Her face must not be seen. Mia opens her bag and looks for a tissue or handkerchief. But she has neither. Do you have a tissue? Mia asks. The Child shakes her head. Blood falls onto the Child's indoor shoes. It also falls on the floor. Hold on, I'll go get some from the bathroom, says Mia. Violently, the Child shakes her head. She tries to say something, but her hand is blocking her mouth. Her missing fingernail. It hurts. She pulls out the hem of her shirt from under her sweater and wipes away the blood.

The bleeding is slowing. The Child swallows the lump of blood that has clotted in her throat. She reeks of blood. Mia pats her on the back. Are you okay? The Child nods. There's blood on your clothes. Your mom might get worried, Mia says. Your mom might get worried. The Child thinks that *mom* and *worry* don't go together. She finds Mia's sympathetic hands oppressive. She thinks about Mia for a moment. Knife. She doesn't shake off Mia's hands. What should I do? she wonders. Knife. What should I do? Her head fills with the sickening smell of blood. Her T-shirt is stained with blood. Her blood is turning from red to brown. Before brown turns to black, she must wash her clothes. Won't your mom worry if she sees your clothes? asks Mia. I can wash it in the bathroom, the Child answers. But you'll have to take off your shirt, says Mia. Oh . . . , the Child trails off. By the way, did you, back there, with the teacher . . . The Child forgets what she's saying. Mia flinches. No. The Child has only imagined it. Did you, back there, did you tell the teacher . . . The Child looks at Mia. The Child looks calm and cold. Her upper lip is smudged with blood. Seeing it, Mia flinches. You should wash your face, too, Mia says, changing the subject. No. The Child has only imagined that Mia changed the subject. You can come over and get cleaned up, Mia says. No one's home, she says. Mia's home. The Child already knows where Mia lives. Mia's mother and fathers are not home. At this moment. The Child stares at Mia. But Mia is closing her bag. Mia puts her bag on her back and gets up from the steps. Let's go, Mia says. To the Child. The Child tucks in the hem of her shirt. Blood has even gotten on the neck of her sweater. Blood is not blood red. It's turning black. Hey, what's your name anyway? Mia asks. To the Child. The Child looks down at the drops of blood that have fallen on the ground. Sorry, I haven't memorized everyone's name yet, Mia says. To the Child. Mia walks down the stairs. Instead of answering, the Child follows her down.

22

The cold Child is cold. The cold Child sheds cold blood. The cold blood is cold. Only statements that repeat the same words are good. Expressions that betray no meaning. Meaning that keeps coming back. Expressions that carry no other meaning. The road in front of the school gate splits into three paths. The road that has split into three paths splits into several more paths. The paths radiate from the school gate. Most children choose the paths they normally use. On these paths are the stationery store, bookstore, video arcade, snack shop, toy store, and all kinds of after-school academies. The children's heads begin to ripen. The children stray from their familiar paths. At last, they learn to hide their shadows in obscure paths, but let the desires of their shadows roam off the paths to their hearts' content. They say that a moment's decision can change the course of your life. But life is composed of moments of decision. Once you pass over this path, you must pass over that one. There are paths everywhere and there are children everywhere. Without warning, a motorcycle or car races out from an alley. At times, the children who had been running after the ball must pick up their own heads off the ground. The very children who had tossed unfinished cartons of milk onto the road. On the road bloodstains spread over the milk stains. Grown-ups think the pavement can be marked with all the milk that has collected in the potholes in the asphalt. Whiter and whiter. Redder and redder. The children lucky enough to avoid an accident aren't quick to understand the absurd sadness of survivors. But accidents are always planned. There must always be someone who is bounced violently off the road. This is how an overpopulated city suffering from congestion survives. The children are violently discarded on the endless path and they fully experience the grind of city living. They say that looking back on the path you've walked is evidence that you're now a grown-up. The children look back on the paths they've walked. That time when they awkwardly steadied their necks, they who picked up the heads that were once their property. When they look back, it's always a dead-end alley. Without knowing how they've slipped out from that place, they must be discarded again with violence, with even greater violence. The asphalt calls up recollections. Recollections are ghosts. Ghosts have no feet. Recollections grab hold of their feet. Memories are also ghosts. But memories cut off their feet. The memories that have been paved with asphalt cut across their past and present at a speed that makes sensation impossible. And so the future also exists beyond sensation, the future that doesn't exist waits for them, and for you and me. A million years later, we will be discovered as fossils in a stratum of asphalt and concrete. We must endure a period of a million years, learning how organic matter crumbles into inorganic matter. No one, not a thing, will be able to rescue us until all the moisture has left our bodies. The cold Child is cold. The Child is a child. The Child stands. The Child hesitates. The Child stirs. The Child moves. Where? The Child moves perilously across the border of a path and what is no longer a path. The hill on top of the path, the cliff on top of the path, the river on top of the path, the precipice on top of the path, the ocean on top of the path, and the bluff on top of the path camouflage themselves as the cityscape and quietly wait for the children to trip over their own feet. Most children return home meekly, but the instant the Child steps into her home, she is shoved out onto the path, and the instant she is standing on the path, she must return home. No one knows where her fingernail shard that has been so violently plucked off has gone. The instant her fingernail was torn off, her pain receptors created an illusion of mice and ants. So that the mice and ants would eat up the fingernail and become her and share her pain receptors. So that the Child, if possible, would lose all ten fingernails and become ten of herself and share out her pain receptors equally between these ten. Fingernails grow and wounds heal. Bruises fade and swelling subsides. Time passes this way. But no matter how long she waited, the mice and ants didn't appear. Even the piper, even Puss in Boots, didn't appear. The Child is neither lucky nor unlucky. She is simply luckless. She has neither fortune nor misfortune. And so her fate must quietly come to an end here. But that's impossible. She must no longer disclose anything. But that's impossible. The odd pairing of *disclose* and *dispose*. The expression "wrong path" signifies nothing. There is no path that can't be wrong. All paths are already wrong. All paths are bad. Paths leave traces. The wrong path that the Child has walked will pursue her someday. If you can't stop, you must move on. At a very fast speed, at a speed beyond sensation. The Child goes down the stairs. Because she has no memory or recollection, her feet are safe. If only someone would grab hold of her feet, if only someone would cut off her feet so that the Child would stop right there, so that the Child wouldn't step onto any path. But that's impossible. The Child is moving. When the Child looks back without thinking, not a person, not a thing, is there. The Child's path of retreat is a dead-end alley. She must retreat at the same time that she advances. The road in front of the school gate splits into three paths. Asphalt is good. Footprints can't be left on asphalt. No trace must be left. But there are too many traces on the Child's body. Every time the Child scratches the back of her neck without thinking, dark red scabs fall and scatter on the asphalt. Without realizing it, the Child has left behind evidence. But these things are barely noticeable. They say that what is unseen can speak volumes. Still, what is unseen is better than what is seen. Other children will soon occupy the path that the Child walks. The evidence the Child has let loose will be kicked and trampled by the children; it will soon be destroyed. The Child, who is following Mia, looks back. No one is there. There must be no one. No one is there.

23

Which one is your building? Mia asks. Mine's 120 . . . , the Child
trails off. Hey, this is the first time we've talked, isn't it? How come
you're always so quiet? Do you get sick a lot? The Child doesn't answer. Are you normally this quiet? asks Mia. Both Mia and the
Child look straight ahead. Their gazes do not meet. Murderous desire pulses suddenly from the Child's eyes. She shakes her head. Mia
doesn't look at her. When they're walking past the bicycle shop, Mia
briefly thinks about bicycles. Over the past two days, Mia has missed
the opportunity to beg for a bicycle. While Mia's mother shook her
head from behind the curtain, Mia's fathers each neglected their du-
ties because they were consoling Mia, who was crying. Who should
get lost? Who should gain ownership over this child? Who should
wield Mia's mother? Mia is lucky. By tomorrow, Mia's face will once
again be as fair as milk, as smooth as a baby's bottom. If not tomorrow, then the day after tomorrow, if not the day after tomorrow, then
the day after that. More than half of Mia's journal is still blank. Mia,
who had possessed two journals, now has only one. The other one is
still in the recycling bin that hasn't yet been collected. Mia's yesterday, the day before yesterday, and the day before that had passed
in total confusion. Mia didn't write about her sadness and rage in
the journal hidden in a corner of her desk. She was unable to write
a single sentence. It's because all the questions she has never demanded answers to—why her mother hides her face, why her fathers
seize each other by the collar, why her father slaps her mother, why
her mother slaps her father—have boomeranged back to Mia. Why?

Mia must be compensated for the weekend that she has lost. If only a bicycle could serve as the compensation. Mia could have anything she wants. If only she wants it, and if only she knew what she wanted, and if only she knew that in order to gain something, something else must be surrendered. From color pencils to a sweater, from a sweater to a bicycle, the list of all the things that she could and must have evolves daily. There is no lack of substitutes. If a bicycle isn't given to Mia because bicycles are dangerous, she could plead for a dog or cat. Dogs and cats are safe. Mia's fathers would gladly place a dog or cat in her arms if only they knew that it would help them win her affections. Although Mia can't clearly express her sadness, rage, or other similar emotions, she knows how to use her head shrewdly, or perhaps innocently, to gain the things she wants.

Mia and the Child pass the supermarket at the corner of the arcade. Mia turns to look at the Child. The Child avoids her gaze. A shadow falls across her face. The music of shadows. She is still unable to shake off her suspicions about Mia. Mia had said, What's that? What's all that under your arm? She remembers that moment in one-second intervals. What's that? All that. Under your arm. Mia from the previous Thursday takes shape in the Child's head. Mia is wearing baggy jeans with a green jacket. She taps the ground with the end of her closed umbrella. The water runs down the umbrella and drips onto the ground. Next to Mia is her mother, who is holding a plastic bag filled with groceries, including eggs. Mother and daughter. A scene like this is awkward for the Child. Do you live around here? What's your name, Mia's mother says. To the Child. In that instant, she comes close to dropping all of the thirty-five journals she's carrying.

Mia looks away from the Child. The Child stares at the back of Mia's head. As they pass the weed-choked flower bed beside the security booth, the Child looks up toward the rooftop of Building 101. Would it have rotted? Would it have frozen? Would it have died? She's certain that it would have rotted or frozen or died. No. They say a cat has nine lives. So it could have been reborn and gone somewhere else. No. It could have been on its ninth life then. That's right. Whether it has one life or nine lives, it's bound to die someday. Someday. Everything. Everyone. All. The Child swallows. As Mia gets closer to home, her shoulders begin to droop. The Child looks at Mia's shoulders. Mia tugs her backpack straps forward. The Child purposely trails several steps behind Mia. They might run into someone Mia knows, someone Mia might have to greet. The Child has never greeted anyone within the complex. No trace must be left. As Mia gets closer to home, she makes barely any effort to speak to the Child. As Mia gets closer to home, she forgets about the Child's existence. Mia slows down. The Child stares at Mia's ankles. Mia's two feet and two legs have been in use for the past twelve years. Mia has passed through many places full of memories and recollections for the past twelve years. And so Mia keeps slowing down. The Child falls farther behind. An overgrown lilac branch that has escaped the flower bed grazes the Child's shoulder. Despite the slackening steps, Building 110 gets closer. It's over there, Mia says. Even though Mia doesn't say anything, the Child already knows that Suite 904 of Building 110 is Mia's home. Mia looks back. The Child is there.

Building 110 consists of three adjoining towers. Located in front of the center tower is the security booth. Each tower has its own elevator, with two suites separated by the elevator on every floor. The fifteenth floor is the top floor. Thirty households live in each tower and ninety households are in Building 110. If on average there are four people per household, around 360 people live in 110. That Friday afternoon, in front of the steps of the center tower, another vulgar family drama unfolds. One of Mia's fathers is waiting for Mia. The Child, who has recognized him, stops in her tracks. Mia's father walks toward Mia. Mia stands still as though she were glued to that spot. Mia turns and looks at the Child. Can you wait for me at the elevator? Mia says to the Child. Mia's face is red. Mia's father spreads his arms to greet her, looking at her awkwardly. His eyes are fixed only on Mia. The Child checks the security booth. No one is there. The empty booth, Mia's father, Mia, empty home. The Child's head fills with the smell of blood. She peers into the booth to see if there is a video surveillance monitor installed as she makes a wide arc around Mia toward the elevator that leads up to Suite 904. But there is nothing. The Child hides in the shadow of the mailbox and observes Mia and her father through the glass door. Although she can't hear what they are saying, she can see that Mia has begun to cry and that Mia's (possible) father is patting her, struggling to console her. Mia's (possible) father doesn't have the key to Suite 904. Why else would he receive the stinging, perhaps burning stares of a third party when he could quietly carry out this scene inside the apartment? Key. Again, the Child thinks about the reason why he might not have a key. Mia's (possible) father doesn't have a key. But she has no way of knowing whether or not this is true. She must simply believe it. No one is home. And no one will be home for the next two hours. Judging by the fact that he has no key, the man standing awkwardly before Mia is probably not her actual father. Which means there is a greater chance that Mia won't allow him into the apartment. Mia knows how to use this situation to her advantage. Tears flow from her eyes. She rubs her eyes with her fists. Mia's (possible) father places a hand on her shoulder. Mia shrugs it off. A woman passes by and gives them a suspicious look. Mia will begin to cry harder. Her tears will secure the promise of a bicycle, perhaps a dog or cat. In a few days, Mia will have what she wants in her hands. In a few days. If only there were a few days left. Mia allows her tears to fall to the ground. Because a parked car is in the way, the Child can't see the tear stains on the ground. The Child swallows. The small blood clot that was stuck in her throat finally slides down her esophagus. The security guard comes up behind Mia. The Child can see the guard's face. As though he were caught in a bind, he merely watches the back of Mia's head and Mia's (possible) father without doing anything. The shoulders of Mia's (possible) father droop. Mia shoves him with both hands and heads toward the Child. The Child hides herself completely behind the mailbox. Mia's (possible) father calls out to Mia. Mia whips her head in his direction and shouts, Go away! Looking defeated, he keeps his eyes on Mia for a long time. The Child has already pressed the elevator button. Mia smiles awkwardly at the Child. Mia is relieved that the Child doesn't say or ask anything. The Child's shuttered eyes and firmly closed mouth gain Mia's trust. Mia is relieved that the Child, and not Inju, has accompanied her home today. Unlike Inju, the Child wouldn't whisper about Mia to others. Just as Mia hoped, the Child doesn't ask anything. Truthfully, the Child has no questions. The elevator arrives. Mia, who first slips into the elevator, presses the button to the ninth floor. With her head bowed, the Child steps into the elevator.

Mia pulls her backpack around to her chest and removes a key from one of the pockets. This is it, Mia says. The Child taps the dust off her shoes at the front door. Strewn before the shoe rack are shoes that belong to Mia's mother. The Child removes her running shoes after Mia, setting them neatly in the entrance facing the door. So that she can slip them on quickly and leave at any moment. The Child's mouth fills with the taste of blood. The small living room is dark and still. Sunlight slants in between the heavily drawn curtains. Dust covers the low table that holds a stack of three or four magazines. Dust is bad. Dust leaves traces. Can feet also leave toe impressions? But the Child is wearing socks. Luckily. Mia, who has gone into her room, comes back with a loose T-shirt. Change into this. I'll wash your shirt for you. The Child awkwardly takes Mia's T-shirt. Can I change in your room? she asks. Mia nods. Mia's room is bright and sunny. A pink blanket lies rumpled on top of her unmade bed. Mia's desk. Mia's dolls. Mia's bookshelf. Mia's wardrobe. Mia's framed pictures. Even while pulling off her sweater, the Child surveys the room. Through the door, she can hear the sound of Mia opening and closing the fridge. And the sound of glass cups being set on the glass table. The Child quietly opens Mia's wardrobe. Clothes that are white, pink, brown, and gray are hung neatly in a row. A green sweater catches her eye. It is folded neatly. Following the fold of the sweater, the deer that's knitted on the front is also folded. She closes the wardrobe door without a sound and takes off her bloodstained shirt. Her bare body is revealed. Her white, red, black, and blue body is reflected in the mirror beside the wardrobe. She turns her back to the mirror and puts on the shirt that Mia had given her. White, red, black, and blue stripes appear briefly in the mirror and then disappear, covered by the T-shirt. Holding the clothes she has removed, she opens the bedroom door and looks back without thinking. The Child, who is dressed in Mia's shirt, appears in the mirror beside the wardrobe. Her face in the mirror reeks of blood. Mia's bright, sunny room. The mold growing in every crevice of the large window is hidden by curtains that hang on either side. The mold cannot be seen. The Child estimates how much time she has left. Will half an hour be enough? One hour should be more than enough. Within an hour, the Child will be sitting in her own room, wearing the freshly washed shirt that had been dried with a blow-dryer. She steps out of Mia's room. On the table facing the living room are two cups filled with juice. Mia sees her and smiles. It looks big on you. Here, give me your shirt. I'll wash it for you, says Mia. The Child hands Mia the T-shirt that has been rolled up in a ball. You can get cleaned up while I wash this. The Child nods without saying anything. Mia turns around. Oh, there's juice on the table, by the way. While Mia speaks, the Child glares at the back of her neck. Today. Mia has tied her own hair for the first time today. Perhaps for this reason, her green hair tie is knotted loosely at the base of her neck. Mia's neck is white. It is small, rather than thin. It's a childish neck. When's your mom coming home anyway? the Child asks. Probably around dinnertime, Mia answers. Where's your bathroom? the Child asks. Across from my room, Mia says as she fills the kitchen sink with water. The Child goes into the bathroom. Mia's toothbrush. Mia's toothpaste. Mia's toilet. Mia's bathtub. Mia's tiles. Mia's mirror. Mia's faucets. Mia's soap. Mia's shampoo. Mia's toilet paper. Mia's hair. Mia's lashes. Mia's skin flakes. Mia's fingerprints. The Child twists the faucets and fills the sink with water. It's cold. The cold water is cold. After splashing her face a few times, she dries herself with Mia's towel. Her reflection in the mirror is pale. She takes off Mia's bathroom slippers and emerges from the bathroom. Just as she expected, Mia's (possible) father doesn't press the doorbell to Suite 904 or knock on the front door. Grown-ups use grown-up ways. Mia's mother isn't home. Mia's (possible) father must not bother Mia. The Child approaches Mia, who is scrubbing the Child's T-shirt with dish detergent. The shirt must first be soaked in cold water to remove the blood. The Child has experienced many difficulties in the past, because she had soaked her bloodstained clothes in hot water. Mia, on tiptoe, looks as though she will get sucked into the sink at any second. The Child thinks all of a sudden that she wants to bash Mia's head into the sink. The Child's face cleared of all moisture dries out. It's not really coming out, Mia says. Sorry, the Child says without thinking. Why are you sorry? Mia grips the T-shirt. The Child looks at Mia's fingers. Hey, the Child says. She holds her breath for a moment. Have you ever . . . , she trails off. Ever what? Mia looks back at the Child. Some detergent suds are on Mia's small, pale cheek. Have you ever wanted to kill someone? the Child asks. Mia's face hardens. She is silent for a moment. How about you? Mia asks. I . . . , the Child says. I have. When she hears the Child's answer, Mia reddens. Actually, me too, says Mia, looking embarrassed. To the Child. And I wish I were dead, too. Because if I died, my mom would cry and say it was all her fault. Because everyone would come to my funeral then and say it was all their fault and beg me to come back to life. The suds on Mia's cheek are white. Mia raises her shoulder and wipes it against her cheek. She doesn't seem at all suspicious of the Child. I'm almost done. Mia turns on the faucets and rinses the Child's T-shirt. We'll hang it for a bit and if it's still wet we can use a blow-dryer. The Child nods. So who do you wish were dead? asks Mia. The Child flinches. In her head, countless faces appear and disappear repeatedly. Instead of replying, she stares blankly at Mia's hands as she wrings out the shirt. Sometimes I wish my mom were dead, Mia says casually. But I shouldn't be like that. After all, if it weren't for my mom I wouldn't even be here. The Child broods on Mia's words. If it weren't for my mom I wouldn't even be here. If it weren't for the Child's mom there would be no Child either. The Child's face crumples. Okay, all done. It just needs to dry. Mia spreads open the shirt and shakes it free of water. Water droplets splatter onto the Child's face. Cold sweat trickles down the back of the Child's neck. What should we do while we wait? Do you want to watch television? asks Mia, who has draped the shirt over the kitchen chair. Well . . . , the Child mumbles, and continues in a low, monotonous voice, Do you want to play the fainting game? She asks Mia, Have you ever fainted before? It feels really good to wake up after you faint. It's like being born again. At first, everything's fuzzy so you can't see very well. Then everything gets really clear. Your head becomes totally blank and you get thirsty. Then all you have to do is drink some water or juice, she says. A smile spreads across Mia's face. She says to the Child, Isn't that game for boys? Who says only boys can play it? the Child says. Let's try it. You go first. Then I'll go next.

24

April. Friday. Close to 5:00 p.m. Mia clutches the Child's throat. Like this? Instead of answering, the Child nods. Squeeze harder. Mia's pinky fingernails dig into the Child's red neck. Harder, harder. Mia's face turns red and the Child's face turns white. Mia's mouth opens and she pants. The Child, who lets herself sink to the floor, bursts into laughter. You really suck at this, she says to Mia. Sulking, Mia looks at the Child. Then you do it. Let's see how good you are. The Child has been waiting for Mia to say these words. She lifts her hands to Mia's throat. Watch. This is how you do it, she says, grasping Mia's throat and applying all the force she can muster. Mia's laughter gets caught in her throat. Her eyes fly open. Her hands flail over the Child's hands. Hold on, you're almost there, the Child says. An expression like laughter or sobs flickers across Mia's face. The inside of the Child's head reeks of blood. She can't see anything. Mia's face, even the Child's hands, evade the Child's gaze. She shuts her eyes and tightens her fingers around Mia's throat, harder and harder, with crushing force. Mia's body begins to go slack. She sinks back, her face white. The Child uses the last of her strength to squeeze Mia's throat. A few indiscernible words escape from between Mia's partly open lips. Mia collapses. Tears flow from the Child's eyes. She lets go. Mia's head falls back limply. She supports Mia's head and lays her on the floor. Mia's body is on the floor. The Child pants. It's not over yet.

She slaps Mia's cheek. The whimper of a small animal escapes from Mia's throat. The Child puts her hand on top of Mia's chest.

But she can't tell whether Mia is breathing or not. It's because her own heart is pounding. She takes short, shallow breaths. The Child's face can't be seen. She looks back. No one is there. But her wet T-shirt is hung over the chair. She looks beyond the T-shirt at the kitchen sink. A drop of water falls from the faucet. *Drip.* No. *Drop.* No. *Drib.* There is no onomatopoeia that can express the sound of a water drop falling into a stainless steel sink. She tries to slow her breathing. Where is it? Her gaze shifts desperately toward the sink. Mia is splayed out on the floor. Knife. Where is it? Knife. I need to find a knife. She takes off Mia's T-shirt that she's wearing and wraps it around her hand. Her hand that is wrapped in the T-shirt violently opens and closes cabinet drawers. Mia's spoon. Mia's chopsticks. Mia's fork. Mia's plate. Mia's cup. Mia's straw. Mia's paring knife. Mia's kitchen knife. Even while rummaging through drawers in search of a knife, the Child keeps an eye on Mia. Mia remains splayed out on the floor where she fell. Finally, the Child picks up the paring knife. She brings the blade to her bare, shirtless body. The knife is cold. The cold knife is cold. Her face turns cool. She removes the rest of her clothes. No trace must be left. She places the knife, T-shirt, pants, and underwear on top of the table. She must move Mia. She puts her arm under Mia's shoulders and sits her up. Saliva pools around Mia's mouth. Mia is small and light, but her weight isn't easy for the Child to handle. The Child's face crumples as she lifts Mia. But there is no time to think about anything else. There is no time. She drags Mia toward the bathroom. There is no time. Truly. The Child must take care of Mia before she wakes up, before Mia's father rings the doorbell, before Mia's father opens the door and comes in, before Mia's mother returns home to avoid Mia's fathers. The Child doesn't turn on the bathroom light. There is a dull thump as Mia's body passes over the threshold. The Child thinks she hears Mia moaning. No. She must have heard wrong. The Child quickly studies Mia's face. White psoriasis has bloomed around Mia's mouth. The Child's thin, naked body appears in the bathroom mirror. The traces of assault. But they are much too distinct to be called traces. She looks as though she is wearing red-and-blue clothing. Her chest shows no traces of development. At some point, she stopped developing.

The Child tries to put Mia in the bathtub but staggers under her weight. She looks around the bathroom and spots a large basin. Mia is crumpled up on the cold tiled floor. Using the handheld showerhead, the Child fills the basin with water. For a moment, the sound of falling water calms her. She comes out of the bathroom and picks up the knife that's wrapped in the T-shirt from the table. The blade reflects nothing. She peers at the tip of the blade. Will this work? Will this be enough? Her hand that's clutching the handle begins to shake violently. She tightens her grip.

The water brims over the basin and soaks Mia's hair. Crouching beside Mia, the Child gazes down at Mia's hand. She thinks, The left hand is better. No, she thinks no such thing. She blindly reaches for Mia's left hand. Mia's hand is warm. But that warmth doesn't reach her. You have to cut the artery, not the vein. But she can't distinguish between a vein and an artery. All she knows is that she has read many news stories about people who cut their veins instead of their arteries and failed to commit suicide. Hesitation wounds. External injuries and internal injuries. Blood vessels. Blood. The depth of wounds. Fingerprints. Water. The Child knows many such words. They're words one can know without understanding them. She presses Mia's wrist but she can't tell which is the vein and which is the artery. The Child picks up the knife she had left on the bathroom threshold. She hesitates and then removes Mia's T-shirt that had been wrapped around the handle. She is no longer shaking. The sound of the water coming from the showerhead gobbles up her silence. Mia's hair sways in the flowing water like a dead fish. Slowly, the Child lets out a long breath. In her left hand is Mia's wrist, in her right hand is Mia's paring knife. The Child looks like Mia's red-and-blue shadow. The Child's body is completely hollow. She has no memory and no past. She has no more tears. Such things left her long ago. Like her missing fingernail. Mia is motionless. Is she dead? The Child looks at Mia's face. Or is she alive? Suddenly, the Child recalls the sentence "I want to kill" that had been written in Mia's journal. She recalls Mia's green hair tie. She shakes her head. Because the bathroom light isn't on, the Child's face can't be seen. But even if the light were on, we wouldn't be able to read her expression. We must not look at her face. When she turns to look back, we must disappear. The Child brings the blade to Mia's wrist. Mia's face, sunken in darkness, is strange and silent. One. A long slash appears on Mia's wrist. Through the torn flesh, blood begins to seep out quickly. Two. She scrapes the blade over Mia's wrist with a little more force. Mia flinches. No. The Child has only imagined it. She nearly drops the knife. Her breath surges up to her chin. She pants. She gasps. She shuts her eyes. She opens her eyes and thinks, if only she could be anywhere but here. She opens her eyes and thinks, if only it were her instead of Mia who's lying on the floor. She hacks at Mia's wrist until the blade nearly snaps. Something cold and wet collects on the Child's face. Water. Perhaps sweat. Perhaps blood. It covers the wounds on her body. Her gasps drown out the sound of the water. The inside of her head sinks and bleaches out. Faster and faster. Harder and harder. Deeper and deeper. She drops the knife. The knife falls on the tiles. *Plink. Clink. Ca-clang.* But no onomatopoeia exists, not in any language on earth, that can express the sound of a knife falling onto tile.

She stands up. Mia doesn't move. Even the tip of her finger doesn't move. Only Mia's loose hair ripples in the water, quietly, in the dark. Somewhere within the Child's body, a nerve strand snaps. Mechanically, she blinks a few times. Mia. Mia is dead. Mia will never reveal anything. The Child slowly flicks on the bathroom light. She shuts her eyes. When she opens her eyes, if only she could be anywhere but here. She opens her eyes. But here is here.

Mia and Mia's things, Mia's world, is marked by Mia's blood. The mark's expression is cold. The Child doesn't scream. She doesn't sink to the floor. She doesn't look at Mia. She can't look at Mia. Mia's small, light body is drenched in bloodstained water. The Child bends over Mia's body and picks up the showerhead. Mia's loose hair is covering her face. The Child rinses herself off. She is shaking. Is it because the water is cold? Mia's left arm is submerged in the basin. The bloodstained water brims over. The Child carefully cleans the blood off her face and body. She is shaking. It's because the water is cold. She works her fingers through Mia's hair. Something gets caught in her fingers. She grabs hold of Mia's green hair tie.

The Child dries herself with a towel. She puts on each item of clothing that is on the table in order. On the table are the two cups of juice that Mia had poured. The Child doesn't take a sip. She puts on her wet T-shirt that is hanging over the kitchen chair. She is shaking. Is it because the wet T-shirt is cold and wet? Her sweater is on the bed in Mia's room. Mia's room. The Child stops pulling on the sweater and looks once more around Mia's room. Mia's wardrobe. The Child rubs the handle with the end of her sweater sleeve. She comes out of Mia's room and stands in front of the bathroom. Mia. The Child looks down at Mia's small, light body. It is no longer small and light. It is no longer anything. She wipes the light switch with Mia's T-shirt that had fallen by her feet. As her hand moves up and down, the light flickers on and off. Mia flickers. Blood has splattered even onto Mia's T-shirt. The Child leaves the bathroom light on. Because Mia might get scared if it's too dark, the Child thinks. No. She thinks no such thing. The knife is by Mia's chest. She might get hurt if she moves around, the Child thinks. No. The Child thinks no such thing. She thinks nothing.

The Child stuffs Mia's T-shirt and the wet towel into her backpack. What else? She mechanically surveys Mia's apartment. Mia is no longer there. Mia is dead. The Child puts on her backpack and her running shoes. From the entrance, she surveys Mia's home for the last time. The sound of trickling water comes from the bathroom. She wraps the front of her sweater around her hand and turns the knob. She does this several times, because the sweater keeps slipping around the knob. The door opens. The elevator is on the ground floor. She climbs the stairs up to the rooftop. From there, she goes down another tower, which can be accessed from the rooftop. She decides to use the stairs all the way down. She doesn't catch anyone's eye. She returns to the ground floor. The fragrance of lilacs suffocates her. She lets out a long breath. Her heart begins to beat violently. Her world goes askew. Where there should be light, there is darkness. To her. Inside her. Outside her. It starts pouring. One, two, three, a hundred, ten thousand, a million of her nerves snap at the same time. She is on ground level, but she's far from grounded. She binds her breath. She opens her eyes wide. But everywhere her gaze touches, the world sinks. Buildings heave. Roads twist. Cars flip over. Blood trickles. It collapses. It's collapsing. No matter how much it collapses, here is here forever. Even in a million years, here will be forever here.

25

Will we ever know the Child's name? Impossible. It's been impossible until now. The incident leaves traces. No trace must be left. But how do you erase the traces of a trace? She doesn't move. She hasn't moved until now. We must avert our gaze. We must not look at her. She must not move. The instant she moves, time will move again. The instant time moves again, she will leave traces again. The instant she leaves traces again, those traces will grab hold of her feet. Therefore we must no longer look at her. Our eyes must not see, not even Mia's hair tie that is clenched inside the Child's fist, not even the Child's wet T-shirt that is rolled up above her belly, not even her empty eyes that are gazing out at the empty world. Do not look at her. Do not read about her. Do not think about her.

But that's impossible.

II

26

Snow is falling. Snow is falling on the two-lane road that stretches darkly ahead. The end of the road disappears into the end of the hazy sky. The end of the end. The end beyond the end. Even the silence has frozen, like breath turning white. One, two. One snowflake, two snowflakes. The drifting snowflakes land on my cheeks. My cheeks are no longer warm enough to melt the snow. My face freezes. I put my hands in my coat pockets. My pockets are full of pebbles. I grab them without thinking and pull my hands out of my pockets. The pebbles are white and transparent. They are lumps of ice. The lumps of ice that my hands are clutching freeze the lines on my palms. The fate lines on my palms freeze. Fate freezes. Fate that has turned to ice influences nothing. I begin to walk. I am alone on the long, black, narrow road. Not even a single car is on the road. Snow falls on top of the asphalt. The black road turns gray. Soon the road will turn white, and then the road will disappear. Already, the road's half gone. The shadows of white. Everything silent. Desolate branches hide themselves in the snow. When I happen to look down, there is snow up to my calves. Someday, the snow will gobble up the entire landscape. I will become buried in snow without even a gravestone to my name.

I begin to walk. Snowflakes fall on my frozen cheeks. Even as I walk, I can sense the futile beauty of snowflakes. The word *snowflake* is beautiful. The word *snowflake* may be more beautiful than an actual snowflake. Snowflake. Word. Footprint. Word. Shadow. Word. One footprint, two shadows. I look back. The footprints have disappeared. Because snow is piling up on top of them. The sky is white and the ground is also white, and so, there are no shadows. Even the crunch of my footsteps on the snow cannot be heard. Is it cold? I ask myself. Strangely enough, it doesn't feel cold to me. Is it because all sensation has left me? Any sensation that remains is overwhelmed by the snow-white color of snow. Is white a color? Snow reveals neither light nor shadow. White snow is simply white snow. I brush off the snow that has collected on my coat. The strength of snowflakes is stubborn. I can no longer recall the color of the coat I am wearing. The coat has already turned to ice. I slow down. I'm surprised to see that snow now comes up to my waist. The snowflakes that keep falling on my forehead and lips freeze. I remove my hands from my pockets that are filled with ice pebbles. My hands have turned to ice. Through my transparent hands, I see the white ground. Snow piles up even on top of my hands that have turned to ice. My transparent hands turn white. I look back again. White snow, everywhere white snow. I turn back around. The road has disappeared. White snow, everywhere white snow. White hill, white slope, white field, white road. The border between earth and sky is unclear. I no longer walk. I simply stand in the same spot and watch the snow that is endlessly falling. When this snow stops falling, perhaps I'll be able to walk on it all the way into the sky. Suddenly, I realize that I've come here to discover the most beautiful snow crystal. But there is snow all around. And all the snow crystals are already beautiful. Therefore, which one am I supposed to take back? But even if I managed to come upon something perfectly crystallized, the road back has already disappeared. And so, therefore. I stand still and watch how a world is buried in snow. Soon my two eyes will become ice. The phrase *snow blindness* comes to mind. A blind world withdraws into snow. Gradually, my vision grows dim. When I look down, snow is up to my chin. I can no longer touch the ice pebbles inside my pockets. It's because my arms have turned to ice. Using the last of my strength, I stare straight ahead. Ice has formed even on my lashes. But the ice on my lashes cannot cast a shadow. Because even the light has frozen. And I can no longer see a thing. Because both of my eyes have become ice pebbles. I should have taken off my coat. I should have checked whether the bones beneath my skin, which has turned to ice, were black or white. And so, before the white snow covered my transparent body, I should have checked whether one bone, two bones, the bones beneath my skin, which has turned to ice, were black ice or white ice. But it's too late now. Time itself has frozen. And I can no longer think. Because even my mind has turned to ice. White snow, everywhere white snow, like the whites of our eyes.

27

I begin to walk again. No. I'm driving in some kind of trance. I'm still on the two-lane road. I look behind me through the side view mirror. On a slope back in the distance, snow is falling. That scene is as small and exquisite as a postcard. I keep gawking at the view and then glancing at the dashboard. The speedometer is pointing to 0 km/h. I look back again. The scene with the falling snow is growing distant. Faster and faster. It is now as small as a fingernail. But I can see each of the snowflakes falling in the scene that is as small as a fingernail. All of a sudden, I realize I've left the most beautiful snow crystal—that perfectly crystallized thing—back in that scene. But I can't turn the car around. Is it cold? I ask myself. It is cold. It's so cold I can't bear it. All the while, the scene is growing more and more distant. It has already become as small as a fingernail clipping. But I can see each of the snowflakes falling in the scene that is as small as a fingernail clipping. A thousand snowflakes, ten thousand snowflakes. I shift gears and turn the steering wheel. All of a sudden, I can't help but think that I don't know how to drive. The car doesn't move forward or backward, it neither floats nor sinks. It's simply going somewhere. Onward, somewhere, onward. I look straight ahead. The scenes on either side of the car move backward. The car is moving forward. The speedometer needle is stuck on 0 km/h. Slope, brick, vallate, glacier, corridor, well. Words I have never seen before parade past the windows. All of a sudden, my vision swells up. I blink, but I can't open my eyes once shut. When I swipe at them with my hands, pointy ice cones burrow into my palms. Is it cold? I ask myself. It is cold. It's so cold I can't bear it. Are these the world's most beautiful snow crystals? But before I can answer, the ice cones on my palms vaporize. Without vapor. My hands are neither black nor white. They are neither smooth nor transparent. I can't sense the color of my palms. Snow blindness. I look back again. Ice scales fall into my collar. The particles of the scene are sinking. The scene as small as a fingernail clipping, ten thousand snowflakes, ten thousand and one snowflakes. I've left behind that perfectly crystallized thing. I must go back and get it. I must confirm what cannot be confirmed. I must go back. But my body doesn't move. My body, my frozen body. There is frost on the glass. I must go back. But my hands have frozen onto the steering wheel. Every time I move, ice scales burrow delicately, sharply, into my body. I can't tell whether the scene I see is the foreground or the background. Probably neither. I must go back. But the scene grows distant. I can no longer recall the names that point to objects smaller than fingernails. A part of a fingernail, a part of a part of a fingernail, a part of a part of a part of a fingernail. From that place in the distance and beyond, countless snowflakes are in bloom. The snowflakes take over. White petals are in full bloom. The scene begins to crack. The cracks spread, and the scene spills over onto the scene. The scene overflows. I am nowhere to be found. Ice scales burrow into my entire body. I glance down at myself. I vaporize. Without vapor. Without vapor.

28

I am erased from the dream. Night is crouching. Before this dream disappears, before it retreats to the far side of recollection, before it retreats beyond the midday shadows, I must put this dream down in writing. But I soon fall back to sleep again and am thoroughly separated from the dream. The dream that has drifted by forgets me. It is forgetting me.

But now I'm aware that I'm dreaming. I'm walking along a road paved with bricks. It isn't snowing. It's probably summer. The sky hangs low. Buttercups grow in the cracks between the bricks. Although I have never seen buttercups before, I somehow know that they're buttercups by their thin green stems. A nag passes by. On the way to a zoo? A farm? A slaughterhouse? It's headed somewhere, wherever that may be. Everywhere, death is being dispatched with speed. The nag that had been passing me nags, That dog was dried out. What the nag just nagged is probably wrong. Dogs don't dry out. Drying out can't be a dog's trait. The nag nags again, Then is it you who's dried out? I look at its face, but I can't tell what it's looking at. I keep staring as it passes by. In the distance, at a point where the brick road ends, there's a brick fence. Beyond the brick fence, there's a brick building. The nag that disappeared is back and is now standing beside me. I climb on and we trot down the brick road. The brick wall looms so close I think I can touch it. That dog was dried out, it nags in a low voice. That's wrong. You can't use the expression "dried out" for a dog, I nag in its ear. It shakes its head. But I can't tell if it has understood my nagging.

Beyond the brick fence, there's a brick building. The nag jumps over the fence. I tilt backward. The world spins. Its hooves trample on the buttercups. The brick building grows larger and larger. The brick door of the brick building swings open. The nag that's carrying me enters the brick house. Brick shoes are laid out in the brick entrance. I've never seen a brick entrance or brick shoes. The nag steps inside, scattering the brick shoes that were lined up so neatly. I crouch so that my head won't bump the ceiling. The nag's mane burrows into my neck. Inside the house there is both everything and nothing. The nag goes up the brick stairs. I don't ask, Where are we going? I don't ask, Where are we? It trots up the steps in no time. Second floor, brick pillar. Third floor, brick hallway. Fourth floor, brick wardrobe. That dog was dried out. The nag stops at a spot where the stairs end. Get off, it nags. I listen to its nagging. I walk forward, groping the brick wall. The brick light shines from the brick ceiling. I walk on the brick carpet past the brick table and draw back the brick curtains and open the brick window. The shadow of the sun falls across my face. All of a sudden, sleep floods over me. I must tame sleep.

I lie down on the brick bed and pull the brick blanket over me. Gazing up at the brick ceiling, I close my eyes. When I open my eyes again, the nag is standing beside me. That dog was dried out, it nags. Yes, I know, I say. The nag is standing beside the brick bed. Aren't you cold? I ask. No, I'm not cold, it answers. Do you sleep standing up? I ask. I don't sleep, it answers. So I don't dream either. The brick breeze blows in through the open brick window. This is a dream, I say. The nag replies with a cold snort. I pull the brick blanket up to my chin and shiver. The brick sunlight crushes the brick pillow. That dog wasn't dried out, the nag nags. Yes, I know, I answer. Do you know the opposite of *confusion?* the nag asks. I don't answer. There is no opposite of *confusion*, it nags. No such word exists. Buttercups are growing in the cracks between the bricks in the pillow. Why did you bring me here? I ask. To ask you if you knew the opposite of *confusion*, the nag nags. What kind of nagging is that? There is no such word, I say. Fine, let's play another game then. Let's find the most beautiful word in the world, the nag nags. I lie on the brick bed with my head on the brick pillow and cover myself with the brick blanket and nod. Buttercup stems burrow into the nape of my neck. They are long and pointy and painful.

Buttercup, I say.

No, the nag nags. Those aren't buttercups. They're lilacs. And *buttercup* isn't the most beautiful word.

I've never seen lilacs before, I say.

You're looking at them right now. See? These flowers are mauve, the nag nags.

The nag gazes down at me. I turn my head and look at the small purple buds. Buttercups have yellow flowers, not mauve, it whispers. How is yellow different from mauve? I ask. Buttercups are poisonous, it says. It blinks and stares at the brick wall for a moment. So the most beautiful word can't be *buttercup* because it's poisonous? I ask. How can a word be poisonous? it says.

I'm cold and I'm in pain, I say.

Wait, the nag nags. Quick, tell me the most beautiful word of all, it urges.

Water, I say.

No, the nag says sternly. *Water* isn't beautiful at all. When water freezes, it becomes ice. Ice is more beautiful than water. But neither *water* nor *ice* is beautiful. Water flows. Ice is slippery. I've run on ice before. No one was on my back. Every time my hooves touched the ice, I heard a strange noise. It was the sound of me slipping, on and onward. So I guess I can't say that I ran on ice. Can I say that the ice slipped? The ice slipped up. I was afraid that the slipped-up ice would crack, I was afraid that water colder than ice would drench me, so on and onward I went. The ice didn't reflect my shadow. I gave a loud cry. The sky was a hexagon. Have you ever seen a hexagonal sky? Have you ever walked on ice that reflected a hexagonal sky?

I shake my head. The corners of the brick pillow graze my neck. But what is a hexagonal sky? I ask. A hexagonal sky—the nag says, glaring at me—is a hexagonal sky.

It's your turn, I say. What do you think is the most beautiful word in the world?

The nag closes its mouth. It then asks, What is the opposite of *confusion?*

What is *confusion?* I ask.

The nag closes its mouth.

A word lingers inside my mouth. I know only that it's just one word. I don't know what the word is. I run the tip of my tongue along my teeth. I feel something. I put my hand in my mouth and remove the buttercup stem that is stuck between my teeth. The instant the stem comes out of my mouth, it turns into a lilac stem. Small mauve flowers vaporize from the tips of my fingers.

Lilac, I say.

The nag shakes its head violently. No, no, *lilac* is beautiful, but it's not the most beautiful word in the world. What kind of nonsense is that, suggesting *lilac?* You don't even know what beautiful is. No wonder you don't know what it means for a word or anything to be beautiful.

I'm cold and sleepy and in pain, I say.

That's a lie, the nag nags. This is a dream. So how can you be cold and sleepy and in pain?

Didn't you say you don't dream? I respond.

I don't dream, but you're dreaming, the nag nags.

When did you become a nag? I ask.

When you fell asleep. When you walked in the snow. When you turned to ice. When your bones were transparent. When your bones were black. When your bones were white. When your bones were red. When your dream was red. When your sleep was red. When your lie was red. I've been a nag since then, it answers.

I'm a liar, I say.

I know, the nag says. But why do you lie and try to tell the truth? Why do you write a lie and try to write the truth? You know that everything is a lie, so why do you try to seek the truth?

The brick pillow clutches my throat. The brick blanket crushes my body. The brick bed undulates. It hurts, I cry. Please let me out of here.

No, the nag says in a low voice. The nag opens its brick eyes and snorts brick air. Brick buttercups grow in the cracks between the strands of the brick mane. The brick buttercups turn to brick lilacs. Mauve buds appear on the brick lilacs. The brick flowers give off a brick scent. The brick word senses the brick tongue. The brick tongue opens the brick mouth. The brick memory erases the brick expression. The brick silence looks at the brick nag.

You, I say.

The brick nag hardens into a brick expression. I heard *you* was the most beautiful word there is, I say. Someone told me that. The nag and I look at each other for a moment, not saying anything. Who are you? we both say at the same time.

Who are you? I ask again. The nag shakes its head. Who are you supposed to be? it asks. I shake my head, but the brick pillow is clutching my throat. Fragments of brick burrow into my throat and shoulders. Brick throat. Brick shoulders. Brick arms. Brick chest. Brick cheeks. The brick nag shakes its brick mane. The brick buttercups give off their poisonous brick scent.

The opposite of *you* is *brick*, the nag nags.

The opposite of *confusion* is also *brick*, I say.

The opposite of *brick* is *brick*, the nag nags.

The opposite of *lie* is also *brick*, I say.

The opposite of *brick* is . . . For a moment, the nag forgets its nagging. The opposite of *brick* is . . . I forget the nag's nagging . . . is *brick*. The nag nods. Then the most beautiful word in the world is . . . The nag stops nagging and looks at me.

Then the most beautiful word in the world is . . . I repeat the nag's nagging. Not *brick*, I say. The nag nods. Then is the most beautiful word *you?* the nag asks. I shake my head.

The opposite of *you* is *confusion*. The opposite of *confusion* is *lie*. The opposite of *lie* is *you*. The opposite of *opposite* is *brick*. And the opposite of *brick* is *brick*. I am cold and sleepy and in pain. The opposite of *I* is probably *I*. This is a dream. The opposite of *dream* is also *I*. I am talking in the dream. And when I wake, I forget. The brick breeze blows in through the brick window. The brick dust flies in, carried on the brick wind. Yesterday I walked in snow. Today I'm walking in brick. How much more does it have to snow before the brick house collapses? If you open the brick door and walk down the brick steps, brick snow covers the ground. Brick snowflakes fall and brick wounds form on the brick cheeks that are struck by the brick snow, making brick blood flow, and the brick ice makes everything freeze, even the brick shadows. You can't nag with a frozen mouth. You, too, are lying. A synonym for *you* is *lie*. Don't ask me for the most beautiful word. Don't ask me for such a thing. Nothing like that exists. No word in the world suits a superlative adjective. All words are antonyms or synonyms. The synonym of *antonym* is *antonym* and the antonym of *synonym* is *synonym*. Brick snow is falling on the brick field. I have never seen brick or fields or snow before. But I know that brick is brick. I also know that buttercups are lilacs. You probably don't understand my nagging. You probably don't even know what kind of nag you are. I've always thought about synonyms and antonyms. But I can't remember any of them now. Do you know what the opposite of *memory* is? The opposite of *memory* is *memory*. Memories are dazed and forgetfulness blazed. Have you seen the opposite sides of a coin at the same time? The fretfulness of forgetfulness. The reputation of obfuscation. The relegation of reputation. Recollections are full of objections and memories are mutinous. So the antonym of *dazed* is *blazed* and the synonym for *blazed* is *dazed*. Listen to my nagging, since you're not nagging. The color of buttercups is the color of buttercups. The color of lilacs is the color of lilacs. So don't go confusing yellow with mauve. Or mauve with purple. Or brick with brick. Or walls with layers. Or stones with stones. Put me on your back. Put me on your back and go. Put me on your back and put me in the fire and just like that chase away my brick sleep once again. There's a nag that carries on with its nagging and forgets its nagging. The crystallization of mystification. The mystification of symbolization.

The nag doesn't nod. It doesn't nag. It doesn't put me on its back. I've seen a hexagonal sky before. A snow crystal is hexagonal. Sharp ice splinters cling to each of its six corners. Six ice, six skies, six fields. Snow falls on the field. Then nothing is seen. Not mushrooms, not souls, not punctuation. Not even beautiful words, not even the most beautiful word there. I went there to find something most perfectly, most beautifully, crystallized. One snowfall, two snowfalls. But that place was full of the most beautiful snow crystals in the world. Because they were all beautiful, each one of them, they couldn't be beautiful in the end. Therefore, the most beautiful word in the world exists and doesn't exist. So don't ask me anything. One snowflake, two snowflakes. Is it still snowing there? Did it stop? Did it melt? Did my body that froze in the snow melt and trickle down? Did I soak the ground? Did my black-and-white bones collapse? The nag no longer nags and I continue to nag. Yesterday was snow and today is brick. If tomorrow is ice, what will the day after tomorrow be? There's something I've forgotten that I'm not nagging. But I can't remember what that is right now. You can't compare that nagging with something like the most beautiful word. Nagging that's been forgotten means that it has disappeared. Things that have disappeared do not exist. Dawn's light, red sky, red cheeks. Tomorrow may not come. Because if tomorrow is ice, it will already be frozen. The brick nag doesn't nag brick. The brick nag doesn't go down the brick steps. Brick I don't look at brick you. The brick curtains don't flap. The brick pillar doesn't lean. The brick walls don't collapse. The brick bed wrings my brick arms and brick legs. The brick world shrinks. The brick dream doesn't shatter. The forgotten nagging and the lost nagging turn to brick and become trapped inside my brick mouth. The brick world sinks. It keeps sinking.

29

I anticipate another failure. In the days I spent writing this, I had many dreams and I put them all in writing. Some dreams were obvious, and some were deceptive. I rewrote them many times. The story became filled with details that were somewhat different from what I had first imagined, but nevertheless the framework of a given incident never changed at all. I don't understand why I tried so hard, so stubbornly, to write this story. This story that may well be about nothing.

My childhood was moderately unhappy, and I was moderately unlucky. I don't believe that the unhappiness or unluckiness of one's childhood creates happiness or luck in adulthood. An unhappy child could grow up to be happy, but once the child has become an adult, he won't be able to forget his unhappy past. But unhappiness is simply unhappiness. Just as happiness is simply happiness. The words *happiness* and *unhappiness* denote nothing. Don't be deceived by these words.

I can package a certain story as a dream and tell it that way. I can disguise my childhood, and as I disguise it I can make allusions, and as I reveal details about the allusions, I can make them appear fictitious, and in this way, I can deceive you all. But you won't be deceived. I hide, stab, hide, cut, hide, kick, hide, hit, hide, strangle, hide, and kill. I must divide all the stories in the world into moments that are short, and shorter still, no longer indistinguishable from one another. Like the fragments seen in a long death scene. Or the long death scenes in a seen fragment. At times the violence in a story bewitched people, and through that bewitching, they couldn't glimpse the details of the story. Even the one writing the story. When I was three years old, I injured my head and suffered minor damage to the frontal lobe. After that, I couldn't understand certain fundamental emotions, perceptions, moods, jokes, feelings, words, and stories. I know how to act so that it looks as though I understand. I learned this only after I grew up.

But certain words—no, to be honest, all words—are still a kind of mystery. For example, after the injury, you were no longer you. The word *you* is composed of countless words that composed your being. Your forehead, your eyelashes, your hands, your face, your shoulders, your fingernails, your index fingernails, your left index fingernail, your torn left index fingernail, the hangnail beside your torn left index fingernail, the pink-red-and-white mark where the hangnail beside your torn left index fingernail was clipped. Your first eyelash, your second eyelash, your third eyelash, and because one fell out, your fifth eyelash that became your fourth eyelash. And so it was impossible to describe you, or anyone, or anything. Because I don't have enough time. Because I won't ever be able to reach the end beyond the end. Because I don't have an infinite amount of time. Your elbow. Your right elbow. The scar inscribed on your left elbow. The scar inscribed on top of the scar inscribed on your left elbow. The memory of the first time you played fivestones, the memory of the first time you played fivestones with two other children, the memory of the fifth time you played fivestones with four other children, the memory of the fifth time you played fivestones with four other children while rubbing the third scar inscribed on your left elbow. In the end, not you, not anyone, not anything, could ever be completely described; not any of this could become anchored in a single word. There were times that I couldn't bear this, no, I often couldn't bear it, no, I could never bear it. But now I have no regrets about all the world's essential elements that can never be known, understood, or accepted. Although I don't see what people say is essential, this blindness has allowed me to see another type of essence. I must remain in an endless state of confusion. The word *essence* is deceptive.

While I was writing this, I read Maurice Blanchot's *Death Sentence* over and over. Eventually, I could practically recite every line, but the book remained a mystery to me nonetheless. Death that is delayed at the same time a sentence is delivered. A death sentence delivered at the same time it is delayed. This book showed me that instant when a long death scene is severed into seen fragments, and when all the seen fragments compose a long death scene. I'd always disclosed the texts that I coveted and copied; therefore, this time, too, I decide not to hide the fact that I've wanted to make a part of, or all of, *Death Sentence* mine and mine alone. I must hide other things. Brazenly, I have hidden many things until now, but I have never gone so far as to hide the fact that I was hiding something. Therefore, even as you're being deceived, you're not deceived, and even as you're not being deceived, you're deceived still. In this way, the sole objective of the stories I want to tell is to throw you into an unclear state, to make you believe while you're not able to believe.

I keep listing, describing, explaining your every detail, all the elements that shape who you are, and I want to forever delay you coming to find me, perhaps forever delay my death and yours. I should never have written from the beginning. I should never have attempted to write from the beginning. But the story has already begun, and a story that has begun must go on. Like every unlucky narrator, I am fated to finish this story. Whether or not I wish to. Whether or not I will it.

30

I begin to walk again. This time it's not a dream. At least I don't think it is. I'm not on a road. I'm inside a room. I take three steps toward the desk. If I turn around, it's three steps to the bookshelf. I take twenty steps. If I so desired, I could walk inside the room forever. Forward, backward, right, left. I have always thought about direction. On top of the desk are dust and electric cords, on top of the desk are dust and books. Dust on dust, dust under dust. There are other objects besides these things, but I decide not to mention them.

I'm writing from memory. Before the memory vaporizes, it will be transferred by pen or keyboard onto paper or laptop. Ideas precede memories, and dreams precede ideas. Dreams precede dreams, and dreams succeed dreams. Last night's dream was cool and fierce. The dreams I didn't dream came looking for me. I couldn't help thinking that I had to put them down in writing before I lost or perhaps forgot them. That compulsion expelled me from the dreams. I used to confuse *lost* and *forgot*. I still confuse them. The sentences are disappearing.

One step, two steps. It's neither spring nor summer and it's neither fall nor winter. I'm not yet thinking about the season. It may be spring or summer. Since I've written a spring and summer story, perhaps it's time to write a fall and winter story. Soon it will begin to snow. I must finish the story before it's buried in snow. One step, two steps. It's 3:00 a.m. It's actually 9:00 a.m. A long strand of hair clings to my pillow. It isn't mine, but it's actually mine. After waking from my dream, I came back to reality. But my reality remains fictional. So 3:00 a.m. is probably fiction as well. The most beautiful snow crystal in the world and the most beautiful word in the world still don't exist. They don't command any meaning. I think of the words I haven't yet discovered. But that's impossible.

The blank page on my desk, the black cage in my head. I'm waiting for someone. I've tried to delay her visit. But one day she'll come and find me. It's not difficult for me to summon her image. But I used to think about how she looked, the expression on her face. Her facial features, the slant of her shoulders. She hasn't finished growing. Right now these are the only details I know about her. In my latest dream, she was pushing herself out of a second-story window. Luckily, my room is on the second floor. She went from the second floor to the first. Perhaps she tumbled down the stairs. I've had this dream before. That time I clutched a throat and this time I cut a throat. Whose throat? I don't know. Perhaps it was my throat that was clutched and my throat that was cut. I'm forgetting the dream. A stranger lives below me in a room on the ground floor. Sometimes I'm curious about where this person can tumble to. I have never seen this person's face. The dream swiftly scatters. But this stranger isn't the one who'll come visit me.

One snowflake, two snowflakes. Buttercups and lilacs. One brick, two bricks. Words that have been randomly extracted from my dreams are strewn on top of my desk. One scrap page, two scrap pages. One blank page, two blank pages. Words seize me. The nag asked, How can you tell a lie and at the same time tell the truth? I can't remember if the nag was white or brown. It was probably the color of brick. It asked, How can you tell the truth and at the same time tell a lie? What is a lie? I can't remember if the nag had four legs or six. Probably five. The nag passed by once in the dream. Then it came back.

Time is passing. The time she'll come for me hasn't been determined. I don't want to meet her. If possible, I want to delay our meeting. She and I will end up talking about someone's death. I'll say that I'm not responsible for that death, and then she'll blame me. But I must finish the story before it gets buried in snow. I must finish it before its bones turn black, before they turn white, before they turn red, before they turn transparent. Now that I've begun, I must finish. Perhaps I began the story in order to finish it. One step, two steps. The thought that I want to see the end collides with the thought that I don't want to see the end. Perhaps I shouldn't finish the story. All of a sudden, the word *lilacs* comes to mind, but I've never seen lilacs before. Was it a dream?

It's neither snowing nor raining. The weather hasn't yet been determined. How do you describe a neutral season? Perhaps not describing anything is the only way to portray a neutral season. My senses don't operate. Nothing has become certain. Not yet. The space between my desk and bookshelf is a cease-fire zone. Here, fiction confronts reality. Across from the desk are winter and spring, and across from the bookshelf are summer and fall. I'm able to summon a summer afternoon without rain. But I could describe a scene where it begins to rain all of a sudden, and the children who had been waiting for class to end look out the window to either discover, or not discover, the faces of their mothers or fathers, and they run out of the school gate, holding their shoe bags over their heads, and they share umbrellas, or get soaked by the rain, as they cut across the school field. I might have already written a scene like this. This kind of scene was only a sketch. Could I give a single raindrop a name? But there is no time. Even a blank page isn't enough.

I begin to walk again. Once again, it's not a dream. I live on the fifth floor, not the second floor. When I descend over a hundred steps and open the lobby door, sunlight spills in. It's daytime. The road in front of the building splits into four paths. No matter the path I take, I always end up in the same place. And so, I set out on any path. People pass by. Cars pass by. The traffic lights blink. Every streak of light and shadow is anchored to the fronts and backs of buildings. Does each ray of light have a name? I realize that I left without wearing my watch. When I glance down at my bare wrist and look up again, it's growing dark. The sun is rapidly burning out. Before me is an enormous stadium. What's the largest building around here? The stadium is too big for my field of vision. People are pouring out of the exits. Could I give each person a name? Is there a name for the top part of the stadium, the top part of the top part? Is there a name for the left part of the stadium? Does the person smoking beside the exit with his head bowed have a name? Could I give each fleck of ash a name? Could I give each plume of smoke a name? Does each fading ray of light have a name? The stadium's scoreboard reads 8:47 p.m. Could I give each flagstone a name? The game is over. What could I call the time after a game is over? There are banners hanging all around the stadium. One player, two players. Written on the banners are unfamiliar names. The next game is in four days at 6:00 p.m. While glancing at the names, I discover among them the name of a friend who died several years ago. This friend and the player share the same name. What should I call the friend and the player? Is there a name for the friend's forehead? Is there a name for the player's feet? Is there a name for the friend's elbows? Is there a name for the player's sweat-soaked uniform? I turn my head and look up at the scoreboard again: 8:47 p.m. Not even a minute has passed. But if I closed my eyes and opened them, it would be a different time again. A time I could not give a name to.

I must go back. And I must wait for her. We will talk about someone's death, and about some things like death. She will come without warning and leave without warning. I must wait for her.

31

No sentence is clear. Or unclear, for that matter. Every time I discovered traces of all of you in the sentences I'd written, I cracked my knuckles as though it were a habit. There were always too many or too few sentences to contain the copied words. Therefore, it was impossible to copy down all the stories that were conveyed to me. There are four sentences on the chalkboard. The king died. The queen died. War broke out with a neighboring country. A plague spread across the entire country. Each of these sentences contains an incident, and depending on the kind of story that is inserted between these sentences, the context changes. Although I have forgotten the name of the person who first composed these sentences, I discuss them repeatedly in the second class each semester. The king died. Why? The queen died. Why? War broke out with a neighboring country. Why? A plague spread across the king's entire country. Why? This is followed by the conclusion. The order of the sentences can be switched as you please. The queen died. It was because the king died. The queen was charged with adultery with a state minister. War broke out with a neighboring country. The queen had been the princess of the neighboring country. The alliance that had been forged through marriage was broken. A plague spread across the king's entire country. The people grew miserable. The plague penetrated even the royal palace. The king caught the plague and died. In this way, one story is composed mechanically. The number of stories you can generate using four sentences is twenty-four. The students in the class nod. I can't bear it.

I make up another story. My grandmother was Japanese. She was born in 1931 and didn't go back home even after Japan lost the war. A harsh period followed. After the Korean War ended, she married a Korean—my grandfather. But he became ill and passed away before the end of the sixties. My grandmother raised my father and his brothers on her own. And then I was born. Although I don't have many memories of her, the memory of the taste and smell of the pickled Japanese plums she often served at mealtime is vivid. It was my mother who taught me that *umeboshi* is the Japanese name for what we call *maesil jangajji*. I've tasted *umeboshi* only once; never since. My grandmother never left for Japan until she left this world. Whenever I see *umeboshi* at a Japanese market or *izakaya*, I can't help thinking about my grandmother. The students nod. I wait a few seconds for the story to sink in.

And then I continue. To be honest, that story was a lie. As far as I know, my grandmother is definitely Korean, and she has never tasted either *umeboshi* or *maesil jangajji*. You all assumed the story I told you was completely true, or at least partly true. Such is the power of story. It was because of one word—*umeboshi*—that you believed my story to be true. The students nod. I can't bear it. On the back wall of the lecture hall, the hands of the clock point to 12:25. Only twenty-five minutes have passed since class began. There's nothing I can do. I must hastily make up a story about a story. During those twenty-five minutes, the only thing that had made me remotely happy was the fact that I was able to work in some wordplay—left for Japan and left this world. I stop there and take attendance. Three students are absent. When I look up from the attendance sheet and survey the lecture hall, I spot an unfamiliar face.

She wasn't here the first day of class. Her name isn't even on the attendance sheet. But I think that I've seen her face before, somewhere, unexpectedly, no, just in time. She looks as though she has just slipped out from the shadows. I look at her, momentarily forgetting what I was saying. She doesn't avoid my eyes, but peers calmly back at me. When I remain silent, several students give me strange looks. Her gaze blends in with the other gazes. I open a book with trembling hands, but I can't remember anything—what page I'm supposed to turn to, what sentence I'm supposed to read. Her face is blank like ice. I begin to rattle on about anything, stories that make no sense unravel from my tongue, and pages turn, carelessly, without method. The story of how a few birds defended an amphitheater, how a nameless man drifted along a nameless road, how the piper didn't play the pipe, stories that were scattered like the stars in the night sky, but you can't really see the stars in the night sky anymore, can you, actually, they say a million, perhaps ten million birds defended the amphitheater, only the horizontal line exists in the world of the romantic novel, whereas the vertical line, rather than the horizontal, is clearly apparent in realist books, the nameless road that the nameless man walked along had neither a horizontal nor vertical line and was instead full of dots, only dots, like the stars and remote stars tens of thousands of light-years away, countless dots that existed like hordes of mice. Mice, where could all the mice have gone? Where could all the human fingernails and toenails that the mice swallowed have gone? Now that the mice, which are no longer mice, have eaten these things and look like humans, where could the rest of the mice who aren't humans have gone? When the piper no longer plays the pipe, where could all the children who followed him have gone?

Her face is cold, hard, and expressionless like ice. She looks at me, but I don't look at her. Wouldn't the story be more realistic if a million, perhaps ten million, birds, all together, held up the stone pillar of a collapsing amphitheater? Wouldn't it be more realistic to hear how the birds smashed their heads, bled, and sacrificed their lives? At what point does a story acquire realism? Or what method must be utilized for a story to maintain plausibility? Fingernails. Toenails. The words I don't speak spill from my mouth. I forget what to say. Wordlessness continues. I spread open a book and peer at the first sentence. I must go on. I go back to when the piper plays the pipe, when the 475,955th bird holds up the forty-sixth brick, when Julien Sorel recites the Bible in Latin. I should probably shut my mouth now. I should probably end class early and return home before the face without shadow follows me. But I can't stop. Mixed-up shoes, mixed-up names, desires that surge vertically and then scatter horizontally, useless objects, cruel people, hat, rope, key, drawer, well, river, pond, sky, power plant, laughter, extinction, coffee, transmission, wire, monopoly bureau and flood basin, consonance and dissonance, hair tie and pencil. The face is still looking at me. The tolling of birds, some people witness such a scene and make up a story. Some people hear such a story and make up a story. But when the birds bleed, an instant like that can never be reduced to a story, but if it must be turned into a story, it must become a story that goes beyond a story. Anyhow, I don't know why I'm still talking about this. The power of a story is sometimes so great that one can't escape its shadows. Asymmetrical desires; desires that can't be covered by even the deepest darkness; fingernails and toenails that can't all be swallowed. Once a thief broke in and flung open all the drawers in my house. The contents of the drawers became jumbled up. Among those things were the first clippings of my fingernails and toenails from when I was a baby. They all disappeared. I sometimes wonder where those clippings went.

I look again at the clock: 12:26. I scan the lecture hall. The back door opens and someone walks in looking embarrassed and sits down. The girl has disappeared. I greet the late student with my eyes and wonder if I'd gotten confused. I'd seen that face before. But I don't know when or where. And because she's no longer here, I don't know how to stop my confusion. The page turns. "Quick, a perfect rose." A line of dialogue catches my eye. A thin line is drawn under the sentence in pencil. I close the book. In fact, I have nothing more to say. I have nothing to say. But it's too late. Therefore this story . . .

Embarrassed, I begin to talk. This story introduces three or four characters. One is dying, and because her illness begins even before the story begins, the story can't heal or cure the patient of her illness, and the narrator, too, can only watch the illness go on, that's right, he can only watch the dying death, the continuation of death. "Quick, a perfect rose." Because it looks as though the illness would lead the patient to certain death, the doctor consigns her to the fate of the terminally ill, and the narrator advises the patient to take her own life. But she continues to die a slow death, since illness doesn't retreat merely because death is near, and she wishes for a perfect rose. Quick, before the illness that's without cause or source flees. Can we understand an illness we don't suffer? Can we imagine it? The patient waits for the narrator, the narrator receives a message saying that the patient is dying, and because death hasn't arrived as expected, the narrator goes to see the patient, while doubting the content of the message. When the narrator arrives, death's already there. The face in bed is that of an effigy, not of a living being. The narrator walks toward death. That instant, death is delayed once more. The patient, who has come back to life, looks at the narrator with a face marked clearly by death. A perfect rose moves across the room. We interpret this as the perfect morphine. The narrator gives the patient, who has come back to life, an injection containing a lethal dose of morphine, death and life burn out at the same time, the last moment disappears, and the narrator no longer mentions the patient, illness, or death. Am I alive or am I dead? Am I living or am I dying? A death sentence delivered at the same time it is delayed. I haven't heard many other stories that are stranger than this. Silence mocks me. I think about the characters that I've killed. I killed them because they had to die. I glance around the lecture hall again. The desk where the girl was sitting is empty. I go on speaking.

Before the Second World War, the author was active in a right-wing organization. The war that everyone expected erupted in a way that no one expected, and after the war was over, the author retired into silence. Can we understand an illness we don't suffer? Can we imagine it? Can we know it through understanding and imagination? Even if we can't know it, shouldn't we know it? Even if we can't ever know it, shouldn't we have to know it? The illness of someone we don't know. The illness we don't know of someone we don't know. Even if we don't know anything about it, shouldn't we draw near? I think about the characters I haven't killed. I didn't kill them because they didn't need to die. They weren't given even an adequate death. I think about the characters that have been excluded from the story. They die or are dying outside the story. Without attracting any attention. As though they had never existed in the first place. Gradually, they're discarded from memory. Then how are we supposed to draw near? How are we supposed to delay our death? How are we supposed to write our own death sentence?

I stop at this point and glance around the lecture hall for the last time. The hands of the clock are pointing to 2:25. Are there any questions? Someone is sprawled over the desk where the new girl had been sitting. I can't see her face. For a moment, I look at the face that I can't see. There are no questions. I hastily organize the books and pens that are scattered on my desk. One student intercepts me as I'm trying to rush out of the lecture hall and asks me a question. I look back at the desk where the new girl had been sitting. No one is there. Relief and uneasiness wash over me at the same time. I have no idea whether I want to see her face or if I want to disappear before it pursues me. I'm certain I've seen that face before. At last I escape from the lecture hall. As I walk down the stairs, I drop the pen that's squeezed under my arm. When I bend over to pick it up, my books cascade to the ground. The pages of the books rustle like leaves. My legs shake. I hold on to the railing and just manage to descend the stairs. That face is following me. But I can't see it.

32

She calls out to me urgently. I hurry down the stairs, pretending not to hear so that I won't have to turn around. As I skip down two, three steps at a time, I banish that urgent voice from my ears. The tip of my shoe catches on the metal lip of the step. I lose my balance. I falter and fall forward. With the marble step looming close, I suddenly recall the many times I've nearly died at the five-way intersection. I've had to cross it two or three times a week for the past several years. The traffic lights at the intersection are complete chaos. Cars and pedestrians stop and go at their whim. I do the same. And so I was hit by a car twice, and had a near miss another time. The instant before I clutch the edge of the cold step, I think that if I had taken one more step at the intersection back then, or if I had been two seconds early, I wouldn't have to tumble down the stairs this way. The books I'd been hugging to my chest crash to the floor once more. A shoe flies off in an arc. My palms and knees thrum from the impact. She calls me urgently. This time I try to turn around, but I can't. I pant, lying prostrate on the floor.

She draws near. She stands above me for a moment before picking up my books and shoe that have fallen on the floor. She holds them out to me. I look down at my scraped palm. It's sore. I place my other hand on the floor and stand up. Warmth flows through me. I put the shoe back on. I take the books she hands me and put them in my bag. I straighten my clothes and then finally look her in the eye to say thank you. The face is unfamiliar. That face watches me in silence. I see myself in that face. It's actually mine. We may have had the same childhood. She's me. You're me. But I'm not me and I don't look like anyone else. But I sense that the writing about me has already begun. We gaze at each other without speaking. I've been waiting for you. I've tried to delay your visit. But I knew that you would find me one day, that you would come find me regardless of what I might wish. It's something you want, but not what I want. Mia. That's not your name.

There's something I want to ask you, you say.

The pain dissipates. I peer down at you. You're a head shorter than me. The bangs that cover your forehead are long enough to poke you in the eye. I notice the sloppy part in your hair. I straighten my bag and begin to walk down the stairs. You scamper after me with small steps. Familiar faces come up the stairs. I greet them with a nod. When I stop to look back, you're gone. No. That's only my vague, unclear hope. I don't even know what I'm hoping for or not hoping for. I don't disappear. Neither do you.

The door is open. At the entrance, I grab a copy of the school newspaper. You watch as I stop walking to gaze blankly at the headline. Darkness is falling outside. I briefly wonder where in this darkness I might hide myself. The headline doesn't come into view. Actually, I can't read anything. I step outside and light a cigarette. I don't look back at you. Your shadow withdraws into darkness. I begin walking toward the main gate. I don't look back, but I know you're there. Five or six students are playing *jokgu* in a corner of the field. When it grows darker, they won't be able to see the net. Then where should they aim the ball? While I guess at the trajectory of the ball, you say, There's something I want to ask you. I don't look back.

How can I delay my death? you whisper. How can I write my own death sentence? Did my illness begin before the story began? Or after the story began? The darkness grows thicker. These are questions I hadn't expected. No. That's a lie. Am I alive or am I dead? Am I living or am I dying? Who am I?

I stop walking and look back at you. There you are. I never imagined what you might look like. No. That's a lie. You've grown, I say. You were smaller then. You nod. The long ash on my cigarette falls to the ground. You extend your foot and step on it. No trace must be left. You gaze up at me. In the distance, a streetlight comes on. Your dark eyes shine with a clear light. Let's go, I say. You nod. You stand beside me. Side by side, we walk down the slope toward the main gate. My footsteps are nearly silent. Yours, too. That habit, you say, with a hint of a smile in your voice. You taught me that. And just like that, the sentence I'd forgotten comes back to life. No trace must be left. Memories shove me violently. Distorted memories cut across my past and present at a speed that makes sensation impossible. That habit of walking without making a sound, you say. I don't nod. How old are you now? I ask. Briefly, you seem lost in thought. I'm probably twelve, maybe twenty years old now, you say.

Because I don't want to attract any attention and because I don't want to run into anyone, I hail a taxi in front of the gate. The taxi stops quietly before us. I open the back door and beckon you inside. You bend your small body and climb in. While I tell the driver the destination, you place your hands neatly on top of your knees and gaze out the window. I feel like I've seen your profile before, but I've never actually seen you. I've never put you in a taxi either. You have only run or darted, hidden or crouched until now. The taxi begins to speed off, and you watch the scene outside sitting straight up, making no contact with the backrest. I try to see what you're looking at, but I can see nothing but your profile reflected in the window. There's something I want to ask you, you say without looking at me. I want to know what that is, I say. You burrow into the seat. The laces of your running shoes are untied. It's difficult to run far like that. You could have a serious fall like I just did. But I say nothing. All I think is that as soon as we get out of the taxi, I will tie your laces for you. So that you'll be able to run again, far, far away without falling, once again to a place I can't see, running and running until you disappear from view. The taxi driver runs the red light. A car about to turn left from the opposite side of the road blares its horn. For an instant, I wish the taxi driver would run all the red lights and speed faster and faster, so that we would collide with an oncoming vehicle, a vehicle as large and heavy as a bus or freight truck if possible, just before reaching our destination, so that my life and yours would be extinguished simultaneously. You're silent. You've probably read my mind. Soon a familiar road appears. I try to guess how many traffic lights we would have to pass before reaching home. Every time the taxi nonchalantly, recklessly, races through the crosswalk, changes lanes, and passes cars, I feel a peculiar regret. My palms tingle. They begin to throb. The driver speeds up, as though he doesn't know how to stop. The red light flickers. The person who had been about to cross the street spews curses, but his words can't be heard from inside the taxi. The taxi barrels through the last intersection. I feel a sudden murderous desire.

I pay the fare and climb out of the taxi. Your small body follows me out. The taxi speeds away and you gaze blankly up at me. Just go. But different words—Let's go—flow from my mouth instead. You nod. When we step into the alley, a cat brushes lazily past me. I flinch. I know what you're thinking. No. It's just a guess. When we reach my building, I check my mailbox. There is a package that looks like a book. I take it out and open the lobby door. You deftly slip through the glass door. Before going up the stairs, you tie your shoelaces. I feel relieved and uneasy at the same time. Going up the stairs is less dangerous than going down the stairs. My knees throb with pain. Today, the stairs are endless. I wish they could go on and on, so that we could climb and climb the endless stairs, until the soles of our shoes wear down and disappear, until our feet wear down and disappear, climbing and climbing the stairs, until our breath wears down and disappears. You pant.

This is it, I say. Here we are.

I know, you say with a smile.

When I open the door and step inside, the apartment smells of dust. You take some time untying your laces. I place the package and my bag on the table and wash my hands at the sink. My palms sting. While I shake off the moisture from my hands, you stand barefoot on the threshold, looking at me wordlessly. I turn on the light. Your face grows dim. Do you want something to drink? I ask. Can I have some orange juice? you say. I've never tried it before. I've never tried oranges or orange juice. I open the fridge, thinking I might not have any. But a half-full container I can't remember buying is there. While I take it out and pour some into a glass cup, you sit at the table and open my package. Before I can stop you, the paper package is torn open and what's inside is revealed. It's a newly published book. You flip through the pages. I put the cup down beside you. A speck of cigarette ash is floating on the surface of the juice. I rummage through the shelf above the table and find some bandages and ointment. The knee of my pants is torn. I'm relieved that I won't need to remove my pants or roll them up. When you see me twist off the ointment cap, you offer your hand. I'll put it on for you, you say. I tell you that it's okay. But you stubbornly grab the ointment from me. I sit in a chair with my knee pointing toward you. You rub the ointment on my knee. It stings. After you apply a bandage, you spread my hand open. On my palm are many crimson lines. After you rub ointment on my palm as well, you bring your hand to your neck without thinking and work what's left on your fingers into your own neck. I watch you. You take the wrapper off the bandage. I take it from you and stick it on my hand. But the lines on my palm spread out beyond the area covered by the bandage. I remove it right away. You smile. Have you read this? You point toward the book that has just arrived. No, not yet, I answer. Is it okay if I read it first? you ask. Sure, I say. I have more books in the back room. Feel free to read whatever you want, I say. For as long as I want? you ask. That's right. For as long as you want. Then you look as though you're about to cry.

You look blankly at me for a long time. Do you have that book, too? you finally ask. I shake my head. No, that book hasn't been written yet, I answer. You reach for the juice. Hold on, I say. I fish out the fleck of ash with a teaspoon. You drink the juice. I'll never forget your expression as you sipped orange juice for the first time. Aren't you cold? I ask. You put the glass cup down. I look at you. There was something I wanted to ask you, you say. I wish that this moment would end, so that I could petrify like a fossil formed by some meaningless death, so that my gaze and yours, exquisite and entangled like veins, could petrify, so that no one could discover or detect us even a million years from now. But time doesn't stop. It keeps bleeding. My pain comes to life once again. There was something I wanted to ask you, you say in the past tense. I don't answer. Already, any answer is impossible.

33

Although I never expected you, you've appeared before me, and I'm now confused. You are tall (taller than I thought), but short (shorter than I thought). You are bright (brighter than I thought) and dark (darker than I thought). You are talkative (more talkative than I thought) and quiet (quieter than I thought). I recall your habits, one by one. You clutch your food with two hands. You drink, taking one small sip at a time. You rub the ointment that's left on your fingertips onto your neck or the back of your hand without thinking. You gaze vacantly out the window. You sometimes look back. You sometimes look back and back again. And I think about your appearance. There is no shade to be found on your face. You look as though you've just slipped out from the cover of the shadows. Although I have no way of knowing what kind of portrait this investigation will produce, this is the only way I can describe you. You look as if you could be twelve years old or twenty years old. You look like a smaller version of me, but I'm probably mistaken. All of your fingernails are cut short. For a while, you won't be able to cut your nails any shorter. You're asleep on a blanket spread out on the narrow living room floor. I peek at you through the crack in the door. By your head is the book that arrived for me today. Did you read it? I'm not curious about the contents of the book, but I'm curious about the contents of your head. Is this a dream? It's not a dream. One snowflake, two snowflakes. Buttercups and lilacs. One brick, two bricks. As always, words that have been randomly extracted are strewn on top of my desk. One blank page, two blank pages, one black cage, two black cages. I sit at my desk and think about the book I haven't been able to finish writing. The black cage captures me. My heart skips. I dim the lamp and lie down on the bed. You came looking for me. I once read in a book a line that went something like: "A certain dream visited me." Like a dream, you visited me. But this isn't a dream. You, who had fled from the story, entered my inner world. I think about the characters I've killed and the characters I haven't killed. I didn't kill you. I only forced you to kill. You and I will talk about someone's death. I'll say that I'm not responsible for that death and then you'll blame me. And that's how this story will go on. From outside myself, I enter the inner story. This is impossible or not impossible. The possibility of a story proceeds only through severance. Yes or no. Therefore, it's not important to identify the possibility. A story always proceeds by impossible means. Whether someone kills or doesn't kill. I'm not responsible for the death you created. That day, the page of death was composed with your hands, not mine. Whether it's a dream or a story. Again, I peek at you through a crack in the door. You're still asleep. You haven't moved at all. I have a sudden urge to shake you awake.

Dreams without origin pass by. Sleep recedes. When I wake in the afternoon, your area is tidy. The pillow is placed neatly on top of the blanket that has been folded four times. On top of the pillow is the book that arrived yesterday. Did you leave while I was sleeping? I feel both anxious and relieved. Perhaps I will never see you again. I feel both relieved and anxious. I pick up the pillow and sniff. I smell nothing but laundry detergent. There isn't even a single strand of hair on the pillow. It's the same with the blanket. It's dark outside. I stand in the same spot by the window for a long time. A long shadow falls near my feet. Soon it will be evening. I must go after you before it gets darker. There is a note on the table. Power plant → Stadium. I sit at the table and try to track your movements.

You probably left the house at noon. When you walked down

the stairs and stepped out of the building, a light flurry would have been falling.

No. You probably left the apartment just before I woke up. When you went down the stairs, the streets would have already been covered with snow. You would have purposely stepped on the spots that hadn't been cleared of snow.

No. No trace must be left. Being careful not to get any snow on your shoes, you would have picked out the bare spots on the ground to set your feet. You would have hesitated, not sure of which way to go. The power plant is located in the five o'clock position. You probably walked toward the power plant along the low hill and the similar-sized houses. You may have become briefly disoriented. As far as I know, you've never been to this neighborhood before. The place that you once knew is hundreds of kilometers from here. Physically and literally. You would have managed to find the power plant without having to ask anyone for directions. To be honest, I don't know why you want to go there. As far as I know, your memories aren't entangled with a power plant. There wasn't one in the place that you once knew. There was merely a hydroelectric dam nearby. To describe the place where you spent your childhood, I used the town I lived in as reference. But you must know that already. The place you went to find was a thermoelectric power plant. You might have gazed at the smoke rising from the five smokestacks. Anyhow, you wouldn't have been able to go inside. Why did you want to go inside? I have no way of knowing. There would have been snow piled on the wall surrounding the power plant. Perhaps you wouldn't have been able to distinguish between the white smoke and the white snow. Both smoke and snow move vertically. But whenever the wind blows, the vertical line moves horizontally. The wind would have been blowing and you would have adjusted your collar. The coat you're wearing is probably mine. Before leaving the apartment, you would have opened the closet and taken out the heaviest coat you could find.

Wearing a coat that was too big for you, you would have gazed blankly at the five smokestacks for a long time.

No. There wouldn't have been any wind. But I'm certain you still would have been wearing that coat. Because it would be cold, because it would be snowing heavily. Because you wouldn't be able to block even a single snowflake with the nylon jacket you had on yesterday. You wouldn't have felt the cold that much. Again the snow would have begun to scatter lightly, and with your light steps, you would have started out toward the stadium. I have no idea why you're trying to go to the stadium. Some of the possibilities are likely and some are not. The stadium is quite far, but you would have gone there on foot. Several pedestrians and several cats would have passed you. Each time, you would have started in surprise. You would have been thinking of a certain scene. When you have no choice but to think of that scene, I'm compelled to do the same. Knife and blood. A cruel life. And while I think about an animal's death I wasn't responsible for, you would have continued walking along the path. You would have crossed the long-defunct railroad tracks. A train once carried fuel from the thermoelectric plant through here, but you probably don't know that. All the streams near the tracks have been covered up by now, but you probably don't know that either. After you cross the tracks, it's a straight path to the stadium. You would have crossed the street when the light turned green and you would have stopped when the light turned red.

No. You would have hesitated for a long time at the red light. Traces of cars that have passed would be evident on the street, their wheels having swept the snow aside. There would have been dog paw prints in the snow. Sometimes the wind would have scattered the snow piled on the power lines or tree branches. Anyhow, you had to have crossed the street. I wanted to leave the road empty for you, but I couldn't. It was entirely up to you to cross the street and make your way to the stadium. Eventually you would have crossed the street.

You would have caught sight of the stadium between the buildings. You may have even been happy that you had found your way.

No. I've never seen you look happy. You would have looked at the stadium once, wearing the same expression from yesterday, or perhaps from hundreds of kilometers before. The shouts of the crowd that filled the stadium would have reached even your ears. This would have been possible if it were Saturday. But wouldn't have been impossible even if it weren't Saturday. The closer you got to the stadium, the louder the shouts would have echoed. The closer you got, the less you would have been able to take in the entire stadium in your field of vision. People would have poured out of the exits, and you may have wondered if you could give each person a name, if there was a name for the top part of the stadium, the top part of the top part and the top part of the top part of the top part, if there was a name for the right part of the stadium, if you could give each fleck of cigarette ash a name, if you could also give the fleck of ash I had fished out for you with a teaspoon a name, if you could give each fading ray of light a name, if you could give a snowflake that just landed and is now beginning to melt on your cheek a name. You wouldn't have gone inside the stadium. Instead, you may have gazed at the ground outside that was paved with flagstones and wondered if you could give each flagstone a name. Tens of thousands of people will have passed before you and while thinking that every single one of them had a name, you may have thought about me or perhaps your own name. There would have been banners hanging all around the stadium. The faces of uniformed players and their names on the banners. Although I had discovered among them the name of a friend who had died several years before, you wouldn't have been able to find a familiar name. You may have managed to discover a name that suited you. No. You already have a name. It's only that I've never called you by it. No one has your name. No one knows your name. And while I don't call you by your name, you would have sensed the hundreds of thousands of snowflakes blowing, the hundreds of thousands of people passing before you, the scores of names hanging before you, the hundreds of streaks of wind shaking you. Is there a name for your forehead? Is there a name for your cheeks? For your arms? For your elbows? For your wrists? For your knuckles? For your smallest parts and the parts that are even smaller? What should I call you? Any name is impossible now. I can't call you by any name. You wouldn't have glanced at your watch. But if you closed and opened your eyes, it would be a different time again, a time I couldn't give a name to. You must come back. You must come find me again. We will talk about a certain death, and about certain things like death. You will come to me without warning, and you may never leave me. I wait for you. I tell you the shortest way back. Without words, without sound. I wrap the warmest coat around you. Without words, without words. I tie your shoelaces tightly for you. Without words, without sentences. You begin to retrace your steps. You go down the stadium steps. Tens of thousands of people disappear at once. The wind no longer blows. There is no snow on the steps. Either someone has already cleared the snow or there happened to be no snow where you set your feet. Still, you are careful and tread slowly, trying not to slip or tumble down the stairs. On the last step, you don't look back at the stadium. You leave no trace. You no longer have to obsess about carelessly leaving a trace. Perhaps there never were any traces. You look both ways as you cross the street. But there are no cars on the road. The green light comes on. You cross the street and the snow grazes your cheeks. You cross the train tracks. Light breeze, you look up once more at the power plant. There is no smoke rising from the smokestacks. People pass by but there is no cat in sight. You no longer need to start in fright. Perhaps there never was a cat. Perhaps there never was a knife, or blood, or a rooftop. You gaze up at the five-story building I live in. You shove open the glass door in the lobby and begin to slowly climb the stairs. I can hear the sound of your footsteps coming up the steps. I fold the note on the table, hide it in my shirt pocket, and stand up to open the door for you.

34

The doorbell rings. I open the door and let you in. Your expression is chilly. With frozen red cheeks, you remove your running shoes and unbutton your coat. The coat is mine. I don't ask, Where have you been? Your running shoes are wet. The pattern on the soles of your shoes becomes stamped on the tiled floor of the shoe closet. I open the window and look down. Everything is white with snow. I don't ask, Did you go to the power plant? I don't ask, Did you go to the stadium? You wait for me to close the window. You spread open the folded blanket and sit down with it wrapped around yourself as you begin to read the book you'd been reading earlier. I quietly withdraw into my room. I watch you through a crack in the door the width of a fingernail. Your face is hidden behind the book. As far as I know, the top corners of most of your books and notebooks are torn. You habitually eat paper. Without being aware of it, you tore the paper into little pieces and put them in your mouth. Paper tastes like paper. You couldn't sense the taste of paper. You don't know how much of the paper scraps you've swallowed, and you don't know how much you've grown up on paper. As far as I know, you finished growing a long time ago. But you still look like you're twelve, and sometimes you look like you're twenty. Although you were half-plant and half-animal, you now look 100 percent plant or 100 percent animal. All your fingernails are cut short, but I notice that the nail on your left pinky is somewhat long. But it's so thin and transparent that I wouldn't have noticed at all if I hadn't looked closely. At one time, your fingernails and toenails grew very slowly, but even before these slow-growing nails had a chance to grow out, they were cut short, so short that the flesh underneath became exposed. You turn the page. I observe the corner of the page. The page grazes your hair. You lift your head and stare in my direction for a moment. Where have all your nail clippings gone? Have the mice or ants eaten them up? And just as you had wished as a child, have the mice or ants transformed into your image to appear before me? You resume reading. I watch you.

Without warning, you shut the book and stand. The blanket drops heavily from your shoulders. You walk toward my room. I straighten up from the door and stand motionless. You swing the door open. The door bangs into my cheek. You stare straight up at me. I step back.

I went there again, you say.

Where? I ask.

The rooftop.

I take another step back.

The rooftop of Building 101. Where the cat was killed. No, where I killed it.

You glare at me.

That place is two hundred kilometers from here. It's not some place you can just get to and back from in a few hours. Especially on foot.

No, it's close. It didn't take even fifteen minutes to walk there. Don't lie.

You're the one who's lying. The bloodstains were still there. I didn't see the cat, but I'm positive it was never removed. It's still there somewhere.

You don't know where that place is. So you can't go there. That's impossible.

It's impossible or not impossible, you say.

Your face twists into a sneer. I can't stop you. You start attacking me again.

You killed it, you say.

I don't respond.

I didn't kill it, you say firmly.

Didn't you go to the stadium? Didn't you go to the power plant? I ask.

No, I didn't go there. I couldn't care less about places like that. I was interested in going to only two places. The rooftop of 101 and . . .

I don't say anything.

You killed her, you say.

You leave the room. The door is still open. You wrap yourself again in the blanket you had flung off and go back to reading. I approach you. You don't take your eyes off the book.

I didn't kill anyone, I say. No one died.

I sit down next to you. You draw your knees to your chest. Your movements are stiff with disgust. On the back of your hand is a small drop of dried blood. It looks like it's from yesterday, or perhaps twelve years ago, or perhaps a million years ago. No, it might not be real. It could be fake blood you've contrived to taunt me. You are about to tear the corner of the book without thinking, but then you stop yourself. Every time I see you enact the habits I've designed, I feel both an unnameable sense of happiness and unease. Every time you speak in a tone that isn't my own, I am both confused and relieved. You brush your hair back over your shoulders. You need a hair tie. I remove the hair tie from around my wrist and hold it out to you. You shake your head. You open your fist. In the center of your palm is a green hair tie. It's a distinct, vivid green. You use it to tie your hair while calmly watching me. Your neck becomes exposed. Your neck is smooth and unblemished. There are no scars, scratches, or marks. I don't know if I should be happy or sad. Even if I knew, I wouldn't be happy or sad. Your ponytail shakes like the tail of a nag. Brick nag and brick mane. Brick buttercups and brick lilacs. Brick bed and brick blanket. I gaze at the green of the green hair tie. Green is green. The green of the hair tie can't be designated as another color. I think about why the hair tie that is securing your hair so firmly must be green. You whistle. It's a melody I've never heard before.

There was no key, you say.

Are you going to go back? I ask.

You nod.

There's someone I must meet, you say. Even if I can't, we'll end up meeting somehow.

Of course there's no key, I say. Because it fell into the drain. Even I won't be able to find it again.

The key isn't important. I'm going to find something else, you say.

What's that?

You don't answer. For a long time, you say nothing.

Even if I can't find it, I'll end up finding it, you say.

I have no idea who you must meet and what you must find. Even if I knew, it would be better to pretend I didn't know. I gaze down at you, at your hair, at your green hair tie. There is a small mole at the corner of your left eye. I've never noticed it before. You tear off the corner of the page without thinking. One blank page, two black cages. I peer at the book you're reading. The book is blank. No words. No commas. Instead of asking, What are you reading? I clutch your hand and lift the cover. The cover is blank. No title, no name. You grip the book. I let go of your hand and stand up. There is a pen in a penholder on a nearby table. I take out a pen and thrust it at you. You shake your head.

Give me a pencil instead, you say. Or a fountain pen.

There are no pencils or fountain pens in the holder. I give you a look that says wait and I walk toward my room. Use a pencil to write what you can't erase and use a fountain pen to write what you don't want to erase, you whisper from behind. I think about the underlying meaning of your words. You talked like me, more than anybody else. I don't know whether I should laugh or cry. Even if I knew, I wouldn't be able to laugh or cry. I take out a pencil and fountain pen from my desk and hand them to you. You put the pencil in your left hand and the fountain pen in your right. What are you going to write? But I don't ask you anything.

I'm going to write what you're unable to write, you say.

I pick up the coat you've removed. A pack of cigarettes falls from a pocket. I open the pack and count how many cigarettes are left. Five are missing. You let out a low breath. There are many questions I want to ask you, but I decide not to ask any. Just like you, I used to have the habit of tearing off the corners of my books and eating them. At some point, I'd started doing this instead of folding the corners down. If I remember correctly, I was around six or seven years old. Dog-eared pages. Gripping the pencil and fountain pen in your two hands, you gaze at me. Is there a name for characters who haven't yet entered the scene? Or the characters who won't ever enter the scene? I've always wanted to begin a story with a concrete setting. A setting so exquisite that it would go beyond the concrete and overwhelm reality. I've wanted to describe you in as concrete a way as possible. But now that you're here, I see that these desires were nothing more than wanting proof about characters. And now you're rejecting my story. My story is becoming neither truth nor lie, fact nor fiction. I once spilled diluted hydrochloric acid on my thigh during chemistry class. It burned a hole through my black school stockings. Because the acid solution was diluted, I didn't suffer a serious wound. If your story had not ended in 1998, you—with your bobbed hair, wearing a uniform of necktie, starched shirt, and plaid skirt—might have suffered a minor burn. And then you, with a faint burn wound on your thigh, would have come looking for me. You would have said that you weren't the one to spill the diluted hydrochloric acid solution, and you would have then accused me of spilling it. My childhood wasn't beautiful and neither was yours. I had poor penmanship and I persuaded you to have poor penmanship as well. And so I can't keep making excuses to you. My memories and yours are muddled together. I can't untangle the tangled-up memories. Memories that were once entangled can't be untangled; they become disheveled. You're right. You have the right to accuse me. Things like a hole puncher, cryptic note, and broken clock were supposed to be given to you. But I didn't use them. Even if I had, you shouldn't have come looking for me. I should have forgotten you. At last, with a pencil, you begin to write something in the empty book. I turn my head, afraid I would see your sentences. The collar of the coat is wet. It smells of snow. The coat must dry. I force myself to focus on the coat. I hear the scratch of pencil on paper. I hear your hair brush against the nape of your neck. Brick nag and brick stairs. Brick ice and brick fire. The most beautiful snow crystal in the world and the most beautiful word in the world. Brick snow and brick nag. Brick buttercups and brick lilacs.

You said that *cheek* was *leaf*, that *bruise* was *wind*, that *fingernail* was *butterfly*, that *sigh* was *whistling*, that *grip* was *tree branch*, you say.

You said that *light breeze* was *blister*, that *thigh* was *cat*, you say.

I close my mouth.

35

The night collides. Inside the refrigerator is a full carton of orange juice that I just bought. You drink some. The juice squeezed from California oranges travels down your throat. Your gulps don't sound realistic. I have never thought of California and you at the same time. The expiration date on the carton is February 2014. A date from the future.

A dreamless night passes. A sleepless night haunts me. I sit up in bed and make sure that the pillowcase isn't made of brick. It isn't. I grope along the wall toward the door. I open the bedroom door I had locked and look at you who have fallen asleep with the light on. Half-covered by the blanket, you're sleeping on the bare floor. The floor is warm. Near your cheek is a white book. The cover that had once contained the title and author's name is now completely blank. I dare not open the book. I simply pull up the blanket to cover you and turn off the lamp. You don't move. You're asleep like a wooden doll. I once compared you to a paper doll. Once a paper doll, now a wooden doll. I'm not using the words *paper*, *wood*, and *doll* in a derogatory way. You're now a three-dimensional figure. You don't talk in your sleep. A doll doesn't speak. Speaking dolls appear only in fairy tales. You sleep, covered by darkness. I go back to my room.

I drift into a light sleep before waking again. Something is touching me. A cold hand grazes my cheek. It's yours. For a long time, you stroke my cheek. Your hand is cold, so cold I can't bear it. I pretend to be asleep. But you know that I'm awake. You clutch my throat. I don't scream. Screaming is someone else's lot, not yours or mine.

You squeeze my throat. I gasp. The darkness bleaches out. You don't speak. You don't whisper. You don't scream. You let go. I sink into darkness. You disappear and when I open my eyes, I'm lying once again in the brick room on a brick bed, covered by a brick blanket. Pieces of brick sting my flesh. I close my brick eyes and try to go back to my brick sleep.

And dreams where no one comes to visit me pass by. Sleep recedes. When I wake in the afternoon, your area is tidy. Your blanket has been neatly folded four times. Leaning against the blanket, you're peering at something. A notebook. The worn cover looks familiar. It's my journal. You glance at me. You pay no attention to my anger. You calmly turn a page. I walk toward you. You don't close the book.

"Nothing is clear. And nothing is unclear, for that matter. Only expressions, no, only sentences exist. I know that clear sentences can't exist, but I don't know why I cling to them with such obsession."

You're mumbling. I can't hear what you're saying. I'm stunned. You begin reading again.

"There are many books and there are many more good books. Adding one more book to the pile of books—that burial mound—is utterly meaningless."

I snatch at the notebook. But you quickly hide it behind your back. I swipe at the air. You resume reading.

"Your name must rigidly designate you even from heaven and hell. Kripke. Refer to rigid designation."

I look down at you blankly. Your face is set in a sneer. You flip through the pages at random. You begin reading again.

"The dog swimming in the Han River. The upper Han River. Submerge the Child or submerge the dog? Disappearance. Wet feet. Or footless, like ghosts that wander the earth. Atonement."

You snicker. I have never once imagined you laughing out loud. I hid my journals in the safest places around the apartment. In places even I could not find, places only the dust could touch. One of these journals is in your hands right now. You stop laughing and begin speaking again.

You think I'm like a dog, don't you?

I look at you. But not in the way I would look at a dog.

In heaven or hell, I'll always be a dog to you, you say.

I say nothing.

It was your plan to have me atone for the sins I didn't even commit. I once heard the phrase "to die a dog's death." I probably heard it from you. Sometime, somewhere.

You face me. Your expression isn't like a dog's. You begin reading again.

"Before going to class, I spend ten minutes writing in my journal. Every day, I am delaying the sentences that I must write today until tomorrow. There are over five pages of notes. But the sentences do not yet exhibit any strength. How about *The Impossible Fairy Tale* for the title of the book—a novel? It's just as good, or perhaps better, than the title I had originally considered—*Under the Aspect of Eternity*. The only thing is, I've already used it before. It would be good to reread Virginia Woolf's diary this week. Will I end up throwing away this notebook? Will I end up tearing out a few pages and saving them separately? I want to keep a better (as in blameless?) journal. It's not that I want to leave behind a journal. Refer to Marcel Mauss's *The Gift*."

There's something I want to ask, you say. Why do you never write down the date?

I don't answer. You begin reading again.

"I was confused and thought it was Saturday when it was actually Friday. The day before yesterday, I went along the bank of the Han River in a wheelchair, and yesterday, I was struck by the wind while on the rooftop of a building. I put on the clothes that I wore the day before yesterday and put on the shoes I wore yesterday. I found several word pairs but forgot them. Memories blazed and forgetfulness is dazed. Tomorrow I'll say that I'll quit smoking and the day after tomorrow I'll forget all about it. Tomorrow I'll write something short and at the end of the year I'll write something long. Today I'll buy a book and I won't read it. Knees and breeze. Suit of armor and suit of mourning. The dream from this early morning—someone asked about Ophelia and Hamlet in class. I said let's continue after a short break."

It's a nice dream, you say. Wouldn't it be nice if this were a dream too?

I don't answer. You continue reading.

"Read Maurice Blanchot's *Death Sentence* again. Words that should be said scatter and words that shouldn't be said petrify. What should I write? In my case, it's clear what I must write. But I'm dog-tired. Returning from daily life to existence. Returning from existence to life. Returning from life to death. Delaying death. I'll probably live a long life. (The previous sentence is similar to the title of a certain novel.) I've always thought you must write while you can, whatever it is, but you must find the time to not write. Empty the mind if possible. Inhabiting a state just before the moment of exhaustion. And delaying exhaustion. Because one day we'll all be exhausted, we'll all be dog-tired. '. . . there is a time for learning, a time for being ignorant, a time for understanding, and a time for forgetting.' These are not the words of Blanchot's narrator.

"It is unquestionably July 6. I read Virginia Woolf's diary. I steal a few sentences. Starting tomorrow, I will begin to write in my notebook. *Under the Aspect of Eternity.* This title is a phrase Wittgenstein borrowed from Spinoza, which I stole again. I feel compelled to finish today's (this hour's) journal entry before the song on the radio is over. The song is ending. The song has ended. The song ends with the word *eternity*.

"It's still July 6. It is a little past 11 p.m. I haven't felt well all day. I felt as sick as a dog. I took maybe three naps, every two hours.

The dream I had during my last nap was so vivid that I confused it with reality. I was lying in bed. My cellular phone and *A Writer's Diary* were lying next to the bed. Blanket. The feel of the crisp sheet. An alarm on my phone went off. I couldn't tell whether or not I was dreaming. I tried to turn the alarm off, but I couldn't reach the phone. My hand kept grasping the air in front of the phone. After that in my dream, I opened the refrigerator and discovered a carton of Minute Maid orange juice that was overflowing. The stickiness of the juice. I thought about filing a complaint against the Coca-Cola Company. And then I woke up. It felt like I had lost a part of my brain. This reminded me of a scene from *The Man Who Mistook His Wife for a Hat*. A woman who could only eat half a pie. The pie that could not become a zero."

This is fun. This has dates, you say. This is very funny.

You begin reading again.

"When it's time to write in my journal again after not having written in it for a long time, I face this kind of problem: There are too many words that I should say, perhaps too many that should be written, and so I just jot down a few nearly useless fragments and then give up. I want to write slowly, I want to write as slowly as possible. A few more lines about *The Impossible Fairy Tale*: The Child killed Mia. From the very beginning, Mia's death was planned—it's there in my notes. I followed that plot and murdered Mia step by step, meticulously, logically. So perhaps the Child was not the one who killed Mia. (And the Child—she will come and find me—will read this journal.) A kind of guilt dogged me when I was writing the scene where Mia is killed. It felt strange that I had no choice but to assign the logic of cause and effect to a murder. As I write this, I have no choice but to recall the (fictional) fact that the Child had added a few sentences to the other journals. The Child may have to write some fatal sentences even in this journal, imitating my handwriting."

You stop reading and gaze up at me. I don't look away. Your face is expressionless.

You already knew everything, you say. You knew everything. I don't answer.

You even knew I was going to come and find you. You knew more than I did. How is that possible? you ask.

I was reading this before you even woke up. You sure wrote down a lot of things. You had a list of all the things I wanted and even my name was there. Even the sentence about how the way to force pain aside was to create greater pain. Some of the handwriting was hard to make out. You have bad handwriting, too. No trace must be left—you wrote this sentence over and over. But why? You don't need to worry about that. No, you've actually left too many traces. I saw that you've written three books. Are you so smart, so brilliant, that you had to write as many as three books? Those are plenty of traces. You can say they're traces that will still remain after they've overpowered you. *Scary, fearful, sickening, terrifying, hideous, frightful, chilly.* You wrote down these adjectives. These were probably meant for me. And below were these adjectives: *premature, immature, unripe, young, delicate, childish.* These were probably meant not for me but someone else. I'm sure of it. You couldn't find more words? You should have been able to find at least a hundred words, easily.

You close your eyes and move your lips.

She doesn't exist. She never did, even from the beginning. Just like her name, she became a lost child. Because she never existed from the beginning, you have to start over and write the whole thing again. From the beginning. The whole thing. Again. I don't care how you knew that I was going to come and find you. You just got confused. You just got confused and thought you were expecting me as soon as you saw me. Just as you say, memories are dazed and forgetfulness blazed. No, did you say that memories blazed and forgetfulness is dazed? Who cares? It's all the same.

You spread open the journal that was once mine but now belongs to no one. And you continue reading. I don't say anything. I simply don't say anything. Even if I had something to say, I wouldn't be able to say it.

"In order to write something good, you need a dissenter. You also need a dictator, pain, and some cruel people. You need a collapsing world and a dying world. A dog-eat-dog world. I would rather be dominated than dominate. If there are no survivors, no one is left to bear witness."

You take your time reading the last sentence. If there are no survivors, no one is left to bear witness. Each syllable rings out clearly. There's something you don't know. I already knew that you were going to read my journal, that at the very end you were going to read the sentence "If there are no survivors, no one is left to bear witness." But I don't say anything. I must not say anything. Even if I had something to say, I shouldn't say it. I simply stay silent. You look at me.

36

I hear you open the front door. I hear the scrape of metal against metal. You close the door behind you and head down the stairs. The woman who had been sweeping the stairs glances at your unfamiliar face, as though making a point of seeing you for the first time. You bow your head and go past her. When you reach the first floor and open the lobby door, everything is white with snow. Your eyes resemble the eyes of a fish. But since rain has turned to snow, you will surely slip. Your eyes reflect nothing, reveal nothing. Your eyes capture neither background nor foreground. Neither lucky nor unlucky, you are luckless.

You begin to walk. If anything is different now, it's that you're no longer pressed for time. You have plenty of time. To be honest, there is an absurd amount of time. For you, I could forever delay the end of this story. The story's crystallization. So that you wouldn't get buried in the story, so that you would go on in the story, forever. The alley stretches ahead. You don't know where to go. But the path you take is always the right one, because you'll arrive at your desired destination no matter what. People don't pass by. Cats don't pass by. It doesn't snow. Every person and object has disappeared; only the backdrop remains. You walk. A fence appears, and then a stone wall. Houses about the same height, and various shops. A bicycle shop, the flower bed in front of a private academy, a wallpaper and linoleum store, and a hardware store. You look around. You've been here before. Yesterday, perhaps several years ago, perhaps in another life you can't remember. Characters enter the scene. A woman holding a plastic bag walks by. The ends of a bunch of leeks poke out of the bag. A woman with a kerchief wrapped around her head walks by. Squeezed tightly under her arm is a bulging wallet. She straightens the kerchief that keeps falling forward. The smell of hair permanent wafts from her. Children around the age of six or seven pass by. In a loud voice, they greet someone off in the distance. Male students dressed in middle school uniforms pass by on bicycles. They're talking about video games or something on television. For a moment, you observe this ordinary landscape. You have witnessed such a scene before. Yesterday, perhaps several years ago, perhaps in another life you don't remember. It begins to rain. But soon it stops. The sun comes out. When you look at your surroundings once again, the snow has melted. There is not even a trace of snow. You suddenly feel warm. You're wearing my coat, which is much too big on you. A woman gives you a strange look as she passes by. You unbutton the coat. The warm spring wind blows. Behind you in the flower bed, royal azaleas burst into bloom all at once. Red and white flowers are in full bloom. You take off your coat and drape it over your arm. You don't look back. No one is watching you. You know where you must go. But you hesitate for a moment.

You falter.

You stand still.

You don't move.

You move.

With the coat tucked under your arm, you enter the apartment complex. Was it Building 101, or 105, or 103, or 109? You can't recall which flower bed you hurled the key into. Probably not 101. You look up at the rooftop of 101, located near the complex entrance. Was it still there? You once read that a cat has nine lives. In a book of fairy tales. But you've never owned a book of fairy tales. You don't call the cat. You may be right: You may not have lured the kitten, you may not have killed the kitten that never existed in the first place.

It is now 2013. Fifteen years have passed since then. It is more than enough time for the cat that died or didn't die to have rotted away. As soon as you pass Building 101, you step onto the brick sidewalk that connects the apartment buildings. The royal azaleas are rapidly losing their petals. Red and white petals fall to the ground. On each branch of the taller trees hang light-green leaves. The light green turns a darker green. The trees begin to cast shadows. You slip out of the shadows and approach the flower bed.

New green sprouts are emerging from the flower bed. When you pace before it, the lilac bushes burst into bloom all at once. A small, exquisite purple shadow undulates on your face. You put down the coat and rummage through the pockets. You find a coin. You don't look around. Those who might have peered suspiciously at you have already disappeared and are nowhere to be found. You step into the flower bed. You manage to find the spot where you hurled the key one Thursday in 1998. There still isn't a single blemish on the large balcony window. There is no stain, mark, scratch, or scar. You pace the flower bed in front of the balcony, below the clear glass that tautly reflects the spring sunlight. Dandelions and pansies are in bloom. The flowers are getting trampled under your running shoes, but when you lift your feet, they spring back to life. As though they had never died, as though they would never die. The key's not there. The drain swallowed it up. But you already knew it wouldn't be there. The drowsy spring air burrows into you. You're dizzy. You feel vertigo. Someone is standing behind you. Startled, you look back.

It's Kim Injung. He, too, steps into the flower bed. He mimics your movements. He tramples the flowers. He kicks aside the grass thicket and the base of the lilac bushes. You look at him. When his eyes meet yours, he smiles stupidly. You back away. You stupid retard, I told you to quit following me, you mutter. But you're surprised. Kim Injung didn't follow you. He was there from the beginning. Key, key, key, he mutters. He draws closer. You step back and a branch scratches your cheek. It hurts. You rub your cheek. But there is no blood. Does it hurt? Does it hurt? he asks you, wearing an innocent expression.

You tug Kim Injung's hand. How long have you been following me? But you don't ask that. Kim Injung hasn't grown at all. He's wearing the same jacket and running shoes from fifteen years ago. The small mole that had been on the left side of his neck is exactly the same. Does it hurt? Kim Injung whispers. Ordinary people are walking past an ordinary scene. An ordinary afternoon, the ordinary sunlight, an ordinary time. The smell of lilacs grows stronger. The spring day is passing. Does it hurt? Kim Injung murmurs. Avoiding his eyes, you don't nod. I'll blow on it for you, he tells you. You clench the coin inside your pocket. Come to my house, I'll blow on it for you. You stretch out your hand and stroke his cheek. Kim Injung's cheek is cold and warm. It's cold enough to terrify and warm enough to make tears spring up. The moment when no one falls into the flower bed passes. The azaleas and forsythia fade, the royal azaleas fade, the lilacs fade, the pansies fade, the dandelions fade, and the moss rose fades. After that, all the flowers on earth come into bloom at once. Your face becomes mottled red, green, yellow, and white. They're the shadows of flowers. Kim Injung extends his hand and strokes your cheek. You recall that you didn't finish teaching Kim Injung the alphabet. *Giyeok*, do you remember? you ask him. He nods. *Gieok, niun, digu, riul.* Kim Injung lists the consonants incorrectly with pride. Now I know all the way to the end, I can even write my name. You nod. *Mium, bium, sium, ium, jium, chium, kium, tium, pium, hium*, he says. That's not right, you say. Kim Injung looks suspicious. It's not *mium*. It's *mieum*. It's not *jium*, it's *jieut*. It's not *chium*, it's *chieut*. Kim Injung's eyes grow moist. You stretch out your hand and wipe the tears from his eyes. His tears are cold and warm. You take the coin out of your pocket. When you open your hand, it's not a coin. It's a key. The key you had lost is in your palm. It's a key, a key, Kim Injung whispers. You grip it for a moment and then hurl it toward the balcony window as you close your eyes.

You don't hear anything. Not the sound of glass shattering, not the sound of metal grazing the glass, not the onomatopoeic sound *ca-clang*, not the sound of the key falling in the grass thicket. You open your eyes. The large balcony window is reflecting transparent sunlight as though nothing had happened. Nothing is happening. Nothing happened. Someone strokes your cheek. It's Kim Injung. You turn to face him. But there is no Kim Injung. No one is there.

You stand in front of the flower bed for a long time. The four seasons pass. But no one passes by. It rains. It snows. The wind blows and clouds pass by. A heavy rain falls and a light breeze blows. It grows misty and the sun shines. You feel neither warmth nor cold. All the world's seasons penetrate you. Frost forms on your cheeks but soon melts and trickles down. And when the last drop of water has evaporated, pedestrians pass by once again. A man with his suit jacket slung over his shoulder walks by. A little girl with a bob goes by on a bicycle. A cat hides in the grass thicket. The woman who had come outside with a dog tugs on the taut leash. A car starts noisily. A woman with wet permed hair walks by. Someone drops a grocery bag. The eggs break. A man passes by, his bag stuffed with flyers. A security guard straightens the sign in a flower bed. A fruit truck drives by. A few peaches fall off the back of the truck. Children with identical piano academy bags walk by. In one corner of the parking lot, two children draw on the asphalt with chalk. A man in shorts with a baseball cap jammed on his head passes by, smoking a cigarette. A woman who crosses his path plugs her nose with an exaggerated gesture. One of her high heels gets stuck in a crack in the pavement. She struggles to remove her heel. Someone sneezes. Pollen flies. A man passes by with a trash bag. In front of the recycling bin are pieces from a broken lightbulb. Cursing, a security guard rakes up the glass shards with his feet. Ordinary people passing through an ordinary scene. You become part of the scene and pick up the coat you had removed earlier. From where you stand, you can't see Building 101 or Building 109. Unfamiliar faces pass by. To them, you are merely a pedestrian. Where should I go? you wonder. Anywhere is good. You think about Kim Injung. I should have taught him the vowels. I should have taught him how to put in the final letters. But Kim Injung will reappear someday. He'll once again write something in his notebook, he'll get the spelling wrong, he'll struggle to write his own name, and below that he'll write your name. Then you'll take an eraser and erase the wrong letters and tell him to try again, you'll tell him to try again and again, until he can finally get the spelling right. You'll see the consonant *kieuk* and no longer think of a knife, and even when you see the small mole on the left of Kim Injung's neck, you'll no longer think of a knife. And like a child who has never once experienced animosity or murderous desire, you'll look at him with affection, and until the moment his brother or mother returns, you'll show him the same letters, again and again. In Kim Injung's notebook are unfinished letters, and with those letters perhaps we could guess at your name. Could we know your name? What will you be called?

I don't say your name. I don't call you. I don't ask you for your name, and you don't ask me for yours. Therefore, it's impossible to call you by name. And perhaps that impossibility is the only possible thing in this story. You don't look back at me. I watch you from behind. You begin walking again. The midday sun is beating down. Your shadow grows short. And so I won't have to step on your shadow. I follow you.

37

Both everywhere and nowhere, the place that I used as the setting is an ordinary residential area in a city outside Seoul, about two hundred kilometers from here. But the physical distance has now been pulverized. You wander this place that is both everywhere and nowhere. No one pays you any attention. The pedestrians are faithful to the roles they've been assigned. They pass through the scene. Once they slip from the scene, no one pays them any attention. Even if we wanted to, we can't. They simply can't be seen anymore. You bump into some of the pedestrians and even make eye contact, but they soon forget you and you also forget them. You must pass two apartment buildings. You may run into Park Jihye or Cho Yeonjeong, perhaps Park Yeongwu or Jung Yongjun. But they won't remember you. You look like you're twelve, and you also look like you're twenty. According to simple arithmetic, you're probably twenty-seven years old now, but no one would be able to guess that. Twelve years old and twenty years old, somewhere in between those two ages, time was torn and crumpled, repeatedly, until it finally disappeared. You rummage through your pockets. Instead of a coin, you feel a hair tie. You take it out and loop it around your thumb and index finger, stretching it. It's still elastic. You tie up your hair with it. The spring sun is warm. Sweat begins to form on your exposed neck. You walk along the pavement that connects the two apartment buildings. Two children are digging up a corner of a flower bed. Beside them on the dirt is a small cardboard box. Really? one child asks the other. You don't think anyone will notice if we bury it here? They don't see you. You shouldn't use a cardboard box, you say. It will rot so quickly that there won't be any trace left. What are you burying? Whatever it is, you need to put it in a tin box. But the children don't even look in your direction. They are engrossed in digging up the soil with their trowels. We'll dig it up next year, one of the children says. Promise you won't dig it up before then, the other one says. You walk away from them. When you look back, the children are gone. All you see is a patch that looks as though it has been dug up and hastily covered. You go back and gather branches and leaves and cover the patch that is raised like a burial mound. And you begin walking again. Your arm that holds the coat hangs down. My coat isn't just big on you, it's also heavy. You fold the coat neatly and place it on top of one of the rocks that encircle a flower bed. You don't worry about losing it. Although a coat placed in the middle of the road in springtime is conspicuous, no one but you will be able to see it. You round the corner of the massive building. Only then does the low-rise shopping arcade come into view. A piano academy and private math institute occupy the second floor, and on the first floor are a supermarket, import grocery store, stationery store, produce market, snack shop, fried chicken shop, real estate agent office, and video rental store. People go in and out of shops purposefully. You watch them for a long time and then walk toward the neighborhood map.

You peer at the rust-covered map. Where to now? You're thinking of a certain day in 1998, and the long and pointy triangle formed by you, Mia, and Mia's mother. The smell of rain fills the air. You begin to move, following after the memory you don't have. The triangle becomes longer and steeper. Except for you, the vertices have disappeared. The triangle collapses into a single segment. A large recycling bin catches your eye. Throw them away, you had once muttered. Throw them all away. You think about the words you had said. Could they still be there? Has someone taken them? You look back. Out of habit. But no one is there.

You walk toward the recycling bin. A security guard is putting plastic containers in a large sack. He doesn't look at you. You open the bin lid and peer inside. The smell of soft, damp paper reaches you. Rain falls on your forehead and patters into the bin. With trembling hands, you dig through the advertisement flyers and newspapers. There are even reference books and Bibles. Did you accidentally throw something out? the security guard asks. Startled, you look up, but the guard is busy sorting the plastic containers. You go back to rummaging through the bin. At the very bottom under the comic books and magazines, you discover a stack of worn notebooks. Thirty-five journals are stacked neatly together, as though someone had arranged them purposely. You take them out. Your hands shake. Did you find them? the guard says. You're lucky, tomorrow is collection day. You look at him, but he's engrossed in tying the opening of the sack that is filled with plastic containers. You carry the stack to a corner of the parking lot. The name Lee Jiyeong is written on the cover of the top journal. You clasp the journals to your chest. I peer at the clock. It's still noon. Your short shadow that is dangling at your feet totters after you. You step into the shadow cast by the building and perch on the rock in front of the flower bed. You place the stack of journals on your knees. Lee Jiyeong, Park Minsu, Yang Yeong-ae, Huh Namjun, Yun Kyeonghui. Your eyes pass over the unfamiliar names. Oh Sora. Kang Myeonghwa. So Yeonghyeon. Lee Jun-gyu. Kim Jongho. The journal covers are all different from one another. Some are a solid color and some have illustrations of robots, animals, or dolls. You look at each journal. Park Yeongwu, Jang Minguk, Song Ho-myeong, Cho Yeonjeong, Kim Taeyong. Underneath Kim Taeyong's journal is Choi Mia's journal. You gaze at each one for a moment. Underneath Choi Mia's journal is yours. You place both journals on your knees and bow your head. I look at you, but I don't know what you're thinking. From where I am, I can't see your expression. All I can see is the top of your head and a bit of your green hair tie.

You stroke the cover of Mia's journal. On it is a picture of a bunny. Dust rubs off on your fingertips. The wind blows. A light breeze, but it's enough to turn the pages. You gaze down at the open journal. I walk toward you. The pages are blank. There isn't a single sentence, a single letter, or even a single stain. You turn the page. The pages flutter. But there is no writing there—no sentences, no letters, either good or bad. Nothing is written, not your writing, not Mia's writing, not Inju's, not Mia's, not the chick's, not the sentence that said she wanted to kill a chick, that she wanted to kill, too. A void is white and clear. It's impossible to read anything in the journal. You close Mia's journal with trembling hands and open the journal with your name written on the cover. Your journal is also blank. *Leaf, wind, breeze, song, stick, ice cream, moon, stars, whistling, tree branch, footprint, dog, cat, streetlight, bird, colors*—your journal contains none of these words. *Cheek, bruise, blister, fingernail, curse, calf muscle, tongue, palm, hair, sigh, grip, shoe heel, spine, thigh, stick, crying,* and *pain.* These are also missing. Rain falls on the blank page. The smell of rain fills the air. You feel the page with your fingertips. There is no imprint of writing. The paper is smooth, as though nothing had ever been written on it in the first place. You recall certain sentences. When I opened the window, a light breeze blew in. I wanted ice cream, so I went to the store. There was dew on the green leaves. I saw the yellow cat's family. It was strange that their eyes were green. You always received the same comment about your journal entries, that there was no concrete story. But your entries were more concrete than anyone else's. She slapped me really hard. It felt like my cheek was on fire. If I lied one more time, she said she would rip out my tongue. I didn't lie. I was beaten on the thighs. On the thighs so that other people wouldn't see. Beaten like a dog. Your journal, which had once been filled with the most beautiful words, is now nothing more than a bundle of blank pages. Blank pages, blank pages with edges that have begun to yellow, blank pages devoid of any writing that would smudge if raindrops were to fall, blank pages in the hand, black cages in the head. Your eyes tear up. I recall the common figure of speech between tears and the rain.

You run. Your breathing grows labored. Mine also grows labored. You run, hugging all thirty-five journals to your chest. It is about a fifteen-minute walk to the school from where you are. You pass the security booth and the shops in front of the apartment complex, and another apartment complex and police station, and then a post office and another apartment complex, and then a park and library. Finally, you turn into the alley. You pass the stationery store, bookstore, snack shop, and arcade, and stand before the school gate. You take a minute to catch your breath. All is silent and still. The redness fades from your face. With a blank expression, you pass through the gate. You look down at the school field. Only a few children are there, kicking a ball or on the swings. The field has turned muddy after the recent showers. You remember where the open window is. But instead of climbing in through the window, you use the entrance on the right side of the building. In the entryway, you remove your shoes without thinking. But you don't have indoor shoes to change into. You wear your running shoes into the school. In every classroom, class is in session. The voice of the teacher explaining Korea's system of government and its division of powers into the legislative, judicial, and administrative branches rings out into the hallway. Hugging the journals to your chest, you climb the stairs. You remember your old classroom. No. You merely find it by instinct. Fifth- and sixth-grade students use the fourth floor. At the end of the hallway on the fourth floor, you hesitate. You hear the sound of the organ. Children begin to sing in chorus. There are eight classes in fifth grade and you must pass seven classrooms. Each of the shoe racks in the hallway is filled with shoes of different colors and styles. You approach the Grade 5, Section 3, classroom. You grow dizzy. Your classroom is located in the middle of the hallway on the fourth floor. You hesitate outside the back door. You stand on tiptoe and peek through the window. It's English class. Your teacher is explaining long vowels and short vowels. *Snow* contains the long *o* sound. Snow takes a long time to melt after it falls to the ground. It's pronounced with a long *o*. Before the teacher finishes speaking, you quietly open the back door and step into the classroom. Several children turn to look at you. Snow takes a long time to melt. It's pronounced with a long *o*.

Your desk is empty. Your teacher gives you a look as though telling you to quickly take a seat. You place the thirty-five journals under your desk. A shoe bag is hanging from the side of your desk. Quietly, you remove your running shoes and put on your indoor shoes. Why are you so late? Yang Yeong-ae whispers to you. You're afraid to answer. Did you get another nosebleed? she asks. You nod. Your teacher now moves on to *cut/cute* and *tub/tube*. Several children shake their heads, as though they can't bear to sit through another explanation. When you put your hand in your desk, you can feel your English book and notebook. You take them out. Yang Yeong-ae lends you a pencil. You gaze around the classroom. You're dizzy. There is no empty desk in the classroom. Thirty-five dark heads, including yours, are bent over their desks. And then you notice a green hair tie. It's firmly holding together a long coil of hair. It's Mia. Mia sits at her desk, wearing a large, loose sweater. Kim Inju whispers something to Mia. You remember Mia's sweater. The one with the deer knitted on the chest, the one that was too large on Mia, the one Mia had gained after pleading with her mother, or perhaps one of her two fathers. For a long time, you gaze at her green hair tie and her small shoulders that are covered in the sweater. When you turn your head, Kim Injung, who had been scribbling in his book, his elbow propped on his desk that's set next to the teacher's desk, sees you and waves wildly. The children snicker. Mia and Kim Inju also laugh. Mia's shoulders shake. Her hair tie shakes, too. You're dizzy. The scene collapses.

38

When I grow up, I'm going to buy a fountain pen, says Mia. Do you know you can kill someone with a fountain pen? It's because of acceleration. It was in a detective story.

Inju opens her eyes wide and looks at Mia. But what's a fountain pen? Inju asks. Mia's gaze, which had been wandering around the classroom, meets yours. While looking at you, Mia says to Inju, It's called a fountain pen, because there's a fountain of ink inside. Inju visualizes a fountain flowing with ink. Her face turns red.

Mia gestures at you. English is over and the teacher has stepped out of the classroom for a moment. You nod at Mia. At the back of the classroom, the bigger boys are playing a coin toss game. The flicking of the coins cuts through the harsh voices. Mia gestures at you again. Are you okay? she asks. You look up at her. You don't understand what she means. Mia brings her hand to her nose. Your nosebleed, she says, her lips becoming small and round and then stretching to the side. You nod. Mia's face brightens.

But is it true? Inju asks Mia. From her desk, Mia takes out a book with a worn, tacky cover. From where you are, you can't make out the title. As Mia taps the spine of the book, she recites a list of words: *icicle, fountain pen, misfired bullet, slender racer snake, poison.* Inju waves her hands. Mia bursts out laughing.

You already know that Mia has no desire to kill anyone, and in fact, she doesn't even understand the words *death* or *kill.* As far as you know, she is lucky. Mia has two fathers, and they each make every effort to win her favor. Mia is only interested in detective novels, but in a year, perhaps even in six months, she may soon forget the cheap books boasting the flashy title *Children's Library*. Because there are more things she doesn't know than she does know, and more things are hidden than are exposed, Mia's world is still safe. Mia is lucky, still. You recall Mia's bright, sunny room, and you recall the mold growing in every crevice of the large window. The mold, hidden in shadow, is not easily seen. Mia, Mia's mother, and Mia's fathers aren't yet aware of the speed at which the white-blue-and-black mold is infiltrating the room, the speed of the mold that may cause Mia to cough or feel a pain in her chest. Her bright, sunny room doesn't allow anyone to foresee that there is mold blooming in a corner. You don't foresee anything. You simply see. You recall the smooth, white porcelain doll that was sitting on a corner of the bookshelf. A porcelain doll with green eyes, a small, pointy nose, and a blond wig made not from artificial hair but real human hair. It was naked. Its cheeks were painted pink. Its face looked realistic, but its body was just a cold lump. Its chest showed no trace of development and it was without any reproductive organs. After she noticed you staring, Mia dressed the doll, as though she were embarrassed. My mom washed the clothes, but I forgot to put them back on, she said to you. That day. You didn't ask for the doll's name and neither did Mia tell you the doll's name. The scene from that day plays in your mind. You look at Mia. Mia, who is whispering with Inju, notices and flashes you a sweet smile.

It looks as though Mia has grown a little. But her baggy sweater is still baggy. Mia will grow. She will shoot up in a year, or perhaps even in six months. Because children grow in the blink of an eye. There is a crash at the back of the classroom. You look back. A door has fallen off the supply closet. The bigger boys are stuffing Kim Injung's head in the closet. Kim Injung shrieks. You look at the clock on the wall. There is a minute left of break time. The bell will ring in a minute and then the boys' rough, violent hands will grow quiet and return to their sides. According to the schedule hanging at the front of the classroom, the next class is biology. After biology is lunchtime. You slip your hands into your desk. You pull out the biology textbook and notebook. Yang Yeong-ae pouts. I hate biology. You once wandered around your apartment complex and ended up quite far away. You lived close to the highway. Carelessly you climbed over the highway guardrail. Or crawled under it, you can't remember. Cars raced past you at a frightful speed. You trembled. And then you saw two skinny snakes slithering through the narrow strip of grass beside the road. You don't recall how you managed to get off the highway or what happened once you went home that day. A minute passes. The bell rings. The boys let Kim Injung go. Kim Injung, his face red, returns to his desk that sits next to the teacher's desk. Coins jingle inside the boys' pockets. The teacher enters the classroom.

You open your biology textbook. The textbook is like new. There are no notes or scribbles scrawled anywhere. All the children's eyes are directed toward the teacher's desk. Still red-faced, Kim Injung is panting. You lean back and feel the stack of journals under your desk with your foot. Park Yeongwu's journal falls to the floor. The teacher begins to write on the chalkboard. You spread open Park Yeongwu's journal on your desk. His journal is blank. There isn't a single letter or eraser crumb. No mention of a chick, no mention of Kim Injung. You close the journal. The teacher is writing about the solar system and the earth's rotation. You jot down the information about the earth's orbit in your notebook. You use a pencil. Words written in pencil can always be erased. You feel as though you're forgetting something. But you don't know what.

It's lunchtime. You put your hand in your desk, but there is no lunchbox. Yang Yeong-ae has gone over to Oh Sora's desk. The children busily open and close the lids of their lunchboxes. Mia sees you sitting at your desk. She calls out to you. Kim Inju also gestures at you. You go to Mia's desk. Did you forget your lunch? Mia asks. You nod. Mia hands you her fork. I can use a spoon. You can have some of mine. Even now, you still feel as though you're forgetting something. Something. Whatever it may be. You take Mia's fork. Mia's fork. Mia's spoon. Mia's lunchbox. Mia's water bottle. Mia's knife. Mia's throat. Mia pushes her lunchbox toward you. Green peas are embedded in the white rice. Mia picks out every single one. Holding Mia's fork, you hesitate. You're forgetting something. But you don't know what. You're confused. Although grains of rice travel down your throat, you're simply chewing and swallowing mechanically. Mia tells Inju what happened on the television show that she watched the night before. Inju isn't allowed to watch television after ten o'clock. Inju looks at Mia enviously. So why don't you come over and we can watch together? Just say you're sleeping over at my place, Mia says. You swallow grains of rice. Should I? Inju asks. Mia and Inju look at you at the same time. Do you want to come, too? Mia and Inju say at the same time. Rice gets stuck in your throat. Without thinking, you wrap your hands around your throat. Mia's face crumples. It's because you're crying.

Can I bring my dog? Inju asks. Sure, says Mia. Inju has a dog. You know the dog's name. His name is Busan. Inju's family began to call him Busan after seeing how busily he ran around in circles. But you've never seen or heard any stories about Inju's dog before. Nevertheless, you believe that you've seen Inju's dog. You recall how Mia had patted him. You recall how Mia had tried on Inju's dress. You recall how Mia had laughed so hard she could barely breathe. You recall how Inju's grandmother had slapped Mia. You recall how Mia had cried, how her tears had dropped to the floor. But these are not your memories. Aren't your parents going to be home? Inju asks Mia. Mia's face darkens. No one will be home today, so you can bring Busan, Mia says. You're coming over too, right? Mia asks you. Slowly, you nod. You recall Mia's journal that is completely blank. Inside Mia's journal, there is no sign of Mia's writing or yours.

The last class of the day is over. The teacher gives the same hackneyed instructions. The children move restlessly. Mia and Inju put their flashy pencils in their cases. Mia's legs fidget below her long sweater, and she clasps together her hands, which peek out from her rolled-up sleeves. After school is dismissed, the children scatter in all four directions from the school gate toward the district 2-1, toward 3-12, toward Suite 303 of Building 109, toward Solar Arcade, toward the Cheongpa Institute, melting their shadows into the afternoon's. In Mia's class there are many Kims, Lees, Parks, Chois, Songs, Kangs, Shins, Hwangs, Chungs, and Yangs, but these children will soon have to rearrange themselves according to their biological classification: species, genus, family, order, class, phylum, and kingdom. The warm spring breeze turns cool in the afternoon. The teacher finishes his lecture and pulls out a stack of notebooks from under his desk. He places thirty-five journals on the desk. Shocked, you look under your own desk. The journals that were there have disappeared. You check many times, but nothing's there. The floor twists and turns. You're crying. The teacher returns the children's journals. He says nothing about the contents. Mia and Kim Inju get theirs back as well. When Mia glances inside her journal, her face darkens. Mia and Kim Inju hurriedly put their journals in their bags. Timid and unsure, you go up to the teacher's desk and are handed a journal with your name on the cover. Your heart is pounding. Violently. You look back. But no one is there. No. Someone is there. You return to your seat. Your legs are shaking. You barely manage to sit back down. The teacher calls up the last student. Thirty-five journals have been returned to thirty-five children. The children slip out of the classroom, some ahead and some behind. You gaze at your journal, which is sitting on your desk. Mia and Inju also get up from their desks. Mia shouts something at you. But you can't hear what she's saying. Kim Injung gets up from his seat. The teacher says something to him. But you can't hear what the teacher is saying. The scraping of the desk legs on the wooden floor echoes harshly. Mia approaches you. You lower your head. She stops in front of you. You don't look up. You know where I live, right? Mia whispers. You barely manage to nod. You clearly recall Mia's address. Mia's balcony, Mia's kitchen, Mia's table, Mia's bathroom, Mia's living room, Mia's mother, Mia's fathers, Mia's elevator—all these things you recall too clearly. The things you've forgotten come to life again. You wipe the tears from your eyes, but Mia has already left your side. Just as she is about to step out of the classroom, she turns and waves at you. She beams. Although her words get buried in the bustle and you can't hear what she's saying, you figure it out. See you tonight. You don't open your journal. You don't change out of your indoor shoes into running shoes. You don't put your textbook or notebooks in your desk. You don't look back at the clock. Time is twisting. The classroom that had been quickly emptying begins to collapse. It collapses. It's collapsing. The building heaves. Time turns. The floor twists inside out. You don't feel dizzy. As though you had been expecting it, you simply sit in your seat and calmly watch how one world collapses. You don't look back. If you look back, I will already have disappeared. It disappears. It collapses. It's disappearing. It's collapsing.

39

The brick curtain flaps. Is this a dream? This isn't a dream. You come home. You hesitate at the front door for a moment before ringing the doorbell. Electronic birds chirp. I, who had been standing in the entryway, open the door. You glance up at me.

Where's my coat? I ask.

You simply point toward the far room. The coat is on a hanger. You take off your running shoes and step inside. The apartment is warm. Your cheeks begin to melt. I don't ask, Where were you? Straightaway, you head for the narrow living room. The notebook you had been writing in, or had not been writing in, is on the chair. You open the notebook and take out the pencil and fountain pen you had placed inside. But you don't write anything.

Where's the book? you ask.

That book hasn't been written yet, I answer. And I smile a little, because you sound like me. When you realize why I'm smiling, you grin.

Write it again, from the beginning, you say.

No, I'm not going to write it, I say.

You gaze at me, lips twitching. Your face contains no rage, remorse, sadness, or shadow. Why me? you mumble. I look down at your wrist. Around your wrist is a green hair tie. There are wet stains on your nylon jacket that's zipped up to your chin. But I don't ask, Did it snow? In your left hand is a pencil and in your right, a fountain pen. I can't help thinking I've seen this image before. With your head bowed, you mumble something. I can't help thinking I've heard those words before.

When I was young, you start to say as you look at me, I found a ring on the street. I was around seven or eight years old. It was a ring with a red gem. I believed the red gem was a real ruby. It was probably plastic, because it was too big to be real. It was bigger than my thumbnail. But it made me happy. I'd never owned anything that pretty before. I'd never even owned any hairpins. My hair was always cut short, but if it happened to be long, it was tied up with a rubber band. The cheap yellow ones you use to tie things like chopsticks. But you already know that. Whenever I took one of those rubber bands off, it pulled my hair out. It hurt. But I've experienced many things more painful than that.

You shut your mouth for a moment. And then you begin to speak again.

I decided to keep the ring. But I didn't know where I could hide it. Because pockets weren't safe. And it's not like I could hide it outside, since someone else might take it. Anyone who saw a big ruby like that would get greedy. So I had no choice but to hide it inside the apartment. I'm sure you already know, but there's no place more dangerous than home. When no one was home, I investigated every corner, but it was hard to find a safe spot. So I picked the dustiest book I could find.

You're no longer looking at me. After gazing at the floor for a long time, you go on with your story.

I still remember how it felt when I began to cut out the center of the pages with a knife. One, two, perhaps a hundred pages. Soon there was a square hole in the middle of the book. I put the ring inside the hole and closed the book. I don't remember the title. But for a few years, until I turned twelve, the ring was safely hidden there. What was I so afraid of? The fact that I had found a ring? The fact that I hadn't looked for the owner of a ring I had found on the street? Or the fact that I owned such a pretty, shiny object? I was seven or eight. As far as I know, children that age don't try to hide things like that. They're not afraid or scared. Was something the matter with me? After that I never opened the book again. I didn't dare touch it. I was afraid the dust piled on top of the book would be disturbed and reveal that I had touched the book. Yes, that's what I was afraid of. But as you already know, many things are more frightening and fearful than that. You obviously know that all too well.

You cry. Your tears fall down your cheeks and to the floor. I begin to extend my hand toward you, but then stop.

So how can you think I don't exist? I can still recall that ring so clearly. I can even draw it and describe it in writing. How can you think I don't exist?

You remove your nylon jacket, your sweater, and then your T-shirt, and show me your back. Your back is marked with red scars and green bruises. I cover your back with a sweater.

It doesn't hurt anymore. But it won't go away, you say.

It won't fade and it won't disappear. I can cover it up, though, you say.

Where should I go now? you ask.

It's snowing outside, you say. When I think back, I've never seen snow before. Why is that? Did I just forget I'd seen it? *Snow* is pronounced with a long *o*. Was that something you said? Or a sentence you wrote? Why have I never seen snow before? But you probably know the answer to that.

Stay. Stay here with me, I say.

You look up at me with brick eyes.

That ring was really pretty, you say with brick lips. I wish I could see it again, brick you say with brick lips.

I rummage through my drawer. After digging through objects like tweezers, a camera, pictures, and key chains, the ring appears. I peer at it. The corners of the red plastic gem are chipped and peeling. I spread open your hand and place it in your palm. You look down at the ring.

This isn't it, you say, shaking your head and smiling a little. This isn't it.

In your brick palm is the brick ring. Brick you shake your brick head. There is a green brick hair tie around your brick wrist. Brick you give the brick ring back to me.

I thought about you sometimes, I say. I don't know why. I thought about you more than I thought about Mia.

You look at me.

I thought about you more than any other character, I say. That's the truth.

Brick you shed brick tears. Brick tears become brick and brick falls to the ground. I close my eyes. Bricks crash and shatter. The brick sweater slips off your brick body. Your brick chest is revealed and the brick scars break open. Brick you glare at me with brick eyes.

There's something I want to ask you, you say with your brick voice breaking.

How can I delay my death? How can I write my own death sentence?

Your brick mouth spews brick words.

Did my illness begin before the story began? Or after the story began?

Your brick lips whisper brick words. These are questions I hadn't expected. No. That's a lie.

Am I alive or am I dead? Am I dead or am I alive? Am I living or am I dying?

The hands on the brick clock are pointing to the brick hour. The brick window opens and the brick breeze blows in. The brick snow drifts and the brick ice scatters. Brick you look at brick me. Your brick tears freeze. Brick spoon. Brick chopsticks. Brick fork. Brick plate. Brick cup. Brick straw. Brick paring knife. Brick throat. Brick knife. Brick objects. Brick you approach brick me. Brick I cower. Brick you seize my brick throat. Your brick fingernails dig into my brick neck. Brick face turns red and brick face turns pale. Brick lips open and spew brick breath. Brick body sags to the brick floor and bursts into laughter. Brick hands grasp brick throat and apply all the force they can muster. Brick laughter gets swallowed up in brick throat. Brick eyes fly open. Brick hands flail over brick hands. Hold on, you're almost there. Brick mouth spews brick words. An expression like laughter or sobs flickers across brick face. The inside of brick head reeks of blood. Brick doesn't see anything. Brick face, even brick hands, evade the brick gaze. Brick shuts eyes and tightens brick fingers around brick throat, harder and harder, with crushing force. Brick body begins to go slack. Brick lips open. Tears flow from brick eyes. Brick pants. Brick words escape at once. Brick words disappear at once. Brick eyes meet brick eyes. Brick scene twists. One brick footprint, two brick shadows. Brick snowflakes fall on frozen brick cheeks. Brick you look at brick me. Brick buttercups and brick lilacs. Brick blossoms and falling brick blossoms. Brick I don't look at brick you. Brick you don't look at brick me. Brick words don't remember brick words. Brick dawn, brick morning, brick evening, brick night. Brick world doesn't shrink. Brick you don't break. Brick dream doesn't shatter. Forgotten words and lost words turn to brick and become trapped inside the mouth. Brick pencil and brick fountain pen fall to the brick ground. Brick words and brick sentences fall to the brick ground. Brick world doesn't collapse. Brick world doesn't expand. Brick you become brick and the brick hour stops. Brick I open my brick eyes and look at brick you. Your brick lips are open and have petrified. Your brick eyes are wide and have petrified. Brick snowflakes land on your brick cheeks. Brick dust lands on the brick snowflakes. Brick story becomes brick and petrifies. Brick you will still be brick a million years from now. What should I call you? I write up to this point and then close my brick eyes and spew out brick breath.

40

And I stop writing the story. When I fall asleep as though I'm fainting and then wake, it's either morning or evening. You're not there. No other version of the story exists. The story stops here.

Footless like ghosts, atonement, all this you already knew. Clearly. When the story wasn't yet written, I thought of an ending in which another character would atone for my actions. Perhaps I had hoped that the sin, the act that I'd carried out, committed, and written, would be atoned for in that way. But that's impossible. There was a time I thought it was possible. I was confused. The opposite of confusion doesn't exist.

The dog and the river. When I began this story, I thought of a dog that drifted along with the river. Several people who heard me describe this said it was impossible to swim downstream. Perhaps it would be possible if it were crossing the river. But they said swimming downstream was not actually swimming; it was closer to floating. But I kept picturing a dog that didn't swim from this side of the river to that side, a dog that didn't swim upstream, a dog that simply followed the current, as though it were being swept down the river, a dog that didn't sink or flail. And now that the story has ended or is in the process of ending, I superimpose you over the swimming dog. There is no connection between you and the dog. It is merely a superimposition caused by confusion. Just as I believed you had come to see me. Just as I thought a dead child had come back to life. Repeated confusion can completely change a story. The dog and atonement. I thought not about your death, but about the death of another character. That kind of character is often called a third party. But I've given up on a story with a third party. Why?

There is no dog, but you are there. You're drifting by. A small, run-down boat moored across the river looks as though it's adrift, but I want to put you on that boat and send you off, somewhere, to a place that will not attract any attention. So that you can escape the story, before you're carried over the dam, before you meet the barrier, before you're cast away, before you drown, before you turn into brick and sink. I've always thought about you. Every time I looked back, you were there. Every time I looked back, you also looked back. Our eyes never met and therefore we have never met. But stubbornly, I remove the boat from the scene. You can't reach the boat. There is no boat. As though you've never even laid eyes on a boat, you move on soundlessly, wordlessly, noiselessly. As you sink. As you rise a little and then sink again.

Therefore, you don't swim. You're merely swept along with the flow of the river, with the flow of the story. No one knows why you don't cross the river, why you don't cut across or sail across, or how you have come to drift with the current. The spot where you should have landed has already disappeared from your sight and is disappearing from my sight. Across the river in a safe place, in a place that actually exists, I'm watching you. I, too, must soon disappear. One current, two currents. Not only is it impossible to name every object, but it's impossible to count them all. The parts of all objects. The parts of the parts. I don't call your name. You came to find me because I named you, and because I never called you by that name, not once. Because of this, I command you to cross the river, I fasten the securest metal collar around your neck, and I push you into the water. On this side and that side of the river, I'm standing safely among the reeds, not entrusting my body to the current, hoping, no, not hoping, that you would cross the river. You don't cross the river, and when your blackness and largeness, your whiteness and smallness, when you and the river, the river and you, are no longer in anyone's sight, you will disappear. You will sink before you sink. It's a strange way to put it, but there is no other suitable expression. Quickly or slowly. All speeds are either quick or slow, one or the other.

Your hair undulates like a plant underwater. Because your soaking wet hair looks as black as black can be and your body is mostly submerged, your blackness and whiteness aren't very noticeable, and therefore you're no longer black or white. You can't speak, and even if you were able to speak, bark, or cry, the noise would get swallowed up by the water, and silently, it would be washed away with you. No one knows how you ended up drifting in the current, but this ignorance is clearly a lie. I keep telling lies. You look as though you're swimming, as though you're following the current, heading toward the dam where two rivers meet. No, it looks as though you're being swept down the river. No, it looks as though you're sinking. Soon you will sink.

You are sinking, following the current of the river.

You are sinking.

You sink.

You are there.

You are not there.

Afterword

I had a dream.

It's summer. Perhaps winter. I'm sitting in a lecture hall among unfamiliar faces. It's the middle of the day.

Someone comes in. It must be the teacher. He sets some books on his desk and looks around the lecture hall at the students. Our eyes meet.

He writes several words on the chalkboard. But the words become severed from each other. It's strange to say that they become severed, but I can't describe it any other way. I realize that I'm dreaming. The severed words are severed into smaller fragments. Those severed fragments are in turn severed into even smaller fragments. Sever, segment, dement, chain, key, calculation, separation. All of a sudden, I recall the phrase *phantom limb pain*. The words on the chalkboard become severed and then divide repeatedly. It hurts. But I can't feel the pain of the words. Despite the fact that the words are being severed, I can still read each word. The teacher says that a collection of severed words is a *bounded component*. To me, the phrase *bounded component* is strange. All the other students nod. And then I wake.

After I wake from the dream, I look up the words in the dictionary.

Bounded: Let R be the set of all real numbers and let A be a subset of R. If A is the set of natural integers, for any choice of a large real number r, there exists a natural integer as an element of A, which is larger than *r*. On the other hand, if *A* is the open interval (0, 1), we can choose a suitable real number, such as 1, which is larger than all of the entry of *A*. A set *A* is called bounded from above if there exists a suitable real number *r* such that any element of *A* is less than or equal to *r*.

Component: in Gestalt psychology, the phenomenon where a part of a whole is perceived independently from another part.

I'd never heard of the phrase *bounded component*. As I read the definitions of these two words, I think about you. Could I explain your face as *bounded* and the parts of your face as *components*?

But what about the parts of the parts of your face?

Han Yujoo was born in Seoul in 1982 and is the author of four short story collections. She is an active member of an experimental group called Rue and also runs Oulipopress, an independent publisher. *The Impossible Fairy Tale* is her first book to appear in English.

Janet Hong is a translator and writer living in Vancouver, Canada. She is the recipient of a PEN/Heim Translation Fund award and numerous grants from the Daesan Foundation, LTI Korea, and English PEN, as well as fellowships from the International Communication Foundation (ICF).

The text of *The Impossible Fairy Tale* is set in Adobe Jenson Pro. Book design by Rachel Holscher. Composition by Bookmobile Design and Digital Publisher Services, Minneapolis, Minnesota. Manufactured by Versa Press on acid-free, 30 percent postconsumer wastepaper.